Praise for *The Boyfriend*

"Another demonstration of Thomas Perry's cool, tough-minded skill at staging battles of wits." —*The New York Times*

"Perry launches another excellent series. . . . The pacing is rapid, Till is an intrepid hero, and the ending is satisfying." —*Library Journal*

"(Perry's) work is characterized by tight, clean prose, well-drawn characters, and heart-pounding suspense." —*Associated Press*

"The strength of the psychological drama lies in Mr. Perry's capacity to develop his characters. Mr. Perry has turned out another riveting mystery." —*The Washington Times*

"While there is plenty of action and tension here (indeed, it may well be Perry's best book to date), it is the moments that Till spends with his daughter—in person and across the miles—that make *The Boyfriend* a memorable book and give rise to a heartfelt demand that we see more of Till sooner rather than later." —Bookreporter.com

"Perry's prose is perfect. *The Boyfriend* is a model for thriller writers and one that should reinforce the reputation of the author of *The Butcher's Boy* and *The Informant*. If you haven't read anything by Thomas Perry, you're in for a delightful surprise." —*Huntington News*

Also by Thomas Perry

The Boyfriend

Thomas Perry

The Mysterious Press
an imprint of Grove/Atlantic, Inc.
New York

Published simultaneously in Canada
Printed in the United States of America

ISBN: 978-0-8021-5512-2
eBook ISBN: 978-0-8021-9368-1

The Mysterious Press
an imprint of Grove/Atlantic, Inc.
154 West 14th Street
New York, NY 10011

Distributed by Publishers Group West

www.groveatlantic.com

13 14 15 16 17   10 9 8 7 6 5 4 3 2 1

As always, for Jo and our children.
And many thanks to Robert Lescher and Otto Penzler.

1

Since Catherine had met Joey two months ago, it seemed she'd never had enough time for the amount of living she wanted to do. But today she wasted nearly twenty minutes standing on the sidewalk outside Ivy at the Shore waiting to have lunch with two friends from college, Caitlyn Raines and Megan Stiles. They arrived together in Caitlyn's Mercedes, a car Catherine thought of as not a real Mercedes. It was the type that was no bigger than a Honda, but it had a three-pointed Mercedes symbol in about five inches of chrome.

Seeing the other two come together in that car started things wrong for Catherine. She'd had to drive alone from the Valley. There was the hint that they had been together for some time and shared information, and that they would be able to talk about her on the way home afterward, or even go on to continue their afternoon without her.

They were the sort of friends who had not been friends out of affection or admiration of one another's good qualities. They had all been attractive—two of them hot, in the argot of that time and place. Caitlyn had been the Scots-Irish girl with coal black hair and blue eyes, big breasts, and an undiscriminating smile, and Megan was the tall natural blond, so they had both been sought-after, but Catherine had not. She had been born with strawberry blond hair, a face that was pleasant but not striking, and eyes that were hazel, not blue. They had all done the work in high school that was necessary to score well on the standard tests and get themselves certified as college material.

At UCLA they had all pursued impressive-sounding academic programs that were genuinely demanding and edifying but were not designed to lead to any sort of future compensation. They had met in a freshman dormitory and been selected together for pledging at Sigma Tau Tau, a sorority filled with young women of similar promise and limitations. Their friendship had been dictated by the situation, the role they were doomed to play in that place. They had competed against each other for three more years.

The competition was unavoidable. If you were in a university program you had a grade point average, whether you wanted one or not. And to refuse to divulge yours was an admission that it was lower than someone else's. And when you went to parties or university social events, it was always painfully obvious who was of great value to the opposite sex, and who was the second choice, and who was the one being settled for by the boy who was shortest or a little bit chubby. These were primal competitions of the crudest sort. The males were choosing on the basis of the females' pure mating potential. Although the males had no idea that was what they were doing, they chose in absolute sincerity. In general, by the time males made any sort of approach they had already been drinking. Nuance was lost. They looked, and they wanted. Or they didn't want.

Catherine's few victories in this competition were due to a particular, odd circumstance. Megan Stiles, the tall blond, was actually over six feet tall in bare feet, a woman whom some short—or even average—men wouldn't approach. She was a golden prize, but it took a man with a great deal of confidence to believe he could interest her. So there were evenings when she stood around a lot, surreptitiously looking over the heads of not-quite-suitors and hoping for somebody of the right height to come into view.

Caitlyn too had her solitary evenings. She had a loud voice, and a louder laugh, so on a couple of occasions a man who had immediately drifted toward the black hair and the white skin and the seductive shape seemed to drift away, his ears battered by the voice.

Usually Catherine had won the GPA and academic achievement events in the competition, but lost the social and romantic events. Having Megan and Caitlyn show up together reminded her of all of those disappointments, and she wished she had said she was too busy for lunch today.

"Hi," she said as they let the valet take the miniature Mercedes and Caitlyn slipped the car check into her wallet.

"Been here long?" That was worse than being late. It showed Caitlyn knew she was late, but didn't plan to apologize.

"Not too long," Catherine said. "I got here right at twelve-thirty." Twelve-thirty was the time of their reservation, and the time they'd all promised to be here.

Caitlyn and Megan leaned in and delivered air kisses. Catherine hoped that her perfume and hair smelled as fresh and floral as theirs, but she couldn't tell what they thought.

"My God, Cathy," said Megan. "It's been how long? At least two years."

"At least," Catherine said. She had arrived at UCLA seven years ago having never been allowed to be anything but a Cathy. She had made a conscious decision to be a Catherine. The refusal of her friends, her supposed sisters, ever to respect or even acknowledge the change had always infuriated her. She'd been sure it was a competitor's ploy to rattle an opponent. If there was a group photograph, she would always be identified as "Cathy" Hamilton. If there was a roster or listing of names, one of her friends would alter it to make her "Cathy." At one time, if they had greeted her this way, she would have said, "Actually, it's Catherine." But she found she had outgrown that, as she had outgrown them. "Shall we go in?"

She held the door and let the others inside. For an instant she hoped they would see some hint of irritation on the face of the maître d'—some disapproval for being half an hour late. But no, as long as they looked the way they did, they would be permitted to behave the way they wished. He was delighted to lead them to an excellent table where they had a view across the street at the ocean, and his other customers had a view of them.

They sat in the light, airy atmosphere of the restaurant and ordered the things that the ocean suggested to the appetite—crab cakes and sole and swordfish, which they ate the way they had eaten in college, sparingly, only tasting, with no bread and salads with no dressing. They drank iced tea unsweetened. The bit of caffeine helped burn off weight, and heavily iced drinks made the body use calories to warm them to body temperature.

Caitlyn said, "Well, here we all are, divorced and unattached almost four years after graduation."

Catherine had never been married, but she felt no reason to correct her.

"I thought surely you two would be the first ones in our class to have it all and do it all."

Megan gave Caitlyn a sly look. "I thought you'd be the first one to do it all, anyway."

Caitlyn gave a little slap to Megan's forearm. "I hope you meant that in some nice way."

Catherine said, "How is the movie job?"

Caitlyn said, "That was two jobs ago. The whole world got laid off two years ago, not just me. I decided that if studio work was that precarious, it wasn't for me. I was taking a low salary and working insane hours, thinking I would pay my dues and then move upward. And it wasn't fun, either. It was always, 'Get this one on the phone,' or 'Messenger this to that one.'"

"What are you doing now?"

"I'm thinking about going to get an MBA."

"Ah," said Catherine, nodding as though she agreed that was a sensible thing to do, although she didn't. "How about you, Meg?"

"I'm getting ready to open a business."

"What kind?"

"Fashion. I found an opportunity to get some things made cheaply downtown, so I'm doing my own line. I should be ready in the spring."

More concrete plans that weren't concrete. Their plans were always specific instead of true, because that was how they had learned to lie. She knew that if she pressed either of them for details they would invent as many as she could listen to.

Megan made it Catherine's turn. "And how about you? Are you still in school?"

"No. I've been working as assistant to a lawyer whose clients are all businesses. It's pretty dull. No interesting details of divorces, no suspenseful criminal cases. It's all just agreements between companies— four copies, signed and countersigned, then filed in the client file."

"Oh my God, Cathy. You poor thing. How did that happen to you?"

"I had been looking for over a year, and didn't find anything. I needed a job. There was no other choice. I had to pay my rent and live while I looked for something else, then tried to keep up with my expenses and put a little away." She laughed. "It's not like I went to prison. I'm getting through hard times. When it's over I'll look some more."

They looked at each other. "Good luck."

Catherine could see that they thought she was making a mistake. To be an unemployed fashion consultant or unemployed business owner was better than being a secretary. Better to be something pretentious and never get a chance to work than to let go of the illusion—the pose—that they were better than other people. She could see them moving her down the hierarchy in their minds.

Caitlyn and Megan talked through the rest of the lunch about "losing" their husbands. She knew that was a lie, like most of what they said. Women didn't "lose" husbands, they threw them away. Only later did they realize what they'd done, and some of them regretted it. What they regretted was losing the person who had supported them, but that wasn't what they felt. They felt the loss of a world where they could behave in any way they liked, and there would never be any consequences.

Caitlyn prided herself on being a "spoiled bitch," and had once owned a T-shirt that said so in sequins. Catherine wondered what Caitlyn would think of a man who had a T-shirt that said, "Overbearing Ass." It became clear that they'd both lost romantic interest in their husbands after a year or so, and, as Caitlyn put it, "stopped acting like a little concubine or something." So the husbands had moved on, and found somebody else. Caitlyn had made up a story about how men were selfish and went after every new woman.

Catherine didn't know if that story ever happened or not. Probably it did. But it had never happened to anyone she knew. The woman had simply turned off the affection like a water faucet. Then she devoted herself to the house, though she didn't clean or maintain it; the children, though she saw them for only a couple of hours a day;

her friends; and her activities. Sometimes there was an enterprise of some kind, an almost-business the women conducted, but usually not. They didn't give much thought anymore to their husbands, so their husbands were "lost."

Catherine didn't worry about Megan or Caitlyn. They would find more husbands. They had already learned that it was possible to make a lot of money in a divorce, and the quicker the divorce came after the wedding, the easier the money. If the dissolution of the marriage came really fast, there was almost no emotional investment lost, and their assets—smooth skin, thick hair, a good figure—sustained little depreciation.

Catherine took the check. There were a couple of feeble murmurs that started as a mild protest, then shaded into unenthusiastic thanks. She had done it because she had heard things in the conversation that she'd recognized as signs of money trouble. She too had once used Caitlyn's "I'm too busy to take a job." It meant she couldn't find one. And Megan's "My ex-husband is late with the check" meant more than late. Catherine didn't care anymore, and so she didn't begrudge them their lies.

In her profession, she had heard a lot of excuses like those. There were very few girls who hadn't gotten started because whoever was supposed to be supporting them had stopped.

She went outside with Megan and Caitlyn and exchanged the usual hugs and near-miss kisses that they had traded since freshman year. She was acutely aware of the way the three of them looked on the sunlit sidewalk in front of Ivy at the Shore. As they were at this moment, three young women who were sophisticated, graceful, and just reaching the late peak of their beauty, they would have made a wonderful painting—one head light blond, one strawberry red, one coal black.

As the valet parking attendant brought the little runt of a Mercedes and the other two got in, Catherine waved. As she watched them drive off along Ocean Boulevard she thought how nobody in LA called the place where the land met the ocean "the shore." And then, without consciously turning her thoughts in their direction, she found herself deciding she would never see those two women again. Everything she had ever wanted to know about them she had known before graduation. Now, four years later, they were the same, as they would be forever.

There was no reason to see them again. She handed the valet her parking receipt, and he ran off to get her car. He came back with the sleek black Mercedes S600. She had felt glad she had arrived first so they hadn't seen the car. Because they were Megan and Caitlyn they would always assume she'd arrived on time because she drove an old Nissan or something, and not a car that cost five times what Caitlyn's had. She heard a set of police sirens just as the car stopped and the valet got out and opened the door. She listened, and decided they were moving away.

She drove along Ocean Boulevard toward the end of Montana so she could get back into west LA. It had been a long lunch. It would be after three by the time she got home, and four by the time she was ready to work. She took out her phone and listened to her messages on the speaker.

The first one was an "I can't help thinking about you all the time" call. She recognized the voice. Billy? Bobby? It was that kind of name. He was sweet, and kind of handsome. She would return his call when she got home. There was an "I saw your pictures on Backpage.com, and I thought I'd call and see if we could work out a deal." No, she thought. If you saw the ad, you saw the prices. Nothing to work out. "Hi. It's me, George. I'll call later to make an appointment." George was in his sixties, older than her father. But he was exactly the kind of regular that made girls rich. He was a widower who missed his wife and loved women. The old ones were gentle and patient, much easier on the body, and George gave her big tips.

She drove into the short driveway and waited while the heavy iron gate rose to admit her, then drove in, pressed the button to close it, and swung into her parking space. Catherine stepped to the inner door and went up into the first-floor lobby. There was a thick carpet, so her high heels made no noise. She stepped into the elevator, and went up to her apartment.

When she walked in, she could sense he was in the bedroom, even though he was very quiet. It sounded as though when he'd heard the door open he had stopped to listen to be sure it was Catherine. "Hi," she said, and stepped into the bedroom.

He smiled. "Hi." He had a great smile—boyish and unguarded, and yet there was a sly, knowing look in the big, beautiful eyes that revealed he was a really bad boy. It made her want to jump on him. She stepped toward him and saw he had a gym bag half open on the other side of the bed, and he had folded clothes inside.

"Are you leaving?"

"I think I've taken enough advantage of your hospitality. Thanks, Catherine. Thanks so much for putting up with me."

"And for putting out with you?" She shrugged.

His smile renewed itself. "That too. No, that especially."

She stepped closer. "I forgot to tell you the meter was running. You owe me seventy thousand roses. Just kidding."

"If I had that much, I'd be happy to give it to you," he said. He sat on the bed and put something else into the gym bag.

"Did you find an apartment?"

"I'd never move out for that," he said. "I finally agreed to take that job in Phoenix. I'll be back from time to time on weekends, and the job will end in the late spring."

"Okay," she said. "Sounds fine."

"It gets a little hot for construction around then, and the jobs taper off." He reached down, picked up a nearly empty two-quart plastic bottle of Pepsi, took a drink, and offered it to her.

As she looked at him it was unbearable to imagine the Phoenix sun shining down on a construction site, ruining his unlined, beautiful complexion. She accepted the bottle, took a drink, and handed it back. "Ugh. That's real. I thought it was diet."

He took another deep draft, emptying it; set it down; then went back to packing his gym bag.

She walked into the bathroom and took off her new skirt, then the expensive silk blouse. "Will you send me your phone number and address?"

"Of course. But you've already got my cell number and e-mail. Those will always be good."

While Catherine was in the bathroom he took a roll of duct tape out of his bag and tore off a long strip. He reached in again and pulled out a Beretta M92 pistol. He pushed the muzzle of the pistol into the neck of the big plastic bottle and taped it there. He said, loudly enough for her to hear, "I also plan to see you whenever I can get back for a visit."

"Make sure you call a couple of days ahead. I'd hate to have you come and be too busy to see you." She regretted having said that. It had just been a way to sting him for leaving her.

"I will."

She came out of the bathroom barefoot, dressed in a bra and a thong, passed by him, and stepped to her closet to hang up her lunch clothes.

He stepped close behind her, raised the pistol and the plastic bottle, and pulled the trigger. There was a smothered *pop* sound, not much louder than their voices. The second shot was slightly louder because of the hole in the bottle, but still not enough to worry him. He watched her collapse onto the carpet, then touched her carotid artery. Dead.

He went back to searching the apartment. In-call escorts didn't have time to rush off to the bank every time they accumulated a lot of cash, and they couldn't deposit big sums anyway. At least Catherine couldn't. She had no way to explain to the IRS where she was getting more than two thousand dollars a day. He had found about thirty-five thousand in the apartment while she had been out with her friends today. Predictably, she had hidden it in her bedroom. He wished he could search the rest of the apartment thoroughly, but the moment he had pulled the trigger, he had given up that option. It was already late afternoon, and as he took her purse from the bed and pulled out the cash in her wallet, he could hear her cell phone buzzing.

While he'd searched the apartment he had been cleaning it too. Now he stopped searching and turned to cleaning in earnest. Lately, he had become extremely careful about the way he left a woman. He made certain that there were no fingerprints, hairs, or fibers. There were people in this world who were too dumb to think of all the devices that were able to prove that a person had been somewhere. He always cleaned out the drains—even opening the traps where there were hairs in the pipes. He vacuumed the floors and the furniture, emptied the canister into a trash bag, and took the bag with him. He laundered the sheets, pillowcases, and blankets. None of the women he left had ever given her apartment a more thorough cleaning than he had.

He knelt behind Catherine's body; unclasped the gold chain around her delicate white neck, carefully freeing a couple of strawberry blond hairs from the clasp; then went to her right ankle and unclasped the matching anklet. He put them into his pocket.

He picked up his gym bag, set it on the bed, unwrapped the duct tape from the gun, and removed the bottle. Then he put them into the bag, zipped it shut, and went to the bedroom door. He looked back once. It was a shame. She was so much more beautiful than she knew, and so kind. He picked up his trash bag, went out to the hall door, stopped there and listened, then opened it a crack and looked out to be sure the hall was clear. He locked the door and walked out the front entrance toward his car.

Once he was on the road, he felt confident. He knew that if the cops found a man's hair, prints, or clothing fiber in Catherine Hamilton's room, they wouldn't know what to do with it. There were probably forty guys a week leaving physical traces of themselves in that apartment, and none of them had any lasting relationship with her.

She had been very pretty, with bright catlike eyes and that strawberry blond hair. She'd had her hair done in a salon that was full of movie actresses who were still perfect specimens and hadn't gotten famous enough to have the hairdressers go to their houses yet. She had fitted in. She was one of those girls who had started taking money for sex because it was so easy that one night the temptation had just pulled her in. She never took drugs or even drank, so that wasn't even a small part of her decision. She had gone to college, and she was smart.

She had been seduced by arithmetic. If she had been a lawyer, she could have charged clients about four hundred an hour, and given back two hundred and fifty on office rent, taxes, secretaries, and student loans. Instead she charged three hundred an hour, and about once a month she'd buy some new thongs and thigh-high stockings. She'd told him once she liked men well enough close-up, so the job hadn't been a huge chore.

Selling sex was a profession that put girls in a position to control men—promising, teasing, coaxing. It made some girls jump to conclusions. Because they could manipulate men so easily, they imagined they must be smarter or stronger. A lot of them died of that. Catherine had been wiser. She had lived within the bounds of reality, not getting overconfident or foolhardy, and not taking anything for granted.

Her only problem was that she had run into him. She had liked him and let him sleep in her apartment for a few weeks while he was in Los Angeles doing a job. He had told her that when the job was done he would move on. He hadn't told her that the nature of his job made it necessary that when he moved on he would have to kill her.

As he got on the eastbound freeway he accelerated rapidly and changed lanes to place his car behind one truck and in front of the next. In a minute, by gauging the speeds of the other cars on the freeway and inserting his between two of them to his left, he found the perfect speed in the perfect lane and relaxed. He did not think of Catherine again. She was gone.

2

Jack Till knew the essential skill was to exert total control over his hands. He held the pistol steady and breathed evenly while he kept the sights lined up and even across the top. At the end of an exhalation he pulled the trigger. The Glock had a long trigger pull, and he knew there was going to be a bang and the gun would jump a little, but he had to pretend he didn't know that—make his mind think past the jump while he completed the squeeze. There was a *Bang!* And then there was the ring of the brass casing that was ejected onto the concrete floor to the right.

It was hard to see a nine-millimeter hole in the paper at this distance. If what you were shooting at was a man, you knew right away. When the bullet hit his body anywhere, it was really bad news for him—about the worst news the body ever got—and it showed. The man went down and became immobile, and there was still a shooter with some more rounds just like the first one in his magazine, and his hands were settling the front sight between the two rear ones right within the outline of the body again. *Bang!* Till got the round off into the center of the target again, but there was definitely barrel drift to the right.

There was no need to adjust his aim. It was his trigger pull tugging the gun to the right. He had to concentrate on bringing the trigger all the way back without letting the sights move. *Bang!* Then the jangle of brass.

As Till went through the next six rounds he knew he had solved the problem, because the pattern of holes in the ten circle in the center was dense enough to show daylight. *Bang!* That was the last round, so he released the empty magazine and set it and the pistol on the counter in front of him. He took off the ear protectors, then reached up and pressed the button, and the target skittered toward him on the wire and stopped. He had carved the center out pretty well, with only the one hit a half inch to the right of the bull's-eye. Gunfights were hardly ever at twenty-five yards. They tended to be close-in and sloppy. Nonetheless, bad habits had to be strangled the day they appeared.

Till supposed he needed some time on a combat range, walking through an unfamiliar course to keep his skills sharp. Most people didn't identify visual cues quickly enough or open fire early enough, so it didn't matter what they might have hit if they had fired. He would try to get around to a combat range soon. Right now he had an appointment.

He packed the Glock, the earphones, and the spare magazines into his aluminum case; locked it; opened the door; and left the range. He put the case into his trunk and drove.

The thing about gunfights was that they were all motion. Nobody just stood there like a dueler. A shooter's eyes and ears were distracted by bangs, shouts, and muzzle flashes. There seemed to be no time, no place to hide, no incentive to stick his head up into all that flying metal long enough to aim and fire. The mind had to insist that he had to do it if he wanted to be the one who went home.

Jack Till parked his car in the municipal lot behind his office and took the aluminum case with him. He didn't want to face even the minuscule chance that somebody would pick today to pop his trunk when it was full of guns and ammunition. He walked around the block to the doorway at the front of the building between the jewelry store and the dentist's office and climbed the stairs to the second-floor hallway. His office was the one just at the top of the stairs, and on the door was a sign, TILL INVESTIGATIONS. He put away his gun case, sat at his desk, and looked at his watch.

He still had a few minutes to kill before the potential clients arrived for their appointment. He wished he didn't feel nervous about this. He knew that they were the parents of a girl named Catherine Hamilton who had been murdered. That meant they probably wanted him to accomplish something the whole police force couldn't. He needed money right now, and the only way to get it was to get a case, but he had to reserve the right to refuse.

He heard them walking up the stairs, the woman's high heels making a sharp sound on the wooden stairs while the husband's leather soles went *shuff,* as each one slid onto the next step. He stood and opened the door. The husband was much shorter than Jack Till's six feet three. He was in his early sixties, barrel-chested, with bristly white hair and a lined face. His wife seemed about ten years younger, with light reddish hair and white skin. They both had the look of people who had been mourning for a month or two and were beginning to sense that the pain would never decrease.

Till said, "I'm Jack Till." He shook Hamilton's hand, then accepted Mrs. Hamilton's and gave it a gentle shake, then sat down behind his desk. The Hamiltons took the two empty chairs in front of it, and told him the story he had expected to hear.

Many times in his life Jack Till had sat across a table from a person who had lost someone to a crime. The experience was always a proof of the inability of speech to comfort anybody and the inadequacy of any attempt by human beings to institute a decent civilization. "I'm sorry for your terrible loss," he said. He had said the words hundreds of times when he was a younger man with a gold badge. He had always meant it.

He was sorry. He felt all of it—the way the death of a beautiful daughter would turn a family to stone, leave all of the survivors wishing they had died too, and make them unable to develop or even change after that. He could feel all the memories cut off at the instant when they'd heard she had died, sealed off as though behind glass. And he knew much more than they did about parts of it. For the first few hundred times, he had gone to the scene and seen the body and the mess, and smelled the coppery smell of all that blood. And as though he could ever forget, he had been duly provided with a full set of color photographs of the body as it lay there, and the whole of the place where it had happened.

He had often been the one to arrest the person who had brandished the gun or surreptitiously held the unseen, often unimagined, knife. And he had heard all the excuses—and the confession and the recanting of it. He was always sorry. And then he had stopped. He had been a Detective 3 in Los Angeles for twenty-three years when he filed for retirement. He had become a private investigator, partly because he never wanted to look across a table again and see the same kind of faces shocked by the cruelty and unfairness of violent death.

"Mr. Hamilton," he said. "I have been a police officer, but that was long ago. I'm only a private investigator now. Almost all of my work is gathering evidence for civil cases."

"Please," said Hamilton. "I'm not under the delusion that you'll suddenly sign up again and fix this. I'd like some advice. Just advice."

"I think your best bet is to try to work with the detectives on the case. Try to make lists of her contacts, her acquaintances. If there's a Facebook page, an address book, the detectives will talk to everybody, and they'll try to develop leads. Finding the perpetrator will do nothing for your grief. But it will make you feel you may have saved someone else from going through this."

"We've already met with the detectives. They were very open about the way things were going to work. Our daughter Catherine was a professional escort, I believe that was the word they used. That means she had a variety of false names. She moved from city to city. She met and made herself vulnerable to many men, all strangers. The police have done four weeks of it. They've spoken with a few other girls. They've got the coroner's report on how she died. They've examined her bank records, credit card bills, and so on. They're done. It was a robbery. She was shot."

"How did she get involved in that work?"

"We don't really know. She graduated from college and got a job. She was very busy, didn't come home much at first, and less after that. She never answered her phone so we got used to leaving messages. We had no idea she was doing this."

"Do you think she might have been forced into it?"

Her mother spoke for the first time. "No. She was capable of calling the police. And she wasn't the kind of kid to be vulnerable to coercion. She knew she had rights, and that there was plenty of help if she needed it."

"What about drugs?"

The father said, "We don't think that was it either. She didn't take drugs in high school. She was an athlete—a gymnast—and they got tested before competitions and at random. She wasn't with that kind of crowd in college. The coroner didn't find any drugs in her system. And he went out of his way to say she looked healthy and well cared-for. No marks, nothing."

"These are the wrong questions," said Mrs. Hamilton. Till could see that she had reached the point of madness. She had listened carefully and answered thoughtfully, but had heard nothing that mattered.

Her husband put his arm around her shoulders and tightened it, as though he were trying to hold a bundle of sticks together. "I'm sorry, Mr. Till. We know those are the usual things. Judy is just . . . getting worn down."

Till moved so he was facing Mrs. Hamilton. "What are the right questions?"

"There are no obvious reasons why anybody would kill her. She wasn't working for a pimp. She was independent. She didn't do drugs, didn't have debts. The coroner says she wasn't sexually assaulted, although she'd probably had sex within a few hours before she died. Look, we know this is awful. Nobody wants to think about it. Everything you learn about it is tawdry and degrading. There is no question at all that for at least the past year, Catherine was providing sex for money. But that doesn't mean it was okay to kill her. I could see the detectives exchanging looks. I could read their minds. 'This woman's daughter was having sex with men who saw her Web site and called her up. What did she expect?' It's all true. Everybody knows it's a risky activity. And it's illegal. But this was a young woman. She was twenty-six years old. She never in her life hurt anybody. But now she's dead. And the police act like she's not human. It's like somebody's scrawny old cat ran away and died. They feel some kind of sympathy for us, and I see it. But the truth is, our daughter's death wasn't a big deal. She should have known better. We should have taught her better." She shrugged. "They're right. Catherine made a mistake. Our family is broken and destroyed."

"The police officers I know don't automatically dismiss the murder of anyone," said Till. "The questions can be insensitive. But I know they'll try hard to find the killer."

"Well, unless some new leads come up, they're finished," said Mr. Hamilton. "So I thought we'd try to develop new leads. We have a list of private detectives who have at one time or other taken cold murder cases and brought them to a satisfactory conclusion. I wonder if you could take a look at it." He held out a single sheet of paper.

Till took it, and looked down the list of names. He ignored his own name, which was on the top. "Yes, I know this one. And this one. And . . . no, not this one."

Hamilton looked at the name he was pointing at. "You mean you don't know him, or wouldn't hire him?"

"Wouldn't hire him," Till said. "He was removed from the police department for cause. I don't imagine he's improved much on his own."

"Which one of these investigators is the best?"

"It's not as simple as that," Till said. "No matter how good he is, this kind of case is very difficult to solve. It's also extremely expensive to pursue, and I'd be dishonest if I didn't say this too. Even if he succeeds, it's not going to make you feel better."

"We're aware of the expense. We accept the futility of it. We're going to do this," said Mrs. Hamilton. "It's a direct question, and we're relying on your honesty. Which one is the best?"

"I am."

"That's what we heard," said Mr. Hamilton. He reached into his coat pocket and produced a check. "Here's a hundred thousand dollars. And here's my card. When you run out of money, call for more."

"Please," said Mrs. Hamilton.

Till sighed. "I'll need all the information about her you can give me—pictures, social security number, bank records, anything that will help me trace her movements over the past couple of years."

Mrs. Hamilton opened her oversize purse and placed a thick manila envelope on the desk between them. "That's all in here. And a few other things we thought . . . you know. A lot of it is personal, things she said or wrote." She began to cry. "I'm sorry. I just can't help it."

"I understand," he said. "I have a daughter of my own."

3

Jack Till parked around the corner and walked to the house, as usual. He had been a homicide cop for a long time and had put some awful people away. Most of them were long gone; a few had been on death row twenty years or more, and a couple had been executed. But there had been some angry, psychotic men he had made more angry over the years, and he didn't want to risk leading any of them to Holly's house.

Holly was twenty-eight years old already, and she'd been living at the house since she had finished school at eighteen. The house had been the idea of a couple he had not particularly liked. They were very rich, and their money had come from one of the many permutations of the film industry. The town was full of people who supplied some commodity or technical service to the movies, and it sometimes seemed to him that they all acted like directors or stars. But this pair had proposed that the parents of all the kids in the class chip in a monthly fee to keep the house going. They had also been generous enough to buy the house and set up a foundation, then pay more of the upkeep than anybody else. They'd been determined to provide a happy home for their son, Joshua, that had a chance of lasting through his life.

It had been a brilliant scheme. The kids had all been attached to each other from the time their parents had noticed that something was different about them and found their way to the school, so they were like brothers and sisters. And the parents had known that they didn't want to die and leave a child with Down syndrome alone and friendless in the world. He still thought of them as children, although they were adults now. In a few years they'd be middle-aged.

He walked around the block and approached the house from the opposite direction to look for changes in the neighborhood and spot things that looked worrisome. It also gave anyone who had followed him a chance to show himself. It had always been one of his nightmares that he might lead one of the monsters he'd met at work to these sweet, defenseless people, searching for Jack Till's daughter.

He stepped up to the front porch, and heard Leah's voice shout, "Hi, Jack!" through the screen door.

"Hijack?" he said. "Hiya, Leah."

"Hialeah racetrack," she said. It was an old joke between them, but she laughed again because she liked him and wanted to make him feel comfortable. She opened the screen door to let him into the living room. "I'm pretty sure I saw Holly come home from work a few minutes ago. Should I go get her?"

"That would be really nice," Till said. "Thanks."

Leah climbed the stairs to the second floor, and Jack sat down in the living room on the couch. He caught himself looking around the room searching for signs that something was wrong. It was much neater than his apartment, partly because the girls in this house were all tidy people, outnumbered the boys, and showed their scorn when anybody left a mess.

"Hey, Dad."

He looked up and saw Holly coming down the stairs. She was like any other twenty-eight-year-old, walking carefully down the stairs, until a sudden attack of exuberance made her jump from the last step to the floor. She came and wrapped a tight hug around Till.

It was impossible not to feel better when he saw her affection and her happiness. "How's the gumshoe business?" she said.

He grinned. "About the way it always is," he said. "It keeps me from getting lazy and going broke. How's the flower business?"

"It's going pretty well," she said. "Mrs. Carmody and I are happy with the way people are coming in this summer. There aren't any big holidays for flowers after Mother's Day, but we've got a lot of business." She leaned close to him and said confidentially, "Mrs. Carmody says it looks like a lot of men are feeling guilty for cheating on their wives." She laughed happily.

There was also that, he thought. The kids, including his daughter, were unembarrassed by sex, and sometimes seemed to him to have a more mature attitude than he did. It was still sometimes disconcerting. He was unable to hide from himself the fact that Holly and her boyfriend Bill had a sexual relationship, because it had not occurred to her to hide it. At first he'd had to say to himself, "She's over twenty-one. Would this bother me if she was like most people?" The thought made him say, "How's Bill?"

"He's great," she said. "He'll be sorry he missed you. He has to work late tonight restocking the shelves for the Big Summer Blowout Sale."

"Well, I guess that happens. Can't have a Blowout Sale without something to blow out. Give him my regards."

"'Kindest Regards from Jack,'" she said, imitating his voice. "You and I can have dinner alone."

"Fine with me. Want to go to Redratto's?"

"No, I can make Italian food myself. We have it a lot. Can we go to Mo's and get a burger?"

"Sure, if that's what you have a taste for."

"I do. With curly french fries. Where's your car?"

"Around the corner and on the next block. It's a little walk."

"Oh-oh," she said. "You're going on a scary case again."

"You know that from where I parked the car?"

"That and how you're looking around all the time while we walk. You're thinking about somebody watching us while we talk. You're paying attention to the rules again."

"The rules. It's funny," he said. "We used to say that when you were little. You remember that?"

"Of course I do," she said. "You told me the rules a hundred times. Don't open the door just because somebody rings the bell. Don't go out without Maria. Don't tell anybody on the phone that my father isn't home. When you were a cop I would be afraid that things were happening every day like they did on TV. Now it's usually better." She studied him. "So what's up this time?"

"It's the sort of thing I used to do in those days. It's a murder. A young woman about your age got shot in her apartment by a man. The police see it as a robbery. Her parents want to know more."

"That sounds okay for you, but poor them."

"I think it's safe. But I have a feeling this might take me out of town. Will you be okay with that if it happens?"

"Sure. I'm not alone. There are ten of us. And when you're not busy you can call me."

"That's right."

They went to the restaurant and got a booth in the bar. They talked about her job and his, the friends she lived with in the house, what a good thing an occasional helping of french fries was. She had the most lively, engaging blue eyes.

He thought about Holly's mother, Linda. The Tills had been twenty-one and twenty-two when Holly was born. The doctors hadn't seen any reason for Linda to have amnio. That was recommended for women in their late thirties. When she'd learned that her child had Down syndrome, she had fallen apart. She had simply been unable to cope with it, to accept the amendment to her vision of what her life should be. She had not accepted it. She had filed for divorce, granted him full custody of Holly, and never come back. In the first years there had been a hundred thousand times when he had blamed her, resented her, or felt contempt for her for bailing out. But in recent years he'd felt a little sorry for her. As he'd gotten older he had realized that she'd probably felt horrible for a brief part of every day. And she'd never gotten to know the person Holly had become.

He took her home, walked into the communal living room, and saw that dinner had just ended. "Come on, Jason," one of the girls said. "It's your turn."

"We can do the dishes later," Jason said. "I just want to see this."

There was a Dodgers game in its eighth inning, and Jason looked as though he were taking a lead off first base. He was sideways, halfway between the television set and the kitchen, his eyes still on the game.

"I'll do it this time if you do it tomorrow," Holly said. "You don't mind, do you, Dad?"

"No," he said. He leaned over and kissed her cheek. "It's a nice thing to do. Talk to you soon."

"Thanks, Holly," said Jason.

Jack Till went out the front door to the porch. He pretended to stop and look at his cell phone's screen, but used the moment of immobility to study the block, searching for men in cars that were parked or moving slowly, any sign of someone watching from a window, or anything that seemed to have changed since last week. There was nothing, so he went down the steps and walked briskly around the corner to his car.

4

Jack Till sat in his apartment, opened his laptop, went online, and looked at the ads for escorts. He studied the ads until he had some familiarity with the services offered and a sense of the prices and the vocabulary. He'd found that his sense of how the business worked dated back to his time as a police officer, so it seemed a generation out of date. When he had last worked on a homicide that had to do with prostitution it had been a world of pimps and madams.

He was ready to look at the material Mr. and Mrs. Hamilton had given him. He opened the thick manila envelope. There were family photographs of Catherine as an athlete—taking a credible starting dive at a swim meet, jumping high in a soccer game to head the ball toward the net. He could tell it was Catherine because of the slightly curly strawberry blond hair. She reminded him of a Pre-Raphaelite painting. And there was her graduation picture from UCLA.

The parents had not been able—never were able—to cull the information they gave Till to keep it relevant. They had probably wanted to include her grades, but had resisted the impulse. They wanted to demonstrate to him that their daughter's life had been valuable.

In a folder inside the envelope, isolated from the material that reflected her real life, was the information that probably mattered—about the life of Tamara Saunders. Tamara was the name Catherine had used. She was five feet eight and weighed 119 pounds. Her skin was very white and, on her shoulders and forearms, freckled. There had to be freckles like Catherine's on Tamara's nose and forehead, but nobody would have known, because Tamara always wore makeup that made her skin look as clear and unmarked as porcelain. Her eyes were hazel, and big. She seemed to appear miraculously each day at four p.m., and continued to exist until around three a.m., when she turned off her telephone and pushed the last client out the door.

His reading of the ads persuaded him that she'd had at least some notion of the danger her work put her in. She said she was available for in-calls only until she got to know a client, and that she did subject clients to "moderate screening." That was unexpected good news. If she had kept some record of the ones she had cleared and agreed to see, the rest of his search would be simpler. He hadn't heard or read anything that appeared to be her notes, but maybe the police had kept them. The more the police knew, the more they kept to themselves. Making a great case in the newspapers would only persuade the killer to run farther and hide deeper.

He looked at more of the material but found no other reference to screening. He stared at the ads again, and then he noticed the necklace. It was a thin gold chain with a gold oval disk at the end; the disk had a row of small diamonds along the rim, and a bigger diamond off-center near the middle. There was a matching ankle bracelet around her left ankle. The smaller diamonds appeared to be about a quarter carat each, so the set would have cost at least a couple of thousand dollars, and possibly much more.

He looked at a list that the Hamiltons had received—the items the police were holding. No jewelry. The necklace and anklet must have been stolen. He looked at the list again. No cash was found in her apartment. He thought about the life of an escort. How likely was it that the killer had just come in pretending to be a customer, looked around, and found all of her jewelry and cash? It didn't seem likely at all. Jack Till put on a black sport coat, slipped a .380 pistol into the pocket, and went outside to his car.

Patrolman Gene Trinicum drove up to the front of his one-story ranch-style house in Simi Valley at four-thirty a.m. He was tired and felt a little bit sick to his stomach from the stale coffee he'd had to keep drinking for hours to stay awake. He'd also had to wrestle with a drunk to get him into the car at two-thirty, and he still felt bone-tired from having all that adrenaline coursing through his bloodstream and the muscle strain from lifting the guy and overpowering his arms while his partner handcuffed him.

He opened his garage door with the remote and drove in, then closed it behind him and got out of the car. He hadn't seen the man standing beside the door, and even as he jumped backward in surprise, he wondered how this could be happening.

"Hold it," said Till. "Don't move."

"You've made a big mistake. I'm a police officer."

Till said, "Stay calm. I haven't done anything to you yet, Gene. I came here so I could talk to you alone without getting you fired."

"Who are you?"

"My name is Jack Till. I was a homicide detective three when you were in elementary school."

Trinicum looked at him, and for the first time made out in the dim light that Till had a gun in his hand.

Till said, "All I want from you is an honest answer to a couple of questions, and then I'll go away."

"Ask."

"Do you remember a homicide from a month ago where a young working girl got shot in an apartment in Encino? Her name was Catherine Hamilton."

"Yes."

"You and your partner were the first to respond to the scene. Right?"

"Right."

"Any paramedics or anybody get there first?"

"No. Some friend of hers got worried, and called nine-one-one. It was a girl's voice on the recording, but she wouldn't identify herself. Probably another hooker. So we went, the manager let us into her apartment, and there she was."

"Here's where we get to the tricky part. I'm asking because I need to know about the guy who killed her—how he does things, what he's got. If you tell me the truth in confidence, it will never get reported. How much money was in her apartment when you got there?"

"It's in the report from the detectives who did the search. I think they said three or four hundred. It's not my case, so I don't have the exact number."

Till said quietly, "I really want to go away now and leave you alone. So tell me what I need and let me."

"What?"

"You know and I know. The detectives on the case might suspect, but they'll leave you alone unless . . ."

"Unless?"

"To make it clear, I was a really good homicide detective, and people remember me. There are guys with stars on their collars who owe me their lives. If I ask them to, they'll toss your house, freeze your bank accounts, examine every deposit and expenditure you've made, and dig up your yard until they find it. And then I'll count it myself. Or you can give me an honest number right now. When you got there, how much cash was in that apartment?"

"How do I know you're not wearing a wire?"

Till moved so quickly that Trinicum was on his back with Till's forearm across his throat before he could tell that anything was coming.

Till said, "You know I'm not wearing a wire because if I am I just made a recording of myself dropping you on a concrete floor and getting ready to crush your trachea. Good enough?" He let up a bit on the pressure on Trinicum's throat.

Trinicum nodded, and Till rose and let him sit up. "There was just under thirteen thousand. My partner and I split it."

"Where was it hidden?"

"In the freezer, in a fake frozen food package. Some civilians might miss it, but we see the latest-model hiding containers every time we bust a house for drugs. We were working on a clock because there was a nine-one-one call, then the call from dispatch, and maybe two minutes after the landlord left, to search. After that I had to call in the body, and the homicide guys would come."

"Good enough. Did it look as though the killer had found any money?"

"Yeah. There were some other little stashes in the bedroom, and they were all empty—a couple of hollowed-out books, a couple of empty boxes in the backs of dresser drawers. She probably had another forty or so."

"Here's the last question. Was there any jewelry?"

"We didn't have time to check, and we wouldn't have kept it anyway."

"There wasn't any on the list of belongings the parents got."

"I really don't know. We weren't going to take anything we had to bring to a pawnshop."

"Drugs?"

"None."

"You're sure? It's happened before—cops, EMTs, firemen," Till said.

"I've heard of that too. The reason I heard is they got caught."

Till said, "I'm done. I'll keep everything you told me to myself. If you suddenly remember something I might want to know, give me a call." He put a card in Trinicum's breast pocket.

"Why would I do that?"

"I figure you'll look at the card and ask around about me. People will tell you that you can trust me."

5

Till dialed the phone in his office and looked out on Ventura Boulevard while he waited. Sometimes this part of LA reminded him of a children's book he used to read with Holly, about "Busytown." There were always a million things happening on each page—cars, trucks, airplanes, bikes, heavy machinery. The phone line came alive. "Vice, Sergeant McCann."

"Hi, Ted. This is Jack Till."

"Hey, Jack. It's good to hear your voice. How are things going?"

"My daughter says, 'How are things in the gumshoe business?' She's a believer in plain talk."

"How is she, anyway?"

"Just great. I'll tell you why I'm calling. I just took on the case of a young woman who was an escort. She was killed in an apartment in Encino."

"Catherine Hamilton. I suppose her parents are getting desperate." He paused. "No offense. You know what I mean."

"It's pretty accurate. Nobody pays for a private investigator until they're desperate. I'm starting to look at the paperwork, and something occurred to me. Is this part of an epidemic or something? Have there been other girls in that line of work who have been shot and robbed lately?"

"No," said McCann. "Not here."

"Somewhere else?"

"Well, yeah. There have been a few over the past year or two in other cities that seem a lot like what happened to her. It's been in the NCIC. I think the way you do. When there's a crime like this, I try to figure out how to get a handle on it. I look to see if there's some kind of a pattern. We're not Homicide, of course."

"I get the hint," said Till. "I just don't know anything about the two Homicide guys who are handling this case—Anthony and Sellers. I don't want to step on any toes or bruise any egos. The parents seem to think they've done everything they can, but it wasn't much, and I knew you'd know what was going on."

"I'll tell you what. I'll e-mail you what I've got on those murders. There are five of them, all young and pretty, all killed in their residences in different cities."

"Not streetwalkers?"

"No. All independent, mostly in-call."

"Thanks, Ted. I'll be watching for it. I'm still walking in a circle around this. Catherine's parents were here yesterday. Anything that I can learn about the landscape is likely to help."

"Just let me know if there's anything useful."

"I will."

"Like if you find Jack the Ripper is now living in the Valley, I'll be the first one you call."

"You will."

Till sat in front of his laptop in his office on the second floor of the building on Ventura. He had once thought he would have a partner in this business, and he'd seen a used desk that was cheap and matched the first one, so he'd bought it. There never was a partner, but the second desk was a good one for the computer because there was no window behind it.

The advertisements on the Web sites were mannered, a testament to the way human beings saw and stole things they liked. The girls were all "hot," even "hotties." One asked, "Is there anything I can help you with?" So fifty others said that too. Generally the women referred to themselves as "providers" when they needed a word. It was a draw to say, "New" or "New in Town" or "Last Day in LA."

The Asian women all wrote about health. They wanted to get rid of the harmful stress for men who worked too hard. They would "re-life" a customer if he gave them a chance. Black women liked jokes and puns. Most of the women included disclaimers to ward off the police: "By calling me, you guarantee that you are not a law enforcement official." When they named a price, it was either in "roses" or in some idiosyncratic version—lilies, diamonds, hugs, kisses. Many weren't good spellers.

There were apparently regulations on the site about what the photographs could show, but almost all the women appeared to have been eager to show everything. Many of them had been photographed in the same studios. Others posted snapshots taken in their own apartments. Just as many were shot with a cell phone by the girl herself in a bathroom or bedroom mirror.

He was taken aback by the range of ages and races and body types. But his biggest impression was that the high-end girls were beautiful. In Los Angeles for two hundred dollars an hour a man could have a twenty-two-year-old who looked like a movie star, and wanted to do things most married women wouldn't. Or maybe they all would, but their husbands didn't ask them to.

Two hundred dollars wasn't very much money for risking disease, being naked and alone with scary strangers, and maybe being arrested. There were a very few who charged three hundred an hour, or five hundred. They tended to be stunningly beautiful, were typically about twenty-six, and claimed to know arts and sciences that couldn't even be comprehensibly alluded to in an ad.

The variety of looks astonished him. There were blonds with blue eyes, Hawaiians, Russians, English, and Australians. There were girls from the Caribbean and from every South American or African country. There were Canadians. There were Chinese, Japanese, German, Italian, Irish, and every possible combination, all described with the frankness of an animal's pedigree and raised in the United States or elsewhere. All of them promised pampering, treating a customer "like the king he is."

Till sensed that enough time had passed for him to expect the information McCann had promised to send. He went to his e-mails. The first one said simply, "This is something you might want to look into." It had several attachments. Till downloaded them, plugged in his printer, and printed all of them before he came back to look at them. Printing without looking was a way of signifying to the universe that he wasn't rejecting any information at this stage.

There were five ads that could have come from the collection he had been viewing. The five were so similar that they could have been posted by the same person. One was from Miami, the others from New York, Minneapolis, Charlotte, and Washington. Always there were one to four photographs of a girl arranged along the right side of the ad. There would be one with a flirtatious expression, with breasts partially showing, one lounging on a bed or chair in lingerie, and one on knees and elbows facing away from the camera.

Judging by price, age, and looks, the women were all at the upper end of their profession. They all said they were "independent providers" or just independent. Some added, "No agency, no driver, no bodyguard," or "I come alone." Reading the words and knowing that these girls were all dead gave him a sick feeling. They had advertised that they were defenseless. He knew that pimps and bodyguards made customers uncomfortable enough to choose another girl, but these girls were dead.

His mind began generating unwelcome scenarios that would account for these five murders. It was too early to make guesses, and he hadn't even read what McCann had sent him with the ads, but he couldn't help running through the possibilities. The girls looked very similar. Maybe this guy had a fixation on fair-skinned strawberry blonds—either hatred or unrequited love. Maybe he was one of the thousand other kinds of nutcase—the ones who heard voices telling them to do bad things, the ones who killed one girl and then got hooked on the rush. This could even be a series of hits, done because all of the girls fit the description of somebody in particular. And whenever prostitutes were killed, there was always the chance it was a religious compulsion to punish temptresses.

He went through the brief dossiers McCann had compiled about each of the women, looking at everything he had included. Each of them had been shot. Till laid the dossiers out side by side. Each had been shot twice. The second shot was always in the head. Each had been an active solicitor, available for at least some period of each day. Each asked for more money than the average escort in her city. Each had been pretty enough in his opinion to be very popular. Till gathered from their surnames and brief résumés that they were of Irish, English, German, or Scandinavian descent. But visually they could all just as easily be grouped with the girls brought in from the Ukraine, Poland, Belarus, or Russia.

He couldn't ignore what their resemblance suggested. Many of the Eastern European girls had been brought into the country by Russian gangsters. As a group, these men hadn't mellowed much since they had first appeared in the 1990s. The few he had met professionally would not have hesitated to kill the competition to increase profits. They usually made an agreement with a girl while she was still in Europe: she would work for two years to pay for being brought here with the proper papers. But at times, the agreement came as a surprise after the girl was here. Either way, the gangsters tried to get as much money out of a girl as possible, because in two short years she would be free.

Till kept the idea in mind, but concentrated on the dossiers. He was puzzled by the fact that each advertisement looked so similar to the others, even though the girls had been killed in different cities.

He finished reading about all of the girls' cases, then drove to the gym up the street. During the day a lot of executives would come in for a half hour or so, but it was empty after business hours. He kept himself lean and toned at all times, but now that he was about to go after a killer, the habit was raised to a level of urgency.

For the next two weeks he trained like an athlete, working for four hours a day lifting weights; working the heavy bag; running on a treadmill; and doing martial arts kamais, practicing set series of blows and kicks until he could do them without thinking. Each day he drove to a firing range in Burbank to keep his shooting skills as perfectly tuned as possible. Now, while he was preparing himself, he thought about the opponent.

He was persuaded that the five girls had all been killed by one man. There had been five strawberry blonds killed this way, but no girl of any other description. He had double-checked with Ted McCann, and all of the other murdered escorts he could find on the NCIC lists were killed in very different ways, usually with more battering and physical abuse. Streetwalkers disappeared and then were found in ditches or empty lots or Dumpsters. Others were beaten or stabbed by pimps. There were a few robberies, mainly on the street late at night, and two drive-by shootings.

Till followed the logic of the killings to learn about the killer. The man killed only girls who looked like Catherine Hamilton. He never killed two in one city. After a killing there was a lull, maybe two to six months. If Till assumed the man was doing it out of some psychological need, then the doses of adrenaline were very irregular. They weren't growing more frequent. If he assumed the man was not crazy, what was he killing for?

Since he always killed only one girl in each city, maybe after each murder he moved on to a new city. Till charted the dates of death and the cities. If the man killed and moved on, then he was not now in any of the five cities where these girls had been murdered. Till made a list of other major cities, then turned on his computer, went on Backpage. com and began to check the ads for his list of cities. He began with Denver. It took hours to look at every ad. Then he went on to Chicago.

He could feel the hopelessness that the police had expressed to the Hamiltons. There were thousands of ads, and he wasn't even sure what he was looking for, but his mind noted everything. He printed the ads of the girls who bore a close resemblance to the five murdered strawberry blonds. He looked at the furniture and wallpaper behind the girls in their photographs, the wording of their ads, the prices, the locations.

There were patterns, but they were all of unknown value. There were parts of each city that housed a great many escorts. There were boundaries and patterns of movement that were as complicated and invisible as the paths of cats. Some did in-calls at an address near the local airport and out-calls to hotels. Others staked out clusters of nearby districts—some wealthy and others not. Some of the patterns were obvious and predictable. Latinas often worked out of Hispanic neighborhoods. The Asians, nearly all of whom said they had just arrived from Japan, China, or Korea, often worked in large massage parlors, probably because their English and urban survival skills weren't yet good enough to allow them to work alone. In every category there were girls who said they were nineteen or twenty but looked thirteen or fourteen. There were girls who said they were eighteen but looked thirty. A woman who said she was forty might easily be sixty.

The sex marketplace was huge and chaotic. The girls used many aliases—some ridiculous, some sweet, some crudely obscene. They often posted multiple ads on the same site with different sets of photographs, as though they were doing market research to see what appealed most to their customers. On every site were many ads that offered "specials" that were very cheap for various reasons—because it was Tuesday, or to celebrate a girl's return to town, her birthday, or the nearest holiday that was coming or had passed.

As Till read, his familiarity with what prostitution was like was brought up to date. There were sites where customers posted reviews of each girl and commented on which acts they performed for their advertised fees, and whether they were cheerful, were polite, and gave fair value. He looked up the five girls and Catherine Hamilton on some of the sites, and found the reviews were still posted, even a year after some of them were dead. They were all highly rated. Could the killer have chosen his victims from these rating services? The company claimed to have no way to identify its customers.

Finally, after weeks of staring at the computer screen for many hours a day, trying to follow every lead, Till found a girl who caused chills to move down the back of his neck.

She said her name was Kyra. She had straight strawberry blond hair that hung down to the center of her back, and showed redder against her paper-white skin. The ad showed her standing in profile, giving a flirtatious sidelong glance at the camera; lying on a bed; and sitting in a chair, wearing a lace bra, staring forthrightly into the camera. She was wearing Catherine Hamilton's necklace.

6

Till went to his apartment and began to pack. He selected two .45-caliber Glock 21 pistols, each with two spare fourteen-round magazines, and a thin razor-sharp folding knife with a blue-black blade. His clothes were the same as always—a black summer-weight blazer and a navy blue one, some wrinkle-free blue oxford shirts, a pair of gray wool pants and some khaki ones, two pairs of leather shoes with thick rubber soles. Anything else he needed he could buy anywhere.

He brought his laptop computer, his phone, and a night vision scope. The last item was a packet containing five thousand dollars in cash and four credit cards that he used only for business. He looked around the apartment to be sure he hadn't forgotten to put something in his suitcase.

He'd had a house in the Valley once, when Holly was small. The yard had given her a place to play, and he had believed it made her feel secure. He had kept it until a few months after Holly had moved into the group house with her friends, and then it had seemed empty and sad, so he'd sold it. When he'd been paid for it he remembered that he had originally saved the money for the down payment because his wife had wanted a place to live and raise children and grow old. He supposed the life everyone lived was a life nobody had foreseen.

Till had invested the money from the sale of the house so Holly would have enough to keep paying for her upkeep after he was gone. He was perfectly comfortable living in his apartment a few blocks from his office. He took a last look around, set the silent alarm, turned off the lights, and closed the door.

He put his suitcase in the trunk of his working car, which was a gray Acura with tinted windows. He had made a few minor modifications, notably a quarter-inch steel plate in the two front door panels. He also kept in the trunk a .308 rifle with a ten-power scope and a twelve-gauge shotgun in a case covered by a second piece of carpet that looked like the one covering the spare tire.

He got into his car, drove out of the parking garage beneath his apartment building, and headed east on Interstate 10. He had no idea how long he might be away, but he had gone off on hunts a few times before.

Till still knew very little about Catherine Hamilton's killer. This killer was drawn, for some reason, to women who looked like her. It was not a completely unfamiliar pattern for certain types of psychotics, and it wasn't incompatible with a different aberration, the habit of preying on solitary, defenseless women. But it had occurred to Till that this man might be a thief trying to give the impression that he was a psychosexual maniac.

Maniacs weren't likely to commit robbery-murders and then give the next woman jewelry stolen from the last. The jewelry meant the killer was making romantic overtures toward these women. If he was doing that, then he wasn't like the usual psycho. Seduction wasn't part of the nightmare fantasy that these men carried in their heads.

Till had been hunting killers for a long time, and he had learned patience. People didn't understand patience. It was very close to humility. It was the capacity to admit to himself that he didn't know enough to act yet. He was prepared to travel and wait and watch and listen, possibly for a long time, before he made a move.

Till had an instinctive sense that this man was something he hadn't seen before. He seemed to be trying to make his killings look like what the cops expected to see, and this suggested to Till that they were something else. If he was a simple armed robber or a psycho, there was no easy way the necklace and ankle bracelet would have ended up on another nearly identical working girl. The man was doing the same thing over and over, but Till didn't recognize it. He was eager to get to Phoenix and get a look at this new girl.

As he drove toward the east the weather was clear and the traffic was moving fast, so he knew he would make the trip in about six hours. He took Interstate 10 all the way, through dry, hot desert with small prickly pear cactus and colored dust. He liked the landscape. It was immense. The eye focused on sights forty miles away and then the hands steered toward them, and there was a restful, unsurprised feeling that helped him to think clearly.

The killer would be young, and he must be handsome. He had somehow managed to ingratiate himself with five very pretty escorts. The way to do that was with money, and he seemed to have used some of that. He had robbed each girl and killed her and probably used her money to win over the next one. But he had shot all of them from the back. They hadn't been on their beds; they had been on their feet doing some mundane domestic activity. One had been reading a magazine with her iPod earphones on her ears, and the others were changing or vacuuming or something. The one in Miami had been cooking what the police thought was a dinner for two people. Was this killer a pimp?

He couldn't be. None of the police forces in any of the six cities had detected any evidence of anyone acting in that capacity. Nobody had arranged the dates or driven the girls to them, and certainly nobody had protected the girls. All of them claimed to be independent, and no contradictory tips had come from anyone—customers, friends, or competitors.

Till's cogitations always returned to the same few issues. What did this man want? He could have killed and robbed any of these women the first time he saw their ads. Why did he always choose girls who looked alike? Did he become a regular customer of one of these girls and later dissolve into a stew of remorse and shame, then kill her in rage? If so, why was he so efficient and practical? He popped each girl once in the back to take her down, and then shot her one time in the head. Crazy remorseful killers didn't rob their victims, either.

He drove on through the desert, bringing back details from the files and trying to use them to build a coherent theory about this man. Till had come to know many killers over the years, but this one didn't seem to be like any of the others. In spite of all of the folklore about senseless killings and wild irrational behavior, most killers were fairly easy to understand if all the facts were known. They got angry, they got jealous, they got greedy. Even the crazy ones were logical. They went to the places where their favorite kinds of victims could be found, watched one of them until she was alone and easy to take, and then took her.

Killers tried afterward to avoid being associated with the crime. Some hid the body, some tried to implicate others, and some cut the body up or sank it in the ocean. All logical. This killer was not.

Till arrived in Phoenix in the afternoon. It wasn't exactly an oasis in the desert. It was more a place where things were brought into the desert and lined up in neat rows—houses, strip malls, even native plants. Till drove to the Biltmore west of Scottsdale, and the impression changed a little. The big hotel was surrounded by gardens and lawns and a golf course, and the greenery supplied a rest for the eye. He liked the Frank Lloyd Wright–inspired design, a construction of individually cast bricks that gave the sprawling buildings the appearance of relics from some lost civilization that the mind couldn't quite identify.

When he arrived he stepped to the front desk at the edge of the cavernous lobby, asked whether a suite was available, and got one. Unless hookers had changed a whole lot since he had last spoken to one, this girl would like that. When he went up to his room he was pleased. The bed and the rest of the furniture were big and dark and solid, and the suite was spacious, with a view of the green lawns, and beyond them the distant rocky hills. He hung up his clothes in the closet and took possession of the place. When he had gotten settled in his suite, he opened his laptop computer, signed into the hotel's wi-fi network, and went down the list of Phoenix escorts to the advertisement he had found at home.

The girl's name was Kyra. She wanted three hundred roses for an hour, five hundred for two hours, or eight hundred for a whole evening. He looked at the photographs. She had exchanged two of the pictures since yesterday for two with better lighting and focus, but she was still wearing the necklace and the anklet in one of them. The ad said she would not respond to text messages or e-mails, and would answer no blocked calls. She began her phone number with *82, because dialing that code would unblock the customer's number for caller ID.

Till called her number on his cell phone and waited. A young woman's voice came on. "Hello. This is Kyra." At first he thought he was listening to a recording because she sounded so professionally cheerful, so he waited for the rest of the recording. Instead, she said, "Come on, honey. Don't be shy."

"I'm sorry," he said. "I thought I was going to be asked to leave a message. My name is Jack. I just got into town an hour ago, and I'm already thinking I could use some company. I saw your online ad."

"What's your last name, Jack?"

"Till. Jack Till."

"Where's home?"

"Los Angeles. I'm here on business, and I'll be around for a couple of days."

"What sort of arrangement were you thinking of?"

"How about this evening? Is your schedule clear for tonight?"

"A full evening? Did you read the whole ad?"

"Yes. I saw the numbers. But you're a very attractive woman, and I find your voice appealing. I thought we could start with a nice dinner, and have a pleasant evening."

"Thank you, Jack. I've got to check my schedule. I'll call you back in a few minutes. Can I reach you then at this number?"

"Sure. I'll be here."

She ended the call, and he wondered if she was checking some list of crazy men and thieves and bad customers to be sure he wasn't among them. If he succeeded in getting to know her, he would ask. A list like that might very well include this killer.

He supposed she would probably run his name through the big search engines. He knew she would find him, and she would turn up a few newspaper articles about his old cases. There were even some photographs of him. He had, for practical reasons, always tried to stay away from cameras. But there were a few shots of him coming up courthouse steps or emerging from a police station, where he hadn't been able to avoid the photographer. If she learned he'd been a cop, she'd also learn he wasn't one now.

The pictures probably wouldn't do him any harm with the girl either. He had regular features, and he was six feet three inches tall, and lean. His habitual dress—a dark sport jacket and oxford shirt with no tie—looked neat and well-fitted, even in the recent pictures.

His cell phone rang. "Till," he said.

"This is Kyra," she said. "I'll be able to see you tonight. Please have the eight hundred in a plain white envelope with the word 'Donation' written on it. I'll want it when I arrive."

"All right. Where and when?"

"Where are you staying?"

"At the Biltmore."

"I can come there if you like."

"That's good for me."

"I'll be there around seven-thirty, and I'll call your room from the courtesy phone when I get there, so I hope you gave me the right name."

"I did. See you then."

Till pressed "End" on his phone screen. He called Wright's, the hotel restaurant, and reserved a table for two for eight-thirty, then set the alarm on his phone, lay on the bed, and slept. The long drive through the desert had tired him, and he could tell he would need to be alert.

He awoke at six-thirty, then showered and dressed for the evening. If Kyra was in a relationship with the killer, then it was possible he would turn up tonight to see if Till was an ordinary client or a threat. He might even serve as her driver or bodyguard. Till looked around the room, and selected two spots. He hid his two Glock pistols, one inside the pocket of a sport coat in the closet, and one under the mattress at the foot of the bed.

Then he sat in the leather armchair, looked out the window at the hotel grounds, and prepared his mind. He carefully erased his hopes, and prepared himself for an evening of questions without answers. Hunting killers took patience.

7

Till was prepared for the possibility that Kyra would simply not show up. Being in a business that was illegal relieved a person of some of the obligation to observe the usual rules and customs. If she had run a more extended search of the Internet and turned up something that said "undercover cop" to her, then she wouldn't come.

He had decided to use his own name with this girl because the Internet explained who he was, including his careers as a cop and a private investigator. If she showed up, it would mean she had accepted him at his word. He had wanted to be sure that the girl never saw him as some kind of deceiver, and withholding information would have made her feel just that. If she knew the facts and he didn't set off any alarms, then he would be far ahead. If she did get worried and talked to her friend, the man who had given her Catherine Hamilton's jewelry, then he might be the one coming for Till.

When Till came out of the elevator into the big lobby he went to the front desk and found a bright-eyed young woman in a fitted uniform, with shiny black hair tied in a tight ponytail. He placed a hundred-dollar bill on the counter. "Could you please call my room at ten-twenty? My name is Jack Till. If I'm not in the room to answer it, can you please have me paged in Wright's?"

She eyed the hundred-dollar bill as though it had nothing to do with her. "Certainly, Mr. Till. If we don't reach you, do you have a cell number you'd like to give us?" He did. He watched her write it down. "Ten-twenty," she said.

"Thank you," he said. He pushed the hundred-dollar bill toward her, turned, and walked away.

There was a bar on the first floor situated at a crossroads where two perpendicular stretches of lobby met. There was a large set of doors on one side that led to the gardens outside, and a long, broad, open promenade big enough to accommodate a parade that led to meeting rooms in another part of the hotel.

He bought a glass of tonic and drank it while he watched the guests walking along the promenade. The dry Arizona air had been dehydrating him for hours. He bought another and went to sit in an armchair in front of a low table. His cell phone rang and he took it out of his coat pocket and slid the arrow across the screen. "Till."

"Jack, honey?"

"I'm in a bar near the end of the lobby."

"Sit tight where you are. I can see you now."

"I hope you're not disappointed."

"This isn't about me. It's all about you tonight. But I'm not at all. I'm pleased. I'm coming toward you right now."

He didn't resist the temptation to end the call and look for her. He turned to his right and saw her. She was wearing a black dress that was very simple and elegant, with a high neckline and bare arms. He instantly searched for Catherine Hamilton's jewelry, but with the black dress she had worn a thin white gold chain with a single diamond. On her feet were heels that were only slightly less than too high. He admired her business sense. She undoubtedly came to the major hotels in the area often. This was the oldest landmark hotel in the city, designed and built in the 1920s. There were plenty of groups and families who would not have been happy about an obvious hooker in their midst. Her outfit was understated, her makeup was subtle, so she didn't raise any suspicions, but lots of eyes followed her as she made her way to Till.

He stood and smiled as she approached. When she reached him she stopped and stood still, expecting, like a model, to be looked at and appraised. Instead, Till took her hand, leaned to her, and gave her a peck on the cheek, and then gestured toward the other armchair ninety degrees from his at the low table. As she sat, he raised his hand to call the waitress.

The waitress came and said, "What can I get you, sir?"

He looked at Kyra. "What would you like?"

"What are you having?"

"This is just tonic. I'd like one now with gin in it, please. Hendrick's with a slice of cucumber."

"I'll have one too," said Kyra. As the waitress scurried off Kyra said, "Unless you don't want me to drink."

Till said, "I don't have a preference. I want you to be comfortable, and I've found that most people feel comfortable having a drink before dinner."

"Thanks," she said. She moved only her eyes, scanning to take in the people around her. A couple passed on their way to another set of chairs grouped around a table. Then it seemed safe for her to speak. "I recognized you from your pictures on Google. You look better in person. I saw you, then called your number to see if you reached for a phone. I was glad when I saw you answer, because it meant you were you, not that guy by the bar."

He followed her eyes. The man was tall and light-haired like Till, but ten years older. "Thank you."

The waitress brought the drinks, and Till paid in cash and gave her a ten-dollar tip. He raised his glass. "Cheers."

"Cheers." She sipped. "Oh. It smells like flowers."

"It does, but fortunately, it tastes like gin."

The waitress moved off, and Kyra looked around again. "When is our dinner reservation?"

"We'll go in after we've talked a bit and finished our drinks."

"Okay," she said. "What do you like to talk about, usually?"

"Let's start with Phoenix. Do you like it here?"

She gave a practiced gesture that looked like a shrug, but was a pose. "I like it a lot when it's seventy-two degrees in February, not so much when it's a hundred and eleven in May." She smiled. "What do you like the best about it?"

"So far, you," he said. "But you're probably not from here originally, are you?"

"Uh-oh," she said. "This is something we should talk about. You're such a pleasant guy, I can tell you're sensitive. You'll understand that I don't like to tell a gentleman a lot of personal information about my history and stuff. I need to protect my family, who don't know what I do for a living. But I don't want to say no to you about anything, so if you'd like, I'll make up a good story to tell you, and it will feel fine, but it can't be true."

"I understand perfectly. I was just forgetting to look at things from your point of view. Sorry. If something like that comes up again, just tell me you're from Jupiter."

"Thanks," she said. "I'm beginning to like you a lot," she said. She grasped his forearm. "Maybe you were a girl in a past life."

"If I had a past life I was probably a rattlesnake or a garbanzo bean."

She laughed. "I don't think so."

53

They chatted for a time, and then he set down his empty glass. "Are you getting hungry?"

"If you are." She set her glass down, although she'd had less than half of it.

"Then let's have dinner," he said.

They stood and walked together into Wright's. It was hard not to be put into a good mood by the room, with its high walls, the tall pillars of distinctive molded bricks, and the windows looking out on green vegetation. The hostess conducted them to a table on the right beneath the big skylight. As soon as she was gone, he said, "Would you like a fresh drink?"

"If you'd like."

"I'm asking sincerely."

She smiled and the candles on the table made two small stars in her blue eyes. "Jack, you don't hire escorts very often, do you?"

"To tell you the truth, I never have before. I was alone, don't know anybody in town, and so here I am. I know it shows, but I'm doing my best."

"You're being great. You just need a little bit of advice. So here it is. I'm in the happiness business, and you're the customer. You're paying me a lot. By the time the night is over you will have paid me like I was your psychiatrist. I won't feel bad, because I'll do you a lot more good than he will. If I didn't like you a whole lot, I would never tell you any of this. You found me online, so you know that my business is very competitive. For a couple of hundred bucks a very young woman who was probably prom queen somewhere will drive to your hotel room and do anything you can think of for an hour. It won't matter to her if it's four p.m. or four a.m. She'll be grateful that you picked her out."

"I did notice there seemed to be a lot of ads."

"There are about five different sites, and hundreds of girls on each listing."

"Okay. So?"

"So when you hire me, I give you fair value. For these few hours, I belong to you. I'm the sure thing. I'm the girlfriend who does everything she can to please you because it's your birthday, and who never says no. If you don't want me to drink, I won't. If you want to see me drunk, I'll drink until it happens, and sleep it off in your room before I drive home."

"Does that go for—"

"It goes for everything until our evening is over. There are very few limits. If you want to do something I don't consider part of our standard deal, I'll quote you a price. If there's something I'm not able to do, I'll try to make it up to you in another way. When this is over, you will be happy. It's how we both measure whether I did my job."

"I'm happy. You showed up looking beautiful, and I've enjoyed our conversation. This is one of the nicest dinners I've ever had, and I haven't thought about the food."

"This talk goes with the service because you're sweet. I don't want you to think about this evening later and feel I cheated you because you're a rookie."

"I'm hardly a—"

"You've never paid before."

"No." He considered. "What if I want to have sex with you right now?"

She pushed her chair out. "Just tell the waiter your room number for the check, and we'll go. We can have a snack later. Come on."

He shook his head. "I was just being theoretical."

"If we were alone up in your room, all you would have to do is lift my skirt or unzip the back of my dress. You get whatever you want, when you want, the way you want it. That's the arrangement."

"It's a very nice arrangement, from my point of view," said Till. "Why is it worth it to you?"

She smiled. It was an imitation of a sly, flirtatious smile, or maybe an echo of an expression that was once real, but it was too expert now. "The business reason is that you'll want to come back to me more and more often, and give me tips and presents. I can tell you can afford it. The other reason is that I'm still an actual woman. Having a tall, handsome older man who has a little crush on me take charge and have his way with me is something *I'd* probably pay for if I had to. When I know I'm going to have a good time later I start to get kind of excited thinking about it. Like tonight."

"Do you have two kinds of dates—the kind that pay the bills and the ones that are for fun?"

"Things are—everything is—much more complicated than that. I can like a person and still try to get him to pay me more. And I can sometimes tell that a person who turns me on is going to be a mistake—maybe be too rough with me, or not pay me enough."

"Do you have a boyfriend?"

"Uh, I told you I don't answer things that are personal."

"I'll tell you what I was asking, and maybe you'll feel more like answering. You were talking about difficult clients. I wondered if there was somebody who would help you if that happened. I should have said a girl roommate, and maybe it would have seemed less personal—just somebody so you're not alone with a psycho."

"You mean a pimp," she said.

"I don't even like the word," he said.

"Neither do I. I have friends. Some are girls who do the sort of work I do. They understand the issues and the problems."

He nodded and kept his eyes on hers. She was holding back.

"And yes," she conceded. "I have some men friends too. One of them stays over sometimes because he travels."

Till had found him. The man sometimes stayed with her. He had to be the one. "Is he there when you're gone, taking messages?"

"No. I don't have a landline. I only use a cell phone, and when I'm busy I turn off the ring and it goes to voice mail."

"Who is he?"

"Just a friend. Friends are good."

"Yes, they are."

"You're jealous, aren't you?"

"That would be pretty stupid of me, wouldn't it?"

She leaned closer and touched his cheek with a hand that felt like silk. "You poor baby. You think your mind does what you tell it to, don't you?"

"Most of the time."

"Good for you," she said, as though she didn't believe him, but liked him for his faith in himself. "Oh, here's our dinner."

He looked and saw the two waiters arrive and set plates down with considerable ceremonial grace and quiet warnings about hot plates. Then the waiters dissolved into the spaces behind them. The food was perfectly cooked and elegantly presented and served.

They ate happily and exchanged samples of food, then said how much they liked it. If Till had not had the sort of mind she didn't seem to think existed, he would have thought he was on an exceptionally pleasant date with a beautiful woman who genuinely liked his company. He let himself feel that way for a while, as he thought about the male friend who sometimes stayed over. She had denied he was at her apartment answering her phone, but she hadn't said he was not there.

He was surprised to see that she ate much of her food and about half the dessert, but he could tell from her arms and legs that she trained regularly at a gym somewhere, so maybe that was enough to burn off the calories. She put down her fork and looked up at him. "I'd like to go to your room now."

"Really?" he asked.

"Yes," she said. "You got me talking about everything—which I almost never do—right after we met, and so I've been thinking about you for about an hour and a half, and staring at you to watch your reactions. And as I was talking about us, I was thinking, 'Do I really want to tell this man that he can do anything he wants to me? That all he has to do is put something into words and I'll do it?' And ever since the answer came up yes, I've been marking time, waiting. And that's like, right out of the secret book of women—get us thinking about it and then wait us out, be patient. Of course, for me, it's even worse. I didn't get into this business because I wasn't interested."

Till caught the waiter's eye and made a writing motion, and the waiter nodded. In a moment he came across the room with the leather folder with the check in it. Till added the tip and signed it.

Till stood and stepped around the table to pull out her chair, then followed her toward the exit from the dining room. He took her moment of looking ahead to glance at his watch. It was only nine-fifteen. The paging he'd arranged was scheduled for ten-twenty.

She walked across the lobby to the elevator. When he joined her she whispered, "Please don't do anything until we're in the room. If I don't act like a lady they'll figure me out and I won't be welcome here anymore."

"Don't worry," he said. "I'm kind of a hypocrite, so I'm pretty good in public."

She said, "It's just that some men think an elevator is more private than it is." The elevator door closed them in. "What floor?"

"Third."

She pushed the button and the elevator began to rise. "Thanks. I'll make up for anything you missed."

Till had been sure he knew how to get out of this part of the evening, but as the elevator rose he sensed his options slipping away. The page from the front desk was still an hour and five minutes away. He could try to play sick so she would leave, but now that he knew her better, she didn't seem likely to believe it. She didn't seem likely to believe an urgent business call, either. He needed to have her trust him after tonight, or he'd never get near her male friend. He thought frantically, and then realized he wasn't thinking of anything new. He considered pulling a fire alarm so the hotel would be evacuated, but the risk would be too great, and he would have to be far from her when he did it. Then he realized that he wasn't thinking of anything because he no longer really wanted to.

They left the elevator and walked the twenty-five feet to his door. He took the key card out of his wallet and slid it into the slot on the lock, and the click told him the door was unlocked. He opened it only a couple of inches before she slipped in ahead of him, then pivoted and pulled him in by the arm. She turned the rheostat on the fixture beside the door to dim the lights. She led him to the bed and made him sit down, then smiled and slowly, tantalizingly disrobed. Under the dress she was wearing a black bra, a pair of thigh-high stockings, a garter belt, and a thong.

Till's mind was racing. *She's half my age. Exploiting and using her isn't something I want to live with. I just need information. I can try to stall for more time.* He could wait for the call from the girl at the front desk. *I can tell her my wife just died a year ago and I'm not ready for this after all.*

She came toward him, and the last of his ideas disappeared with the last of her clothing. She stood in front of him and unbuttoned his shirt, then knelt to unbuckle his belt, and he stopped pretending that he wasn't going to go through with it. When he was naked too, she suddenly said, "Just a second."

She stepped to the desk, picked up the hotel telephone, pressed a button, and waited. "Hi, Beverly." She listened for a few seconds, then said, "Thanks. Cancel Mr. Till's call." She put the phone in its cradle and returned to him.

She began to kiss his neck, his cheeks, his throat, his chest. "You paid the same person I do," she said. "If you want to call this off, we can."

"I changed my mind after I met you," he said.

"I'm so glad you're not a cop. They're the ones who back out. It looks better in court."

After that the time was no longer real. He had some idea that it must still be early, and then he caught a glimpse of the clock on the nightstand and it said nearly twelve. Briefly he wondered when his evening would be over, his time up, and hoped it would last until morning. The thought that kept returning was what would induce a girl like this to become a prostitute? But some self-protective part of his mind told him the answer could only be unhappy or tragically stupid, and should be avoided for now.

Then he saw the clock had moved to three, and sometime after that he fell asleep. He woke to some kind of disturbance among the birds outside and saw Kyra sleeping too, the fiery hair like an aura around her head on the white pillow. He pretended to be asleep as he watched her wake up. He saw her get up, gather her clothes, and make her way to the bathroom. In a few minutes she came out fully dressed.

He saw her notice his pants with his wallet in the pocket hanging on the straight chair by the desk, and he waited for her to reach in and take it out. She didn't. He closed his eyes again.

A few seconds later he felt her hand, the same silky hand, make a swirl in the hair on his chest.

He opened his eyes.

"Hey, cowboy."

He smiled. "Is that a good thing?"

"Yes. I'm too sweet to speak more plainly than that."

Till could see that while his eyes had been closed she had opened the curtain a little bit, and now the sunlight poured in, making the room seem beautiful. Her white skin was luminous. He said, "The evening seems to be over."

"I'm afraid that happened a while ago, lover," she said. "If you don't mind, I'm going to go brush my teeth and my hair. You can get my money ready while I'm in there."

"Okay." He watched with regret as she scooped her purse off the desk and went into the bathroom.

Till got up, went to the safe in the closet, pressed the four digits, opened it, and took out twelve hundred dollars. Then he put the rest into his suitcase. He picked out the clothes he would wear, moved them to the right side of the closet, and shut the closet door. He collected the two Glock pistols and the rest of his belongings and put them in his suitcase.

In a few minutes, she emerged with light daytime makeup on and hair brushed straight. "Too chicken to run off without paying, huh?"

"That too. And partly the fact that I'll sincerely remember this as one of the most amazing nights of my life."

She patted him on the cheek. "I like you too, Jack. But now it's day, and I've got to go."

He handed her the little stack of hundred-dollar bills, and she shuffled through them like a bank teller. "A fifty percent tip. A night for the record books." She put her arms around his neck and kissed him. Then she reached into her purse and produced a plain white business card that said "Kyra" and a telephone number. "Don't lose my number."

"I won't," he said.

She opened the door, blew him a kiss, slipped out, and let the door swing shut.

Till was already at the closet. As he threw on his clothes, he mentally gauged where she would be—walking down the hall toward the elevator, stepping in, descending. He grabbed the phone and dialed the garage. "This is Mr. Till in suite 311. Can you please get my car out right away?"

"Certainly, sir."

Till ran to the bathroom, snatched up his toiletry kit, put it into his suitcase, latched it, and took with him the instant checkout folder and a pen. In the elevator he filled out the folder and put his key card into it. When the elevator door opened he put the folder in the little brass box beside it and went directly to the valet station beside the covered entrance to the building. He looked outside warily to be sure Kyra was still there.

When Kyra's car arrived, it was a silver Jaguar. She handed the parking attendant a tip, got into the car, adjusted her sunglasses in the mirror, and then drove off.

As soon as Kyra was past the driveway, Till stepped out, saw his car already waiting on the circle, hurried to it, tipped the parking attendant, tossed his suitcase onto the backseat, and went after her.

8

Till pulled out onto Missouri Avenue just as Kyra turned south on 24th Street. In a moment she turned right on Camelback Road to go east. As a young man he had been trained at the academy to follow cars, and over the years he had gotten better at it. He kept two or three vehicles between his car and Kyra's Jaguar. When he could find a truck or an SUV he stayed behind it for a time. He wasn't looking at the Jaguar. As long as she kept going straight, he didn't care how far ahead she was. He was watching the lanes on both sides of her, waiting for her to make a turn.

At last she turned right on Scottsdale Road, driving past a six-foot stucco wall and then into a quiet housing development full of twisting roads and abrupt curves. The houses were all recently built one-story homes without much room in front for lawns that would have been burned up by the sunshine. He gave her a little more space, watching the direction she took, and followed cautiously, avoiding the chance of being caught face-to-face on a cul-de-sac. When she turned into one and pulled into a driveway he went past. He turned around in the next one and drove out of sight, waited for a few minutes, then drove out onto the larger street and coasted slowly past the cul-de-sac where she had gone. The door of a two-car garage was open at the house where she had pulled in, and he could see the silver Jaguar.

As he drove on he considered how to watch her without being seen and how to pick out the man who had given her Catherine Hamilton's necklace and bracelet. Kyra was clearly a girl who would have no trouble attracting customers. For all he knew, she might have ten a day.

From the way she had spoken, he was almost certain that the male friend had stayed in her house last night. She'd been up most of the night with Till. The friend, presumably, had gone to sleep. Till was tired, but he didn't want to miss a chance of seeing the man. A day from now, he might have no way of distinguishing the boyfriend from one of Kyra's customers. This morning, the only man who would be coming out of the house would be the boyfriend.

Till parked his car two blocks from Kyra's cul-de-sac, and began to walk. When he'd hastily dressed in his hotel room he had thrown on a polo shirt, khaki pants, and rubber-soled loafers. Now he had added a baseball cap and sunglasses. As he walked toward Kyra's street, he kept his mind unfocused and his eyes moving, scanning the area while he listened to the sounds. The birds here had different calls from the ones in Los Angeles, and they seemed to be much more active in the morning before it got hot. From here he could hear no sounds from the major road outside the gate, and inside the gate there seemed to be nobody driving yet.

Kyra's house had surprised him. He had pictured her living in an anonymous apartment in a large complex, not a freestanding house in a middle-class neighborhood. It indicated to him that she was probably making lots of money, and that she had wanted an investment. Secondary thoughts floated in. She must have a good cover story. Banks didn't like to approve mortgages for young women who didn't have jobs and were vague about where the money for the down payment had come from. It occurred to him that she might not have applied for a mortgage. She might have paid in cash.

He finally came to the conclusion that he had misinterpreted the place. She didn't do business here. The neighbors in this little village of quiet tangled streets would never put up with male visitors arriving at all hours, slamming car doors and rapping on Kyra's front door. He had made a mistake. He turned and walked briskly back toward his car. He managed to get inside behind the tinted glass and put his key in the ignition before he saw the silver Jaguar again. He kept his head low and caught a glimpse of the driver in profile as the car slid past his. It wasn't Kyra. It was a man.

Till couldn't tell much about him. He appeared to be in his early twenties, with dark hair that was wavy rather than straight or curly. He wore the sort of wraparound sunglasses that major-league baseball players wore. It was frustrating to Till that he couldn't tell whether the man was tall or short, thin or fat. And he hadn't really seen the shape of the face from that flash of a side-view glance.

In his rearview mirror he watched the Jaguar glide a couple of blocks into the distance, then swing toward the gate. The car reached the gate at Scottsdale Road and turned left before Till pulled away from the curb, made a U-turn, and followed.

Till was even more wary as he followed the Jaguar a second time. Kyra had been exhausted and lulled into a calm, end-of-the-shift mood. This man had probably been awakened when Kyra came in. She would probably be going to sleep now in her house. He was up and alert and out in her car.

Till's mind was generating theories, but he was not able to eliminate anything he thought of. He knew only that he must learn the man's identity. Till had spent quite a few hours with Kyra, and she had made a great deal of progress in getting to know and trust him. But he had not yet dared to ask who had given her the necklace and ankle bracelet that had belonged to Catherine Hamilton. He had nearly blown all the progress by asking personal questions, so he had held off on a couple of the crucial ones. He was betting on the hypothesis that the man was living with her, and the fact that she let him drive her car made this theory more likely.

No, he thought. Even that was a guess. The Jaguar wasn't necessarily hers. It was a fairly expensive car. Maybe it was his, and she had driven it to the Biltmore to help ensure that she wouldn't be suspected of being an escort and asked to leave. He was tempted to go back to her house, look at the second car in the garage, and have both plates traced.

At last the Jaguar pulled over. When he caught up, he saw that he was at a large plaza. There was a supermarket, a big garden store. Till passed behind the car, took a phone-camera shot of the plate number without coming to a stop, drove to the side of the lot near the stores, parked, and saw the man get out. He was young. He wore a gray T-shirt that revealed well-developed arms and shoulders and a thin waist. He was perhaps six feet even. Till got out of his car too and began to follow the man.

The man disappeared into the market. Till got his cell phone ready, pressed the camera icon on the screen, and stepped into the market. He went to the right, looking down the first aisle at the vegetables along the wall and the bright fruit in bins. There were several shoppers with carts in that aisle, but the man was not one of them. Till kept walking to the back of the store, but the man wasn't visible along the line of meat and fish cases. Till looked up each aisle he passed—the dog and cat food, the paper products, the alcohol, the water and soft drinks, the canned goods, the freezer cases.

Till turned into the alcove leading to the restrooms. He put the phone in his pocket and shouldered the door open, prepared for an attack. The men's room was empty. He stepped into the ladies' room and stared under each stall for feet, then realized he was alone. He went out and looked for the swinging metal door that would lead to the loading docks in back. He found it and moved through, walking straight and quickly without appearing to look either way. There were three young men engaged in stacking produce that they must have just unloaded, but they didn't challenge him, probably because he was moving purposefully and was dressed like their bosses. When he got to the loading dock he looked in every direction. He jumped down from the dock.

Till walked around the side of the big building back toward the front. Maybe he had simply missed the man. Maybe he had not been aware that Till had been following him, and he had just gone to get some groceries for Kyra.

As Till went around the front, he saw what he had been looking for. The man was in the driver's seat of the Jaguar, and he was just closing the door. Till stayed at the corner of the building and moved back out of sight. In a moment, Till looked out again to see the man turning right out of the parking lot. As soon as he was gone, Till ran to his car, got in, and followed.

He drove much faster this time, trying to catch a glimpse of the Jaguar. Another three minutes went by, and then two more, and he began to realize that he was not just *physically* behind. The man had been trying to lose him from the start. Till sped up to fifty. Seven or eight minutes had passed at forty and now fifty miles an hour in traffic.

There it was. The Jaguar had been pulled off the boulevard and was parked in front of a Mexican restaurant. He swung off the highway into the lot, got out, and walked up to the Jaguar. He touched the hood. It was hot in the center and cooler around the edges. He kept going.

He knew the man would not be in the restaurant but would have gone through it. Till walked in and went through the empty dining room to the hallway that led to the kitchen. He went past it out the rear door and saw the place where the second car must have been parked. There were seven spaces outlined by white paint stripes, and an empty one marked RESERVED.

Till went back inside. He endured the inquisitive stares of the cooks and waiters. He called out, "Did anyone see the unfamiliar car parked out back in the reserved space?"

There were a few thoughtful looks and a few people who ignored the question, but a young man said, "It was a Toyota Camry, about a year old. White."

"Did you see the guy who came for it? He would have walked through the restaurant and out the back door."

"No. People come through doing deliveries and stuff all day. He was in my space when I came to work at five in the morning. Overnight they tow your car if you park on the street here, or in the mall. Maybe now I'll go move my car to my space."

"Might as well," Till said. "He's sure gone now."

Till went back through the front of the restaurant and looked at the Jaguar again. The guy had been pretty impressive. Though he'd had no reason to imagine Till was after him, he had stopped in the supermarket to find out. But the restaurant had been a different sort of maneuver. He had left his car in the back of the restaurant overnight so he could switch cars. He had prepared, but prepared for what? What had he been worried about?

Till got into his car and drove. He went back to Scottsdale Road, found the right housing development, and drove to Kyra's house. There was no year-old white Camry parked nearby.

Till had a worried feeling as he approached the front door of Kyra's small, neat, adobe-colored house. He knocked loudly. He heard no movement, so he rang the bell and knocked again. No response.

He walked around the house to the back, which was a small gravel garden of desert plants and a Jacuzzi under a roof. The curtains were open, so he looked in the windows. The dining room had a big old-fashioned maple table and chairs but looked as though nobody had ever been invited into it. He suspected Kyra had put the furniture there as a replica of something she'd been brought up with. A home had a dining room.

He moved to the kitchen door and looked in. The cupboards were all open. Pots and pans had been taken out. In the sink were a couple of pint ice cream cartons that had been emptied. Till's bad feeling intensified. He moved to the next window and looked into a bedroom. The closet was open; drawers had been pulled out of dressers; the mattress had been lifted and leaned against the wall. As Till walked toward the window of the corner bedroom, he prepared himself.

He couldn't see in, because the plantation shutters were closed, and behind them was a dark curtain. Apparently this was where Kyra slept in the daytime. Till went back to the kitchen door, picked up a stone from the garden of succulents, and smashed one pane of glass in the kitchen door. He reached inside and turned the knob to open the door.

Once inside, he closed the door, then walked to the hallway leading to the bedrooms. He found the corner room, pushed the door open, and looked. Kyra wore a pair of pajama pants and a tank top. She was lying in the bed under the covers with the air-conditioning cranked up to keep the room at around seventy degrees. The electric hum of the fan and the whisk of air must have been nice for her, like white noise. She looked peaceful lying there with her eyes closed, but when he took two more steps he could see that the boyfriend had shot her through the left temple. Most of the blood came from the exit wound on the right side of Kyra's head onto the pillow.

9

The boyfriend must have begun searching the house before Kyra returned from her night at the hotel, Till thought. The rooms that Kyra could be expected not to enter on her way to bed had probably been thoroughly searched before she got home. The boyfriend had undoubtedly left her bedroom untouched until after she was dead, and then scoured it. Her purse had been dumped out onto the floor, the drawers pulled out of the dresser, the closet opened and clothes thrown around.

Till looked down at Kyra. He had seen many dead people in his life. It was always a terrible thing, the utter, irreversible destruction of a hopeful, busy, eager, selfish, sensitive, thoughtful, gregarious, lonely creature, already decomposing as soon as the heart stopped. An hour ago this corpse on the bed had been a lively, beautiful, generous young woman.

Till studied the room, but touched nothing. There was no point in making things hopeless for the crime scene people. He knew that the boyfriend had done at least a fair job of staging a meaningless crime scene already. He could see that there were no visible signs that anyone other than Kyra had ever slept here, let alone lived here on her generosity. The boyfriend had proceeded this way before, and the results this time would be the same. The cops would make nothing of it, build no leads, get nowhere.

Till saw the jewelry box lying open and on its side on the dresser. He looked inside and around it for the distinctive necklace and anklet, then on the floor and behind the dresser, but they were not there. He turned and went down the hall to the kitchen. He reminded himself that he shouldn't wait too long with Kyra. He stopped, picked up a dish towel to keep his prints off the kitchen telephone, and then called 911.

"Your name, please."

"Jack Till," he said. "I'm at the home of a young woman who has been shot to death."

"Did you shoot her?"

"No, ma'am. I did not. I just came to speak with her, looked in, and found her dead. I believe the person who shot her is a young male Caucasian driving a white Toyota Camry, about one year old. He is probably heading out of town. He drives fast." He said, "I'm at 9344 North Murietta Terrace."

"I'm dispatching officers. Are you at the residence now?"

"Yes, I am."

"Please remain there, because the officers will need to speak with you."

"I will."

"Are you positive that she's dead?"

"Yes, I am. I've seen a number of bodies, because I was a homicide detective for many years. She has a bullet fired through her left temple. She was right-handed."

"The officers should be reaching you shortly, Mr. Till. Are there any other people in the house?"

"No. The only one I know of who was here this morning was the gentleman I saw leaving. Presumably he shot her."

"I'm getting word that the officers have reached your location. Do you see them?"

"They're parking in front of the house now. That's incredibly quick. They must have been nearby."

The two cops who emerged from the car were both adjusting their utility belts as they came to the door. Till opened it and stepped aside so they could enter.

"Are you Mr. Till?"

"I am."

The first cop put a strong arm on his forearm. "Could you please put your hands on the wall and let me check your pockets?"

Till leaned against the wall, spread his arms and legs while the cops verified that he was not armed. The cop said, "Thank you."

Till said, "I know this is a little tricky for you, but if you could call in a bulletin right away on a male Caucasian about twenty-five years old driving a year-old white Toyota Camry, you might get him before he goes too far. He speeds, so that might help him stand out a little." One cop walked deeper into the house while his partner spoke to Till.

"I assume you think he's the shooter?"

"Yes."

"Does he have a name?"

"Not yet," Till said. "I think he was a live-in boyfriend. I saw him leaving when I arrived. His hair was dark, cut short and neat, and he was wearing wraparound sunglasses. He drove the girl's new silver Jag a few miles, parked in front of Tio Fernandito restaurant, walked through the place, got into the white Camry, and drove off."

"So if we go to this restaurant, the silver Jag will be there, but the Camry won't?"

"That's right. I think this girl also had an apartment somewhere, and he could be on his way there now, or heading out of town."

"Why two places?"

"She was an escort. This doesn't look like the sort of in-call place she would use for business. She would have problems with the neighborhood. I think the guy searched this place for money and valuables. He might wonder if she had money or jewelry hidden in the other place too. He has a history of killing girls like this and then robbing them."

The other cop came out of the hallway. "Beautiful girl."

"Yes," said Till. "She was."

"Tell me about you. What are you?"

"I'm a private investigator out of LA."

"You on a case?"

"The parents of a girl named Catherine Hamilton hired me to find out who killed her. She was working as an escort too. This guy seems to form a relationship with a working girl for a while, then kill and rob her, and move on." Till paused. "I don't want to get irritating, but I can prove all of this, and I really think it would be worthwhile to try to have this guy pulled over right away."

The younger cop looked at his partner.

The older cop said, "Mr. Till. Haven't you heard a radio, or seen a paper yet today? When I came on duty, there had been a call that two city councilmen had been murdered last night in their beds. All morning there have been dozens of tips and leads that have had to be followed up on. We're not a huge police force. There's not much extra manpower to look for a car—the most common model in the country, by the way—when we don't know more than this. Give us a chance to find out more."

Till was looking at the floor. Suddenly he looked up. "Why do you think the councilmen were killed?"

"It could be a lot of things. We're in southern Arizona. There are a lot of people with guns and opinions. There are people who smuggle drugs. We'll sort all that out, but it's making everything else drag. Right now, I think we've got to get you to the station and let you give your statement there. We'll pull some crime scene people off the councilmen, so they can get started here."

"All right," Till said.

"I'm afraid we're going to have to ask you to tolerate wearing handcuffs, Mr. Till. My partner is going to transport you alone."

He turned around and let the cop cuff his wrists behind him. When they were in the car, the younger cop said, "Were you close to her?"

"No. I hired her last night so I could get her to tell me about her boyfriend, but she took her personal life off the list of topics. She didn't tell me his name, or give me any details. So here we are."

"What do you mean?"

"I mean all I accomplished was to arrive the day before she was going to be killed. The next time I get close I'll concentrate on going for him instead of trying to be cagey and learning everything from the girl."

At the station Till gave his statement, then waited in an interrogation room drinking coffee while the cops made a few telephone calls. He knew that they had hoped he might be the one who had killed the two city councilmen. When they realized Till was what he said he was, the detective who had been assigned the case came in and told him he was free to go.

He got a ride back to Kyra's house, where technicians were still going over the whole property. He didn't talk to any of them. He knew they wouldn't tell him anything, and even if they did, what they found would not be of interest to him. He had missed his best chance at this man, and all he could do was start again at the beginning and give the boyfriend time to surface again. He stopped beside his car and watched the coroner's people moving Kyra's body out on a gurney. Then he got into his car and drove.

10

Till began his drive back to Los Angeles after the sun went down, staying on Interstate 10 all the way, hoping the boyfriend was aware of him and ready to come after him. He wanted to be easy to find. Till stopped occasionally at diners and truck stops for coffee. He always sat facing a window so he could watch his car in the parking lot. Even as he watched, he kept hoping the killer was out there thinking about going to the car to ambush Till.

After he arrived at his office on Ventura Boulevard in Studio City, he went back to work gathering information about the murders. He searched jewelry outlets and manufacturers' catalogs for the distinctive necklace and anklet. The gold disks had not been circles. They had been ovals. The little diamonds around the edge hadn't been unusual, but the big diamond on each had been off center. He spent days looking, but he couldn't find anything like them. He drew a picture of them with approximate sizes and descriptions, and drove downtown to the jewelry district. He walked from building to building, entering every store, every design and manufacturer's workshop, and asked if anyone could identify the maker or the meaning. When he got home he scanned an enlarged and cropped photograph of the jewelry into his computer and sent it to dealers in estate jewelry and designers of custom jewelry all over the country. Then he kept looking.

He went back to study the information Sergeant McCann had sent him about the five girls who had been murdered before Catherine Hamilton. He was struck even more, now that he had spent a night with Kyra, by how similar all seven girls looked. It was as though the boyfriend kept browsing the escort ads until he found the same girl, and then he killed her again, over and over.

The necklace and anklet didn't appear in pictures of either of the first two victims. They seemed to have originated with the third, three murders before Catherine Hamilton. He spent more time trying to concentrate his efforts on jewelry sellers in the Miami area, where that girl had died. She was Jenny McLaughlan from Savannah, Georgia. She had appeared in Miami at the age of twenty-two last June, and had found an apartment near the ocean. She had apparently taken to the beach life and then catered mainly to tourists who checked into the big hotels. It was almost impossible to guess where the jewelry had come from. No custom jeweler he could find had any knowledge or opinion.

He studied each girl's murder. The police reports varied in their detail and in the intensity of the inquiries that they reflected. Some of the investigators seemed to see the murder of a prostitute as a simple cause-and-effect matter. Young women, usually small and thin, who were doing something illegal, for which they collected money in cash, were going to be in exceptional jeopardy. Any customer could see the opportunity, and sometimes one took it.

There were hundreds of fingerprints belonging to unknown males in each of the first few girls' apartments. Nobody had found any set twice. There were also complicated mixtures of DNA. If there were relationships, rivalries, resentments, they remained unknown because the girls would stay in a city for a few months at a time and then move on to the next city, like migrating birds. If the victim was foreign-born, the police would try to find out if she had been trafficked, but in these cases they'd had no success. They wrote the report, signed it, dated it, and filed it.

Dated it. He looked again at each of the police reports and noted the time and date of death and the city where it had happened. Then he went back to the Web sites of the local newspapers to find out what else had happened in each of those cities in the day or two before those murders.

It took Till three days to be sure he had picked out the right events to correlate with the deaths of the five women. On April 17 of last year a strawberry blond who called herself Lily Serene was shot in the back of the head in her Minneapolis apartment, and the place was ransacked. The night before, William Rossi, the owner of three restaurants in the Twin Cities area, had disappeared. Rossi was found four days later in his car, which had sunk to the bottom of a lake. He had been shot to death.

A girl named Wendy Steffens was found dead in her apartment in Washington, D.C., on the night when a retired assistant district attorney had been shot in his home. He had been a successful prosecutor for thirty-two years, a man with a great many enemies.

On September 27, a woman named Jenny McLaughlan was found dead in a condominium in a desirable area of Miami near the beach. Two nights earlier, the president of a regional bank and his wife had been killed as they walked to their car after attending a play.

On December 29, Terri Hanford, a strawberry blond, died of two gunshot wounds in her apartment in New York. The same evening a wealthy man who owned a large number of Manhattan rental properties and a horse breeding farm upstate was murdered in the art gallery he owned.

On January 25 a contractor in Charlotte, North Carolina, was killed on the way home after a meeting with potential lenders. A strawberry blond named Karen Polenko was murdered in her apartment early the next morning, apparently while she was asleep.

Jack Till called the Los Angeles Police Department, introduced himself, and asked to speak with Detective Anthony or Detective Sellers. He called the number he was given, expecting to leave a message that would be returned when one of them got around to it, but instead, the phone was answered by a male voice that sounded calm and businesslike. "Detective Sellers."

"Hello, Detective. My name is Jack Till. I was a homicide detective with the LAPD for twenty-three years, and now I'm working as a private investigator."

"Nice to hear from you. What are you working on?"

"Catherine Hamilton. I wondered if you or Detective Anthony could spare me about fifteen minutes anytime today?"

"I think so. Can you be here around two-thirty today?"

"Sure. I'll see you then."

He drove to the Burbank Boulevard station in North Hollywood, where they worked; parked on the street three blocks away; walked in; and went to the front counter to identify himself. Then he sat down to wait. At four o'clock he went to the counter again to let the officer know that he wasn't leaving, just going to the men's room. At four-thirty, the two detectives appeared in the lobby.

Anthony was a woman about forty years old who was about five feet three inches tall. She wore a gray suit that looked boxy, as though it had been made for a small man, and a pair of men's shoes. She wore her gun in a holster at the right side of her belt, and that further filled out her silhouette. Her black hair was pulled back into a tight bun so from the front it looked like a man's hair combed back. "I'm Anthony," she said, and shook his hand.

Sellers was tall, but soft-looking, wide at the waist and hips with narrow shoulders. His lips were fleshy, and looking down to talk to other people gave him a double chin. He smiled. "Sellers. Come on back where we can talk."

Till noted that they had no inclination to mention that they were two hours late. He simply said, "Jack Till," and followed them to the big communal office where they had desks side by side. He took the chair that Anthony pushed his way. The two sat in their swivel chairs and waited for him to speak.

"I've been spending a lot of time trying to catch up with Catherine Hamilton's killer."

"So have we," said Anthony.

"Of course," Till said patiently. "I caught up with him in Phoenix just before he killed his next victim, but I didn't read the signs in time. I saw him leaving her house and, because I suspected he was the man I was after, I followed him. He lost me for a minute, switched cars, and got away. When I went back to her house, she was dead."

The two looked at each other. Neither seemed pleased. Anthony said, "Who are you working for?"

"Catherine's parents. The Hamiltons."

"And how do you know the two murders are connected?" asked Sellers.

He reached into his manila folder and produced two ads for escorts: Catherine Hamilton's and Kyra's. He handed them to Sellers. "Notice the resemblance. And notice the identical necklace and anklet. Both were killed in their homes by a shot to the head. If you get in touch with the Phoenix police you can probably compare the bullets."

The two detectives looked at the two copies of the ads. Anthony said, "Interesting. Can we keep these?"

"I brought them for you."

"Thank you," she said. "Of course, there are many possible explanations. There could be a jeweler who is popular among sex workers, or even one who pays the girls in jewelry. And there are enough sex workers killed that you can get lots of correlations that don't mean very much." She looked as though she was about to stand and offer her hand so she could shake his and terminate the meeting.

Till didn't budge. He reached into his folder and produced the other five ads. "Here are his previous five victims. New York, Minneapolis, Miami, Washington, D.C., Charlotte." He looked at them. "Hard to tell them apart, isn't it?"

"Again, so many of these girls become crime victims that you can draw a lot of correlations," Anthony said. "We could collect five black-haired girls killed in those cities during the past two years too. That wouldn't mean it's the same man."

"Three of these girls are wearing the same necklace and anklet too."

Anthony said, "So it would appear to be a fad."

Till looked down at his feet for a moment, then said calmly, "I've searched the country for more of them, and so far, no manufacturer or designer has recognized them. The consensus is that they're a custom set made for somebody and the design meant something to this person. Now, the reason I came here was so I could share with you a development that might help. I think I figured out what this guy is doing."

"You mean besides killing pretty girls?"

"I think he's a hit man who has figured out a way to be invisible while he's setting up a hit and then avoid leaving a trail afterward."

"He's killing all those girls for that?"

"He seems to have realized at some point that he could get them to give him a place to stay. What is safer than living in an apartment rented by a hooker who uses a false name? Each girl probably rented her place under her real name and gave the landlord some bullshit job information. But she doesn't use her real name when she starts working. She makes up a new name."

"So why do the girls all look alike?"

"He becomes a boyfriend. That's why they let him stay. Maybe he has a strong preference for girls who look that way, so that makes it easier for him to seem interested. Maybe they're a type who seem to like him, so he sticks with the tried and true. Who knows why women pick one guy instead of another? I read one time it's that they subconsciously like the smell of one guy's sweat. The point is that the girls aren't the point."

"Then what is the point?" asked Sellers.

"The girls make him invisible. He stays with them for a month or a few weeks or three months while he gets his killing all planned out and studies his victim. Then, one night, after he's killed whomever he's been hired to kill, he gets ready to leave town. That means he kills the only witness who knows that he's ever been in town. And before he leaves, he takes whatever she has—which is always a lot of cash. He uses that to pay expenses for another month or six months, and maybe to impress his next girlfriend. Then he does the same thing in the next town where he has a hit to do."

"That's a pretty wild theory."

"I know. But in each of these cities we have a high-end killing that happens just before one of these girls gets shot."

"Intriguing," said Sellers. "And what person do you connect with Catherine Hamilton's killing?"

"I'm not sure yet. Hit men don't usually get hired to kill middle-class suburbanites or poor people. There were three murders here on that day that might fit the pattern—important people who seem to have been killed by strangers. I can't pick one on the little information that was in the papers about the method and circumstances. And it doesn't matter to me. What I'm doing now is trying to move ahead and figure out where he turns up next."

Anthony said, "Why did you come to us?"

"I guess it's professional courtesy," said Till. "I can't sit on what I know about a murderer because for a lot of years the homicide detective who needed to have a lead fall out of the sky into his lap was me. I'm also telling you because the guy is good at this. He's well-trained, disciplined, and decisive. He moves quickly. He's not some kind of mental defective who will say, 'Okay, you've got me.' If you get close to him, he won't surrender, and he won't go without a fight. He's done too much for that."

"What are you planning to do?"

"Catch him, if I can."

11

Joey Moreland couldn't go on this way much longer. After two years moving from place to place, crossing names off lists, he had become very good at staying invisible, but that wasn't good enough. His method would work for only a couple of years longer. It required that he still look handsome and unthreatening, but, especially, boyish. That was the most important part.

He was twenty-eight, but he looked much younger. His smooth skin, blue eyes, long dark eyelashes, and wavy black hair made him look like the kind of young actor who was on the cover of teen movie magazines. He was lean and sinewy, and six feet tall, but his muscles were long and stringy, so he could still give the impression he was a teenager just by sprawling when he sat and letting the physical energy he felt find its way into his movements.

Moreland was just pushing into Boston on Route 93. He wasn't a fan of the Ted Williams Tunnel, which he had to take under the Inner Harbor. Down in those close quarters he was always vulnerable to some stupid mistake one of the other drivers might make. He hated to be subject to accident and random proximity to five lanes of people with inferior brains, nervous systems, and muscular control.

He thought about where he was going. He would come up out of this hole in a few minutes and get himself to the Four Seasons on Boylston. The hotel was right by the Boston Common, and overlooked the Public Garden and Beacon Hill. There were lots of MTA stations—Arlington, Boylston, and Chinatown were all a five-minute walk away. The only drawbacks were all the employees kissing the asses of the guests and the high price of the rooms. He'd have to find another girl soon.

Moreland liked coming into each new city and starting to plan a new job. He had spent a couple of weeks since he'd left Phoenix resting in various out-of-the-way Midwestern resort hotels as he slowly made his way east. That was an expensive way to travel, but there was another reason why finding a girl was a top priority. Boston was going to be his toughest job this year. He would have to defeat the most elaborate precautions, and afterward the kill would probably attract the most attention.

While he was living in Arizona he had come up with the idea of the Barrett .50-caliber rifle. He had seen the rifle on television and fallen in love. The version on television was the M82 Long Range Sniper Rifle, fired by a marine sniper. The guy had used it in Afghanistan, where he had fired a shot that traveled a mile, went through a brick wall, fragmented, and killed the three men standing behind the wall.

Moreland hadn't been able to buy the actual military-issue .50-caliber rifle. Nobody was selling those to civilians, maybe because there were two wars going on where there weren't many trees or buildings in the way and maybe because the authorities didn't want a lot of them in the United States. But Barrett made a general production model called the M107A1 that could be bought in gun shops.

It had cost more than twelve grand, including the optics. Moreland was glad he had taken the time to search Catherine Hamilton's apartment in Los Angeles before he'd shot her, because the money he'd found had covered expenses like the rifle. The twelve grand included a Leupold 4.5 × 14 mil dot scope and six ten-round magazines and a carrying case. The price didn't include ear protectors, but those weren't expensive, and they would save his hearing from 180 decibels of sound. He had also estimated that it would take five hundred rounds of .50-caliber ammunition for even a fine marksman like himself to move from being competent with the new rifle to highly skilled to lethal. In all, he had spent nearly twenty thousand dollars to buy and master the Barrett M107A1 while he was in Arizona. The Sonora Desert was perfect. Moreland had met a man named Dave Bright in a shooting club, and learned that Dave had built a range on a vast piece of land that he owned outside Tucson.

What building a range meant was putting a bench rest on the highway end of his property, shielded from the highway by a hill, and then pounding a few white posts into the dirt to mark off each hundred meters to a distance of two thousand meters. There was nothing on the desert end of Bright's property but the side of a small mountain. Bright owned both sides of it, but the only side he ever looked at was the side he could see through a rifle scope. On the first day, when Moreland came to test his new purchase, Dave Bright had taken out his own Barrett M107A1, and said, "Come on. Let's go break some rocks."

The recoil was like a trip-hammer pounding his shoulder. The bullet, a streamlined spinning metal projectile the size of a man's thumb, streaked across the two thousand meters of desert in four seconds, smacked into a chunk of sandstone, and exploded it into dust and flying chips. Once Moreland had experienced the power of the weapon, his interest in it intensified into a passion. He became a fanatical convert, a true believer.

Moreland's excitement grew as he picked out targets at the far edge of the rifle's range. He adjusted the clicks of the sight for fifteen feet of elevation, and experimented with windage to compensate for the complicated and changing air currents over the long distance. Between the bench and the final post there were winds blowing left, right, and in eddies rising from the hot desert floor. As he kept firing and refining his aim he felt himself gaining power. A man who could project his hatred a mile downrange, punch through a car or through a wall, and kill his enemy was like a god.

Moreland kept firing that day until he had fired forty rounds and his right arm felt painful, wrenched, and bruised. He was reluctant to relinquish the power, but he knew he had to put away the rifle or it would be much longer before he could use it again.

He was sore after each practice session, and his head pounded from the noise, but he kept coming back. Sometimes it would take four or five days to recover from the pounding before he could go back. Between visits he worked at the job of killing two Phoenix city councilmen. He had known from the beginning that the councilmen would be a simple job. The only thing that was challenging was that there were two of them. He didn't want to get one and then have the police put the other under protection. Both men had to be done quietly in rapid succession, and right after that he had to be gone.

Getting out of Phoenix had been complicated. He had originally planned to kill Dave Bright before he left, but Dave had conveniently died in a car accident a month before Moreland had planned to leave. Then, on the final day, Moreland had almost run into a problem with one of Kyra's customers. The man—her overnight date—had apparently chosen that one day to follow her Jaguar to her house. He had seen Moreland leave in her Jaguar, and apparently had not been able to see that Kyra wasn't driving it anymore. Moreland couldn't let this man catch up and see him, because by then the councilmen and Kyra were all dead. He had tried to lose the john at a supermarket, then had gone on to switch cars and get out. He had been right to leave. If he had stopped and shot the john, it would have pushed the already odd story of the night of shootings into a bigger story.

Moreland didn't feel much anymore when he pulled the trigger. He killed each person because it was necessary, and he did it in the most effective and humane way—a surprise shot through the back of the head. He wasn't especially squeamish, but he didn't like noise, and he didn't like having to move bodies around. He didn't want to dig holes for them. Everything a man did after taking out that gun was best done quickly.

Moreland traveled most of the time. He was like a fish that kept moving to keep the water flowing through his gills. He could easily find everything he needed in any large city in the country, and if he stayed near the major highways most places were about the same. In any city he could find a good restaurant and a good coffee shop, a luxury hotel, a store that sold clothes that looked good on him, and a beautiful girl.

Joey Moreland liked escorts, maybe because they were like him. They weren't people who had been babied all their lives. Nearly all of them had started turning tricks before they were eighteen, so there wasn't much drama about it by the time he met them. He liked spending time with them. In their professional lives they spent all their time faking and lying, but after they got to know Moreland, they would begin to reveal what they really thought, just because he didn't judge them. He didn't really like killing them, but it was necessary. If he hadn't shot Kyra when he'd left Phoenix, she would be talking to the police about him right now.

The Internet had changed everything for escorts. There were very few who worked for pimps now. All they had to do to get customers was strip to their underwear, use a cell phone to take a few pictures of themselves in a bathroom mirror, and upload them to an ad with a phone number on one of the sites that had "adult services" sections. The money didn't seem that great, but it was cash and they got to keep all of it. If a girl attracted a few regulars she could stop advertising, schedule their visits for convenient times, and spend the rest of her life shopping. If she charged $200 an hour and had two customers a day, she made $2,800 a week. If she was pretty enough to charge $300, it was $4,200 a week.

There were a lot of middle-class women in the business now—a few graduate students, lots of divorcées, and a lot of women from other countries who figured nobody back home would ever find out.

As soon as he was settled in his hotel and could get a shower, clean clothes, and a good dinner, he would get his laptop computer onto the wi-fi network and begin shopping for a girl. Boston was an important, delicate job. The sooner he got out of sight the better.

Moreland was good at scanning the ads. The ones he wanted would often mention their strawberry blond hair in the ads. Red hair was rare, so they would call it red, but sometimes they said blond, so he had to be patient, click on the ad, and see the photographs. Some described themselves as "the girl next door." He often clicked on those, even though he thought the description was misleading. The real girl next door when he'd been young had been reddish blond.

He had been fourteen when he first became interested in Mindy Jones. She was already out of Jamestown High School and working as a waitress in the restaurant down by Chautauqua Lake. He used to see her outside her parents' house, most of the time dressed the way she always was, in blue jeans and a T-shirt and sandals, her long strawberry hair loose down her back. She picked colors that set off her hair and green eyes. She had been coming and going this way for as long as he could remember. A few years earlier, when he was only about eight, she had stopped being a skinny kid, like the other girls in the neighborhood. He remembered thinking that all of a sudden she looked like a movie star.

At fourteen he found it hard not to watch her walking to her car carrying the clean, crisp white waitress uniform on a hanger. She would open the back door of the car and then bend to lean inside and hang the uniform from the little hook, slam the car door, and turn. A couple of times she turned fast, and he saw the green eyes focus on him for a half second and then pass on as she got into the driver's seat.

Joey often saw her on her evenings off getting picked up by young men for dates, and more rarely, usually in the summer, he would be awake when she came home. The street would be silent and deserted, and he would hear the radio first, playing music that was audible because the car windows were open and so was his bedroom window. As the car came up the block somebody would turn off the music and then he'd hear only the hissing sound of the tires moving along the pavement. Joey would watch to see if the boy walked her all the way up onto the front porch, if they then put their arms around each other and kissed. Most of the time the car would just stop and she would be out the door and up the steps by herself. She was very light-footed and quick. Once, when the car moved off again, instead of going inside she walked to his side of her porch as far as the railing. She stood still and looked up at his window for about thirty seconds.

Joey had been sure that nobody could see him in the window, watching her and her date like a voyeur. He had his bedroom door closed and his lights off, but she seemed to be looking right at him. He stayed absolutely still, not even breathing for fear of confirming her suspicion—and suspicion was what it had to be—not only that he was watching, but that he had done it before. At last she turned, but as she did, her face was caught in the porch light, and she was smiling.

Then it was a Friday night, just a day before his parents planned to drive to Milwaukee to visit his grandmother. He couldn't go because he had summer school on Monday. He had to make up a math course. His mother was worried about his grandmother's health and didn't want to put off the visit, so they had convinced themselves that he was mature enough to stay home and take care of the dogs.

His mother woke him up next morning at six and took him around the house explaining all the self-explanatory items on her lists of things for him to remember. He nodded at the right times and then waved to his parents from the porch as they drove off.

It wasn't until late afternoon that he heard the knock on the back door. When he looked out, he could see it was Mindy. She was wearing a white summer dress. He opened the door and she stood there on the steps, smiling. "Hi, Mindy," he said.

She was beautiful. Her strawberry blond hair was shining in the sunlight and the dress fitted her perfectly. It was the kind that made him stare, because he was sure he could almost see through it. He didn't do that now. She said, "Can I come in, Joey?"

"Uh, sure." He stepped backward and she came in and shut the door and relocked it. Her movements were always so quick and graceful that he almost didn't get out of the way quickly enough. He tried to compensate by stepping backward, but she seemed to take that as an invitation to advance, so he was still within the danger zone, where his adolescent clumsiness would be evident if he didn't stay alert to her movements.

"You had to think about that for a second, didn't you?"

"No," he said. "It's just that my parents went to Milwaukee, and I figured you wanted to talk to them."

She shook her head, then stepped past him, put her arm through his, and walked, pulling him with her out of the kitchen and into the living room. "I already talked to them. They asked me to come and check on you. They said you were grown up enough to handle everything. I guess they just didn't want you to be lonely. You don't have a girlfriend, do you?"

"No," he admitted.

"Ever had one? Oh, maybe you're too young for that—to even think of it."

"No, I don't think I am. I just haven't found the right one."

"I know how you feel," she said. "I'll tell you a secret about girls. Boys never seem to figure this out, but what you're thinking about them, they're thinking about you, too." She looked at him closely for a few seconds while he thought about that, and then brought her face close to his with an imitation of his wide-eyed naïveté. "They wish they could get your clothes off and fool around with you too."

He felt himself blushing, his cheeks hot with embarrassment, and felt grateful when she kept her gaze ahead and kept walking with him. He wondered for a second why she was walking him up the stairs. He formed a theory, couldn't think of an alternative theory, and noticed he was sweating now. A familiar change was taking place.

He edged slightly behind her so she wouldn't be able to see him while they climbed the stairs. But after she reached the landing she took two more steps and stopped, and he bumped into her. She half-turned and looked at him with mild amusement. "Don't feel funny. That's what's supposed to be happening. Which is your room?"

"Down there on the end."

She took his hand and walked with him to his room. When they were inside she closed the door and locked it, then turned. "I've never been up here. I was going to ask you to show me around, but that can wait." She stepped so close that they touched, as though they were dancing, and then she kissed him gently on the lips, just as though he were her date taking her home, and they were on the porch. Her arms were around his neck, and his hands had found their way to her slim waist. She pulled her face back a foot and looked into his eyes.

She said, "I can do something really nice for you. It's a big favor. But you have to be able to keep a secret. Can you keep a secret and never tell anyone as long as you live? If you can't, I'll understand, and I'll respect you just as much for being honest with me."

He looked at her beautiful white skin and saw her clear green eyes studying him, waiting. He decided. "Yes, I can. I will."

"I believe you," she said. "If you're not telling the truth, I'll go to jail. You know that?"

The thought had never occurred to him, but he nodded. He remembered that a young married woman had been caught with a teenager and sent away. Was that what she meant? He smelled her perfume, a very subtle scent that seemed to be natural and reminded him that a woman was not made of regular flesh and bone and muscle like a man.

She raised her face and kissed him again. It was the first time he had felt anyone's tongue in his mouth, and then he imitated what she had done, and that was the first time too. After a few minutes of kissing and feeling her hands on his back and her body touching his, she pushed him back a foot. "It's a lucky thing you're a good kisser, because you haven't had a lot of practice. We'll fix that, too."

She stepped back another foot and pulled her dress up over her head and off. She was wearing a half-slip, then stepped out of it so she wore only a white lace bra and matching panties, with the same pattern of lace along the edge. It was no less than what girls wore on the beach, but it had an entirely different meaning, a different intent, and so the sight made his knees weak.

All of her movements were quick, almost birdlike. Suddenly she was back, kissing him with her arms tight around him. As he embraced her, his hands were now on the bare skin on the small of her back, and he was amazed at the beauty and the sheer rightness of the way she looked and felt. As she kissed him, she unbuttoned his shirt and pushed it off his shoulders.

Then she whispered, "Don't be shy," and she knelt in front of him, undid his belt, and pulled his jeans and underwear to his ankles. He was embarrassed at the way his penis was jutting upward, uncomfortable that it was beyond his control, but she gripped it with her hand and kissed the end of it, then ran her tongue along the bottom of it, and stood up.

She kissed him softly as she took the rest of her clothes off, and then gently steered him onto the bed. As he freed himself of his shoes and socks, he looked at her standing in front of him.

She said, "You're wondering what I'm thinking, and whether you're handsome enough, and grown up enough, and all that. I'm thinking that you are. And we're going to have such a good time."

The only part of what she said that confused him for a second was that the good time was in the future. He was already having the best time of his life, lying here naked with this completely naked woman who was as pretty as any woman he had seen on television. She had that shining reddish blond hair against the ivory white skin that made her seem more naked than anyone else could be.

And then she distracted him by turning and stepping to her white dress, taking a strip of three little square packets wrapped in a hand-kerchief out of the pocket, sitting beside him, and tearing one off the strip. She held it up. "You know what this is, right?"

He had gone to a school where he'd had teachers waving them around in sex education class about once a year since fourth grade. "Sure."

"You're going to wear it. You're always going to wear one."

She tore open the packet and handed it to him. He held it, turned it around, and prepared to put it on, but she snatched it and deftly but slowly unrolled it onto him. They came together, and the feelings were all intensified. They began slowly and gently, but soon he began to move faster.

She whispered, "Lie still for now. Let me do the moving." And he did. His hands touched and explored and everything he did was welcome, even received as though she had been eagerly awaiting him for some time. He lasted for a while, but when her movements began to quicken, and she uttered little cries, he felt himself swept along and he let go.

After that everything stopped. Slowly, in the profound stillness, the world began to come back to him. She lay motionless on top of him for a couple of minutes, then stirred, and they were separated. She lay naked beside him on his bed with her eyes closed, and he slowly kissed her from the top of her forehead to her toes. She said, "Better take the rubber off before it drips. Wrap it in toilet paper and leave it on the sink in your bathroom."

When he came back they cuddled on his bed for a time while she talked. "That was way, way better than I ever imagined. For such a young guy, you're great."

"Thanks. You're—"

"I know I am," she interrupted. "We're going to have an amazing time this summer. Just keep our secret. Never tell. Never talk to me in front of anyone."

Every day that summer he woke up remembering the last time he'd been with her and feeling overwhelmed and grateful that it had not been a dream. After his parents returned from Milwaukee, he and Mindy had to find other ways to meet. He sometimes pretended to go to summer school but slipped back to the house next door while Mindy's parents were at work. Other days he pretended there was some reason why he had to stay late at school for extra help. On days when there was no school he went on bike rides and met her at prearranged places, where she would be waiting with her car.

As the summer went on, she helped him learn things. "Want me to show you something I really like? Do this and it will make me go completely crazy. I can't control myself when—yes, just like that." Maybe because he was so much younger, and because he worshipped her, she was not uncomfortable controlling what they did and teaching him. He paid close attention to anything she was willing to teach him, thought about it between meetings, experimented and studied her responses.

By the beginning of August, he was so thoroughly enthralled that she was the central and only essential part of his life. He woke up from dreams about her to think about her. In silences he heard her voice. While his parents and Mindy's were at work, they had the run of both houses. They had sex in every room.

There was never a slipped word, a revealing look. He never told any friends or acted as though he had been doing something they didn't know about. He never made a mistake. When she walked from her house to her car, he didn't even seem to notice her.

Their affair didn't end when she'd said it would. It continued through the fall, winter, and spring until the following summer.

One day Joey saw a new man arrive at her house in a black Audi. He got out, walked to her door, and rang the bell. On later reflection, Joey Moreland realized that what he had seen was Eric Coates's homecoming from the army. When the doorbell rang, Mindy flung open the door, threw herself on him, and kissed him.

The next afternoon as soon as Joey came home from school, Mindy arrived, came in through the kitchen door, and met him inside his room. He looked at her beautiful green eyes and the tentative posture and knew there was trouble. Most days as she came in the door of his room she was already unbuttoning or unzipping. Today she was standing looking at him with her hands knitted as though she suddenly didn't know what to do with them.

"What's wrong?" he asked.

"Eric came home."

"Who's Eric?"

"My boyfriend."

"Oh. Where'd he come home from?"

"A lot of places. He was a soldier," she said.

"So you and me—you know—is this going to be a problem?"

She nodded. "You knew it wasn't going to be forever. The first time I came over I'm sure I told you it was just for then, just for last summer. I'm, like, eight or nine years older than you."

"I love you."

She put her arms around him and kissed his forehead, his cheek, his eyelids. "I love you. You know that. But if word of what we did got out, I'd be in jail, and your life would be ruined. It's not normal. At first this was just going to be me having some fun while Eric was deployed, trying to keep myself from dying of loneliness by playing with the cute boy next door. It would keep me from cheating on Eric. But by the end of the summer it was, like, the best sex ever. And I feel closer to you than I've ever been to anyone. But it's got to end now so we can fit in with other people and have okay lives. Do you understand?"

He was devastated. He just felt deprived, rejected, and sad. He didn't know what to say to change her mind. "You can't just do this. I don't want any other life."

The time he had devoted to Mindy he now devoted to Eric. He began to learn about Eric. He got the license number of the Audi and used it to get the name and address of the owner. He rode his bicycle to Eric's apartment, hid it in a carport behind the building, and walked past, recording the hour and the people who came to the apartment building. He wrote everything he observed in a pocket notepad. On weekends he sat at his bedroom window and watched for Eric's car to arrive and pick up Mindy. His preparation took sixty-two days. Summer had already become fall before he was ready.

He visited his uncle Dave's apartment across town while his uncle was at work. He got in using the key his uncle kept with his parents in case of an emergency, and he didn't spend long inside. He examined his uncle's guns and settled on a compact .38 revolver, partly because it was way in the back of the drawer, where Uncle Dave probably seldom checked on it or took it out to fire, and partly because it was simpler than the semiautomatics, and he had no idea how to clear a jam.

The next night he rode his bike to Eric's apartment. He wore black jeans, a navy blue hooded sweatshirt, and black sneakers. He hid the bike in the back of a different carport, it seem that had been vacant during the whole time since he had been coming to study Eric.

The rest of the job was not as difficult as he had expected. He waited in the bushes near the lot in the back of the apartment building where Eric parked his car. At a little after two a.m., when the bars closed, Eric drove up the street, turned into the driveway of the apartment building, and parked his car in his assigned carport. Before he could get the door all the way open to get out, Joey was beside him, firing over the driver's-side door into his head.

Joey put away the gun, walked two carports down the row, got on his bike, and left. He rode fast along the route he had planned. It went down a pedestrian path across a large city park, along the side of the high school athletic field, and along the route of some old railroad tracks that had been torn out. His ride crossed a quiet street and then led right up to his house. He was never on a street that the police patrolled, and never passed a house with a light burning. He was upstairs in his bedroom by two-forty-five, hid the gun inside the box of a Monopoly game, and was asleep by three.

The next day he unloaded the revolver, did his best to clean the surfaces with a soft cloth made of a worn T-shirt, and then pushed some strips of the cloth through the barrel with a new, unsharpened pencil. Finally he rode his bike to his uncle's apartment and returned the gun to its box in the back of the drawer. There was now one more round missing from the already-opened box of ammunition, but he was sure his uncle wouldn't notice.

A few days later, he overheard his parents talking about Mindy. She had always been such a lovely girl. Nobody could blame her for moving away from Jamestown after what had happened, but losing her struck them as a tragedy for the neighborhood.

12

Joey Moreland opened the laptop again that night, signed onto the hotel's network as a guest with one of the accounts he sometimes used, and began to move down the titles of the escort ads. He moved quickly past "Busty Latina, 21" and "Sexy MILF, 35" and "Platinum Blond Hottie, 23" and the others. He was still searching for the right girl. It was like holding a mask in his hand, and trying to find the face that would fit it perfectly.

When the boast was vague, like "Stunning Beauty, 22" or "You will never forget me, 27" he would often click to see the ad. He didn't like to do it, because about half the pictures reminded him of what an unappetizing business this could be. The ads were often misspelled and ungrammatical. There were girls claiming to be eighteen who looked is if they belonged on a playground, and others claiming to be thirty who looked a hard-worn sixty.

Most of the pictures were shots taken by the girls themselves by holding a smart phone up to a mirror while they assumed a pose that they hoped would be titillating, but was often just a grotesque contortion that reminded him of cubist paintings in which the front and back of a model were shown simultaneously. The reflected backdrop would be a bathroom in a cheap hotel or an apartment bedroom so cramped and cluttered that a client would have to move clothes and shoes just to get to the narrow bed.

He saw another ambiguous title: "I promise to look my best and be on my worst behavior, 24." He clicked on that title, and there she was again, just as she had been in other cities. It really was only a matter of searching for her. The same strawberry blond hair; the smile; the skin that looked like porcelain on her breasts and buttocks but was so heavily freckled on the shoulders that the freckles nearly melted into a tan.

He enlarged the picture and looked more closely. The eyes were bright blue, and the eyelashes that he knew were blond had been covered with black mascara. Her expression was just the right combination of amusement at the human condition—the absurd set of common needs that were about to bring them together—and a hint of the longing she was feeling for a man like him. He was sure. He copied the number and called it on his cell phone.

When the recording prompted him, Moreland said, "Hi. My name is John Carter. I saw your ad on Backpage, and I wondered if you had time to see me tonight. I'm at the Four Seasons and my room is five ninety-two. You can call the hotel and get connected to me. I'll be here for a while." He hung up and turned on the television.

It took her two or three minutes to call back. He lifted the phone. "Yes?"

"Hi. This is Kelly. You called me?"

"Yes, I did. How are you?"

"I'm fine. You said you'd like to see me tonight."

"I would."

"Do you want to come to my place?"

"I'd like you to come to the Four Seasons."

"It's a little more expensive if I come to you. An extra hundred."

"That's okay."

"What time?"

"Can you come at ten?"

"Yes. Please have my gift ready. All right?"

"All right. I'll be looking forward to seeing you at ten."

In the fourteen years since Mindy had disappeared from his life, he had continued to learn what he could about women. He was a good listener because he was listening for vulnerabilities, for ways he could exert power over them. He had to charm them into wanting him to win, even though winning was getting them to abandon self-protection and common sense. He had become highly skilled at satisfying women sexually. His face was unlined and boyish even though he was twenty-eight, and that helped. Many escorts liked his unthreatening face.

He showered, shaved especially close, and met her coming in the doors to the lobby. "Kelly?" he said.

She looked at him, and he could see her eyes focus on him as her mind worked rapidly to see if she recognized him or if he was a cop. He was smiling, so after that instant she smiled too. It was a simple trick. Smiling released endorphins. She would begin feeling good in a few seconds. "I'm very pleased to meet you." He said it into her right ear because that was the shortcut to the left brain, which was the side that needed to be alerted that he was the one. He took her arm in the first couple of seconds and walked her into the bar, because a touch gave a woman the subconscious impression he was a strong, confident man taking charge of her. They sat at a table in the bar, and he said, "I'm going to have a martini. Would you like one?"

Kelly might or might not have ordered a martini if she had been left alone, but once he had said it she seemed to find herself wanting one without thinking about alternatives. She said, "Yes, please."

"You're very beautiful," he said. "And you have perfect taste in clothes." His smile broadened and he leaned close to her right ear again to whisper, "I'm very pleased."

She could hardly not have known she had beauty, because her livelihood depended on it, and she probably heard it every day. But perfect taste was a form of intelligence, and the compliment made her feel even more desirable, and that made her more likely to desire.

He said, "Are you Irish? I can't help wondering."

She said, "I'm part Irish, with a little German thrown in."

He kept her talking so he could mirror her expressions. "Did you grow up right in Boston?"

"No. My family is still in the South," she said. "I still have the accent when I let myself have it." She said that part with the accent. "You can't be from here, or we wouldn't be in a hotel."

He appeared delighted by everything she said, and never took his eyes away from hers. "I was born in California," he said. "I travel around a lot on business. I just got here a few hours ago."

He noticed that she was already beginning to mirror his expressions and his posture. Everything was working already, without much effort on his part.

The waitress arrived with the martinis, and she gave him a chance to take out his soft leather wallet and open it to flash a thick layer of hundred-dollar bills while he found a fifty for the drinks. He noticed that Kelly was not the only woman whose eyes focused for a millisecond on the wallet and then flicked back to his eyes. The waitress gave him a smile to rival Kelly's, and as she thanked him her head gave a little bow. It was aphrodisiac to a woman to notice that other women acknowledged the value of the man she was with.

He carefully lifted his glass and clinked it against Kelly's, then leaned back in his chair and sipped it while he studied her over the rim. "That's good, isn't it?"

"I like it," she said. "I don't drink very often, though."

"Why not?"

"It's bad for my figure and my complexion."

"No wonder you're so beautiful." Alcohol also made women less likely to be critical of men's failings, and less inhibited. He estimated that she weighed about a hundred twenty, so one drink would be enough to make her feel good, but two would make her sleepy. He asked her to have dinner with him.

At dinner he made an effort to learn more about her. She was smart, and seemed to have some education. She knew what artists had exhibitions in Boston museums at the moment. "You might go and see the Newman show at the Hibble Gallery tomorrow," she said. "If you can keep yourself from hiring another girl for one afternoon. And if you haven't been to the Isabella Stewart Gardner Museum on one of your trips here, you should go. The concierge will arrange it for you, and the doorman will tuck you right in the taxicab."

She was intrigued by and grateful for the delicious and expensive dishes he ordered for her, but as he'd expected, only tasted them and left them unfinished.

He asked her about the books she liked, and she was vague about that. He told her honestly about his own preferences. "I travel most of the time, so I read a lot. Lately I've been driving, so I listen to audiobooks on the road."

He expected her to ask which books, but instead she said, "Why do you travel?"

"I'm a consultant. I go to businesses and I tell people what to do, then go away and let them take all the credit."

"I'm sure you're good at it. You eat at very expensive places." She leaned forward and said quietly, "I've been wondering. What are you expecting tonight?"

"Pardon me?"

"It's okay. We're not talking loudly, and nobody's close enough to hear."

"You mean, do I have a fetish or something unusual in mind?"

"Well, you might. And that would be just fine. I'm not at all judgmental. But you've been very nice to me, and I don't want to disappoint you."

"I'm sorry," he said. "I'm pretty ordinary in every way. I hope I'm not too dull. I'm not a married guy whose wife won't do what he wants, or something. I'm just a single man who isn't in a relationship right now."

"Okay," she said. "I'll just have to work harder to make your wish come true—you don't know what it is."

He called for the check, signed it, pulled out her chair, took her hand, and walked her out to the lobby and into the elevator. By the time they reached his floor he had decided she might be the right girl.

He was gentle, romantic. He made sure Kelly felt unrushed and unpressured and appreciated. He touched her softly and didn't speak, so she could imagine whatever she liked. But slowly, gradually, he began to use the techniques he had first learned from Mindy when he was fourteen, and had perfected in the fourteen years since then with many other women. He made the experience about Kelly's feelings, sensations, and desires. He prevented her from reverting to habitual actions that her mind would associate with work, and unrelentingly aroused and stimulated her until, after about two hours, he knew she was his.

They lay still for a long time, and he watched her fall asleep. When she was sleeping deeply he got up and turned on his laptop computer. He bought two admission tickets for the Isabella Stewart Gardner Museum and made reservations for an early dinner at Clio, then climbed back into bed and went to sleep.

When he awoke Kelly was dressing. "Have to go?" he asked.

"I'm afraid so. It's morning."

"I guess I'd better get you your money." He got up and went to the dresser, counted out twenty hundreds, and handed them to her, then lay back on the bed.

She folded the bills in half and put the wad into her purse. She smiled. "I should be paying you."

He shook his head. "Please don't."

"What?"

"Say things like that. I know I'm no different from the last guy or the next. I don't want you to think I'm an egotistical jerk that you have to flatter."

"I don't think that at all. You're a great lover, and you know it." She jumped onto the bed beside him and tickled his ribs. "Admit it or I'll tickle you until you pee. Admit it, Mr. Don Juan. Admit it."

He flipped her over onto her back and held her wrists. "That was the best money I ever spent. You don't have to lie to make me happy. I'm happy."

"Good for you. I'm happy too," she said. "It reminded me of what I like about men. If they were all like you I'd do this for nothing." She struggled to free her hands, but gave up and lay still. "Give me one kiss."

He gave her a long, gentle kiss.

"Now let me go before the staff sees I've been here all night and figures I must be an escort."

He sat back, and she got up and picked up her purse. She took a step, then stopped. "How long are you in Boston?"

"I haven't decided." He went to the desk and opened his laptop.

"If you want to see me again, I'll charge you half price. See? You must be Don Juan."

He said, "I have tickets for this afternoon at the Gardner. Will you go with me and show me around?"

"I don't know."

"That can be the half-price date."

"Done."

"And I have reservations for an early dinner at Clio afterward."

"Clio?"

"Massachusetts Avenue and Commonwealth, across the bridge from MIT. Kitchen opens at five-thirty, right when we'll be starving from walking around and looking at paintings. Okay?"

"You're spending an awful lot of money at once," she said. "I don't want to get you in trouble."

"No trouble. I can't always spend thousands of dollars a day, but I don't often find much that I want. Can I pick you up at one?"

"Make it twelve-thirty. There's a lot to see." She stepped to his laptop and typed Google Maps and her address. "There. That's where I live. I'll be waiting."

She left, and he looked at the map on the screen. It wasn't a bad place—outside the congested areas in a quiet suburb. He wouldn't mind living there for a while.

Joey Moreland had learned patience. He had no reason to rush Kelly into anything, or even to bring up the idea of living with her. If she thought of it, then she would never suspect his motives in accepting her invitation. He made sure he called her once a day, either to make a date with her or to tell her that he was too busy with his consulting job to see her. He always made sure that he included something in every conversation that made her think of money. He said today that the next time they met, he would drive her to Providence for the evening because there was a lobster restaurant that was highly recommended. Since that first night, whenever he'd seen her he'd brought a present, small but expensive—a silk scarf, a pin, a pair of gloves, lingerie; always the right brand, the best quality.

He had not needed to say that she must never call him, because discretion was standard procedure in her profession.

His profession took up much of his time. The man he was being paid to kill was Luis Salazar Cruz, a Mexican federal prosecutor who had become famous for his success against the Sinaloa and Gulf cartels. The broker had told Moreland that Salazar was fifty-one years old, six feet two inches tall, with wavy coal black hair and a small, neat mustache. He wore very good suits, most of them charcoal gray. It was a reasonable expectation that he would be protected by his own bodyguards, and by people from the Boston police. Because Salazar was a high-risk visitor, the police would probably station a couple of snipers nearby. Killing him and getting away afterward would take thorough planning and calm, efficient execution.

This job was why Moreland had decided to buy the Long Range Sniper Rifle and become expert with it. He could set himself up in a high place two thousand meters from Salazar and shoot him. A police sniper would be armed with a .308 rifle with an effective range of one thousand meters. It would be a deeply uneven match, one that would give Moreland enough margin for error to make the kill and easily get away.

Joey Moreland was a reliable assassin who could be expected to stay in the trade forever. He had been recruited ten years ago by Dick Holcomb. People outside the trade didn't know that name, but once it had meant something. Dick Holcomb was a former soldier and a former mercenary who had become one of the people to call for unusual and difficult wet jobs.

Moreland graduated from Jamestown High School at the age of seventeen and realized that there was no practical reason to stay in the southern tier of New York. There seemed to be little left to do there that didn't involve construction, and nothing was being built. He went to Southern California. At first he tried to live by doing odd jobs, but had no success. He stole a few cars and helped chop them for parts, and then delivered a couple of shipments of drugs and money for a crystal meth lab in Tujunga. When the police found the lab, he became a burglar. He had been introduced to a pair of fences, the Hurtz brothers. They would meet him at a bar in Van Nuys called the Eagle, and tell him the sort of thing they were buying at the moment. He would go to a neighborhood where those items were likely to be, and steal some. One night the inevitable happened. A home owner woke up and met Joey Moreland in a dark hallway. Joey killed him with the crowbar he'd brought.

The police never figured out who had killed the man, but the Hurtz brothers were never in doubt. The brothers—Ron and Dale—made most of their money on the simple premise of buying things cheap from people who had not paid for them and then reselling them for more. But on this occasion Dick Holcomb paid the brothers for an introduction to Joey Moreland. When Joey sat at a table across from Holcomb, the first thing he noticed was that Holcomb's eyes were an odd color. They were almost yellow, like a cat's.

"What do you want me for?" Moreland asked him.

"I don't know if I do," Holcomb said. "I have a job to fill. It pays more than boosting things from houses—any houses—but it's not for everybody."

"I guess you want somebody killed."

Holcomb's yellow eyes showed nothing. "I'm offering a tryout. I'll give you some training. It'll take about three months. I'll pay you a thousand a week while that's going on. Any day you wake up and want to quit, you quit. No questions asked. If you last three months I'll decide whether I want to give you the next course or just shake your hand and give you your last thousand."

"Why no questions?"

"I said the job's not for everybody. It's nothing against you if it's not for you. I won't have a problem with you as long as you keep your mouth shut."

"I'll try it," Moreland said.

"Fine. Meet me at the big mall down the street at eight in the morning. Be near the Sears store."

Joey Moreland showed up at the mall at eight. The mall's stores didn't open until ten, so the other people arriving in the lot were a few floor polishers and some trainees in the fast-food places in the food court. There was a big turnover in those jobs, so none of the others, who were about his age, was curious about a newcomer.

At two minutes after eight, a black car with tinted windows drove up about a hundred feet from the others and stopped. After a moment, Joey Moreland walked over and prepared to look in through the windshield, but the passenger window rolled down before he got there. He could see Holcomb in the driver's seat. "Get in."

He got into the passenger seat and Holcomb drove off. "It'll take an hour to get there," Holcomb said. "When we get there we'll spend the day. Who's waiting for you at home?"

"Nobody."

"No parents?"

"They live in another state."

"Which one?"

"Why do you want to know?"

"No girlfriends?"

"Not at the moment."

"Keep it that way for now," Holcomb said. "I figured since you do night work you probably aren't tied down. But we may want to do a little traveling, and it's better if you don't have to explain anything to anybody."

"Okay."

"You don't seem inclined to argue."

"Not about that. Anybody can see the sense of it."

"Good start," said Holcomb.

They drove out to what Holcomb called The Ranch, which was a vast expanse of land northeast of Santa Clarita that was all steep canyons and spiky peaks, with rocky shelves the size of houses jutting from the ground at a forty-degree angle. There was a tangle of dirt roads, or maybe one road that wound around to various places on the property.

The only excuse that Moreland could see for calling the place a ranch was that there was nothing on it but two buildings. One of them was a cinder block rectangle with a large sloping canvas tarp stretching a couple of feet above it on poles. That kept it in shade and provided a shaded area beside it where Holcomb had placed a picnic table. The second building was long and narrow like the first, it had a steel door at each end and no windows. It was buried in dirt and gravel nearly to its roof.

They began with firearms instruction. Holcomb went to the long, narrow building and selected a pair of .22 rifles, two .22 semiautomatic pistols, earphones, and some paper targets. He put two paper targets up on posts a hundred feet away, handed Moreland a rifle, and said, "We begin at the beginning."

Holcomb could rapidly place ten rounds in a one-inch bull's-eye from a standing position. Joey Moreland was less consistent, but not a bad marksman. Holcomb said, "This is the cheapest and simplest way to learn the basics. Do everything right today, and you'll still do it right in a month when it's harder. There's no recoil to speak of, and not much noise. With the rifle, learn to concentrate and control your breathing. What makes you shake is carbon dioxide. Before you fire take a couple of deep breaths, blow the last one out, aim, and fire."

They fired for a couple of hours. Then they switched to pistols at fifty feet. "Keep your trigger pull steady and sure, so you don't drag the sights off target. Know at what point it will fire." After each magazine was emptied, they walked to their targets and examined them.

They stopped every half hour and drank water from a large cooler. Holcomb said, "You're doing okay. Just make sure that no matter how tired you get, you're keeping all of your attention on willing that bullet through the bull's-eye."

In late afternoon Holcomb taught him how to break the rifle and the pistol down and clean them. He was watchful to be sure Moreland did everything as it should be done, that the weapons were truly clean, and that each had the even gleam of a thin layer of gun oil on it. As with the shooting, he did everything Moreland did.

Next Holcomb took him inside the rectangular building. The inside was like the interior of a house, divided into a few rooms with white plasterboard walls and imitation wood laminate floors and powerful air-conditioning. He turned it on and said, "Now we start getting in shape."

There was an exercise room at the back of the house, and they went in and began lifting weights and doing pull-ups, push-ups, and various strengthening exercises. As the sun was showing signs of disappearing over the next ridge, Holcomb took him outside. They jogged along a narrow, winding trail that took them up to the top of the ridge. By the time they descended, the sun had set, and the shadows below the hills were chilly.

Holcomb drove Moreland back to the mall where his car was parked. As Moreland got out of the car, Holcomb said, "You can leave the car at home tomorrow. I'll pick you up at the bus stop around the corner from your apartment at six."

The daily instruction continued and grew more demanding. After Moreland mastered the .22-caliber guns, Holcomb replaced the pistol with a nine-millimeter Beretta and the rifle with a .308. After they had lifted weights for a week, Holcomb added more weights to the bar. After they had jogged the uphill trail to the ridge for a week, Holcomb turned it into a race. Everything they did the first week got harder the second, and kept growing more demanding after that.

Moreland learned to fire a shotgun effectively and became aware of its limitations. Forty yards was about the top range for a kill; but close in, there was nothing with more power. The spreading of buckshot didn't do anything to make up for a poor aim at any range. Next Holcomb began the long process of teaching Moreland hand-to-hand combat. They began with techniques for fighting another unarmed opponent, then moved through disarming a man with a knife or a club, then settled on the more common task of using those weapons to kill a man.

Each week on Friday evening, Holcomb would hand Moreland an envelope with a thousand dollars in it. The next morning they would go to work again at six. After a few weeks they drove to a combat target range a few miles away, and practiced firing at pop-ups and silhouettes that skittered across their line of sight. Every day included the strengthening exercises, the aerobics, and the fighting practice. Day by day, Moreland grew stronger, faster, and more tolerant of minor discomfort. He became better and surer at clearing jams, taking apart weapons, and assembling them.

After six weeks Holcomb changed the starting time to early afternoon and the end of the day to three a.m. so they could engage in what he called "night maneuvers." He simply said, "Suppose you're hired for a hit. You want to do it at noon or two a.m.?" The answer was obvious.

Holcomb taught Moreland about night vision goggles, infrared scopes. They ran in the dark. Moreland noticed immediately that for everything he did in the dark, he was slower, required more concentration, and was more prone to accidents. Holcomb said, "The trick is to make the dark work for you, not against you. The only way is to practice." The longer they worked in the dark, the more comfortable Moreland became. He learned to "cheat the dark," as Holcomb called it, by taking a look at a place while it was still light and making a mental map. He learned to use his ears and to deny an opponent the same sense by moving in silence.

At the end of the twelfth week, Moreland was a formidable fighter with a variety of weapons, who could operate comfortably in difficult environments. On Friday of the twelfth week, Holcomb drove him to his apartment, and handed him an envelope with a thousand dollars in it. He said, "I'll call you."

Joey Moreland waited. He waited a week, expecting the phone to ring at any moment. He considered driving out to the ranch, but he was sure that Holcomb would not be overjoyed that Moreland had decided to get in touch again. After the first week he pretended he had stopped waiting. He resumed his strenuous exercises, ran in the city at night to keep his senses sharp, and began going to a local firing range for pistol practice.

At the end of two months, Holcomb called him. "Are you alone? I'd like to come see you." An hour later he was at the door of Moreland's apartment. When Moreland opened the door, Holcomb looked him up and down, then strolled into the apartment. He looked around him, and walked into the bedroom, where Moreland's pistol lay on top of the dresser. He picked it up, removed the magazine, cleared the round in the chamber, looked down the muzzle, sniffed it, closed the chamber again, and set it down. He said, "The lessons weren't wasted. You ready for a job?"

The next day they began the drive to Santa Fe, where Moreland killed his third man while Holcomb watched from his car. When Moreland asked what his cut would be, Holcomb said, "It will always be fifty-fifty, no matter who pulls the trigger and who watches the street."

The partnership lasted for over two years. The jobs came from a man Holcomb talked to only when the man called him on the telephone. He was called "the Broker." Moreland answered the phone once when he called. The voice of a man in late middle age said, "Are you Joey?"

"Yes."

"Then take down this information. The target is Ronald Miller. No special problems for you. He lives at . . ." and he gave an address in Denver. "He needs to be gone by the fifteenth of this month. The price is forty thousand."

When Holcomb drove his pickup truck along the narrow road to the ranch buildings, Joey came outside to wait. Holcomb pulled up next to him with the truck window rolled down. "What's up?"

"The Broker. He called with a new job."

Holcomb nodded. "I told him it didn't matter anymore if he talked to me or you. It's the same and it saves us time." He got out and began to unload groceries from the bed of the truck.

After a second, Joey pocketed his note and helped. As they stepped into the house, Joey said, "He asked if I was Joey."

"Makes sense."

"I didn't know he knew my name."

Holcomb set his bags on the kitchen counter and stopped. "It's the way the business works. He has to be able to tell his middlemen that he knows the person who will do the job, so he can guarantee they're competent. He'll never tell them who we are, or us who they are, because that's what makes him important. It would also piss off people who kill for a living. But he has to be sure we're good enough. If we get caught or leave a target alive, his middlemen might kill him to cut their only connection with us."

"I guess it's okay," Moreland said.

"It's got to be," Holcomb said. "Without the Broker and the middlemen, we'd have to deal with customers. They're the most dangerous part."

"Who are the middlemen?"

"People somebody might ask about getting somebody killed. Bartenders in the right kind of bar, lawyers, a few low-level guys who run businesses for the Mafia, a few cops, gamblers, fences. Just guys who run into unhappy people sometimes."

After each job they went back into training while they waited for the next job. Holcomb was approaching fifty, and he claimed to be trying to fight the passage of time. He said that each year that passed without his noticeably losing strength, speed, stamina, or nerve was a great victory for him. Training with him gave Joey the body and mind of a fighter.

Most of their assignments were in Southern California, Nevada, or Arizona. They drove to most jobs in a small SUV, stole a set of license plates from the state they were visiting, did the job, and drove home the same night. Sometimes they would have to spend a week or two stalking the target.

From Holcomb Joey learned that the safest way for two men to operate was to show up at the target's house at night, take him from his home quietly, drive him off to a remote area in the desert or the mountains, kill him, and bury him there. They buried a dozen men in various parts of Joshua Tree National Park during this period, and others in other wilderness areas. But most of the time there were complications that made such simple and direct methods impossible. They had to spend time watching a man until he was alone and vulnerable, and then shoot him.

They worked together for over two years before Holcomb made his mistake. They were in downtown Los Angeles waiting in a car for a man named Lewis Hartmann to come out of the Bonaventure Hotel. The Broker had tipped them that Hartmann had a meeting set up with an associate for that evening after midnight. Moreland and Holcomb saw him at the same time. He came to the doorway and handed a ticket to the valet parking attendant, who trotted off to bring the car up from the parking levels.

The idea was that Joey Moreland would wait until Hartmann was in his car and driving off. Then he would pull up beside Hartmann at a red light. Holcomb's side window would already be open, and he would extend his arm and fire a round into Hartmann's head. Holcomb would jump down from the SUV, set Hartmann's transmission in park, and open the car's trunk. Joey would help him put the body into the trunk, then get into Hartmann's car and drive off. Holcomb would get into the SUV and follow. All this would take no more than ten seconds.

Moreland pulled up beside Hartmann's car. He saw Holcomb lift his pistol from his lap and extend his arm toward Hartmann's side window, but then something happened. There was a scrape and a clatter. It looked as though Holcomb had hit the gun against his door on the way up, but the sure thing was that Holcomb had dropped his gun. It fell from his hand and out the window between the two cars. Holcomb flung the door open and jumped out to pick it up, but Hartmann had seen all of it too. He produced a gun of his own and fired three rapid shots into Holcomb, then raised his gun to fire at Joey.

Just as Hartmann's eyes and his arm rose, Joey fired three shots through Holcomb's open door into Hartmann's upper body. Hartmann slumped over, half in and half out of his car, and the car began to drift into the intersection. As he struggled to free himself from his seat belt, the car gained a little speed, so it was going about five miles an hour when it went up over the curb and hit the railing of the freeway overpass at Temple. Hartmann flew out of his seat toward the windshield; the air bag inflated and punched him out onto the ground.

Moreland dragged Holcomb into the back of the SUV, slammed the door, and drove. He could hear Holcomb's labored breaths hissing in and out, a raspy sound that was almost a groan. By the time Joey was driving the SUV up the long dirt road onto the ranch, he couldn't hear Holcomb anymore. When he opened the hatch and touched Holcomb's carotid artery, there was no pulse. He used Holcomb's bulldozer to dig an eight-foot trench, then pushed him out the back of the SUV and covered the trench.

It wasn't until two nights later that he heard the police cars coming up the dirt road. He looked out, saw the red and blue lights in the distance, and set out on foot along the trails he and Holcomb had used. When the trails ran out, he kept going into the backcountry. Before dawn he reached a road he knew led to the freeway. When he reached the freeway he turned right and followed it all the way into the city. He was on his own, but he had learned a profession.

13

As Moreland worked to get Kelly more interested in him, he remembered things he had learned from hookers, the most important being that women who were paid to have sex got tired of men. He didn't blame them. There were johns who would call a girl up and talk dirty from the first sentence. Some would try to take control. So many escorts had had men take their cell phones away that nearly all of them carried two. Nearly every escort got beaten up by a client once or twice a year. Even if clients weren't brutal, they were often rough and impatient and demanding.

The first time he had called an escort was right after Holcomb had died. He had been living with Holcomb for months while they worked their way down the latest list from the Broker. They had killed six men on the Broker's latest list over a period of sixty days. During that time they had never left the ranch except to kill somebody.

Moreland had never stopped paying rent on his apartment while he'd worked with Holcomb. At times he thought he was doing it because he didn't want to move his belongings. But when he arrived there this time he stayed indoors, sleeping and eating beside his computer. He read all the references to their botched hit outside the Bonaventure. After a week he was sure the police had a theory that involved Holcomb's shooting the victim, taking off in the SUV, and stopping at his ranch to change vehicles, but dying before he could do any more.

Moreland spent weeks in his apartment, leaving only to get food. Finally he went on one of the big Web sites that rated escorts by city, and began to search for the right kind of girl. It took him only a few minutes of looking to find Rebecca Coleman. She had the same strawberry blond hair, the white skin, and the long legs that he liked. He called her and asked if he could make an appointment. They met at her apartment.

Later she told him she'd liked him because on that first appointment he had surprised her. He was quiet and polite on the phone. When he arrived he was clean, wore clean clothes, and was a little shy. He made love to her the way Mindy had taught him. It never occurred to him to try to bargain her price down, and when he left, he gave her a tip and said, "Thank you."

He called her again a few days later and made another appointment. She told him to come at nine, which was early for her. When he got there, she seemed to have been thinking of all the ways to try to please him. She made an unceasing effort from nine until nearly midnight, when he asked if he ought to leave. She kissed him and said, "Please don't leave. I haven't got any other clients tonight."

It was then that he realized that these girls had lonely lives. The reason they were escorts was that nobody cared about them enough to make that work uninviting and unnecessary. No matter how beautiful they were—and a surprising number really were—they didn't get much joy out of it. A good experience with a client was an exception.

He left the next morning while she was asleep. He placed a note on her kitchen table that said "Call me" and gave the number of the cell phone he carried.

It rang at noon, but when he answered it, the voice on the other end was the Broker. "I guess Holcomb's dead, huh?"

"It was a freak accident. He dropped his gun out the window. When he went to pick it up, the guy popped him."

"What happened to the target?"

"Well, I wasn't going to let him go just because he got lucky."

"You killed him?"

"Of course."

"Then I owe you money," said the Broker. "Sorry about your partner."

"Thanks," Joey said.

"He was a son of a bitch," said the Broker.

"I know."

"At least you're still alive."

"Yeah."

"Want me to deposit your money in a bank account or send it to you at your apartment?"

"I guess the apartment this time. "

"I'll also send you a clean phone."

"I can get a phone."

"Not like this. It's scrambled. After you've had it for a few days, I'll call you."

"Okay."

They hung up and his phone rang again. He heard Rebecca's voice. She said, "When I woke up I was sad to see you were gone." She added, "When I saw your note I was happy again."

"I'm happy you'd feel that way." It was true. He could feel the power flowing from her to him.

Two nights later she said, "I wish you didn't have to go home."

"I wish I didn't too."

"I mean at all."

He gave a chuckle. "I can't afford to see you every night."

"I wouldn't charge you. I won't. Starting now, everything is free. I just want you to be with me when I quit at night. Sleep with me, so I'm not alone. Then spend the morning with me."

He moved some of his clothes to her apartment, but he kept his own apartment in case the arrangement didn't work out.

After a week his money arrived in the mail at his apartment and so did his new cell phone. After a second week, it rang. He was just walking in Rebecca's door. The Broker said, "Listen carefully."

"I am."

"I'm going to give you a list of ten targets and their addresses. You can do them when you're ready. Your schedule is up to you. I'll give you fifty thousand for each one. Open a couple of new bank accounts in fake names in different states—nothing that might be associated with Holcomb. When you cross off your first target, wait forty-eight hours and then call me with your bank information. I'll get the money transferred right away."

"Why forty-eight hours?"

"It's the news cycle, kid. By then I know it's done and you got away with it. After the second hit, you do the same. Kill the guy and call me. Tell me what to do with your money. This all okay with you?"

"Sure."

"Just have the last name crossed off by January first. Ready for the names?"

"Give me a minute to find a pen."

He found one on the kitchen counter where Rebecca made her grocery lists. He took the pad and wrote down the list of ten men. He was pleased to see that the first couple of addresses were in Southern California.

Moreland spent a week finding the first target, and studying the area around his neighborhood. He contemplated different ways of getting him alone. At the end of each day, he went back to Rebecca Coleman's apartment. She changed her online ads so she was available from noon until nine p.m. At ten he would arrive at her apartment. By then she had bathed and cleaned the apartment. They would go out to a restaurant and return around midnight.

The first name on his list was Thomas Hennessy. His address was a bar in Bakersfield, which was about a hundred miles from the ocean, but the bar was called The Captain's Table. The biggest sign on the building was an ancient one that read UNDER NEW MANAGEMENT.

When Moreland was inside he ordered a draft beer and nursed it while he studied the other people at tables or perched at the bar. The customers were nearly all men, most of them about forty to sixty, with a group of six in their twenties at a table in the corner near the front door.

The place was too popular at midday for him to think of taking out the owner and walking out the front door. In a dive like this he couldn't even be sure a few of the other daytime drinkers weren't carrying concealed guns.

Moreland watched and listened while he finished his drink. He was about to leave when an older man emerged from a room behind the bar. He was muscular, wearing a black T-shirt with "Gold's Gym" on it. He was about fifty-five years old with a short, bristly gray beard and a balding head. He was carrying a case of whiskey bottles that was heavy enough to make his biceps bulge. When he set the case down behind the bar he went back to the door, picked out a key on a ring, and locked it again. Moreland saw tattoo script on his arm that read "Hennessy."

Hennessy's face was expressionless, but his eyes scanned the room as though he was looking for something in particular, and that was not a good sign. He knew he was being stalked.

Moreland regretted coming inside the bar. It had been a foolish, lazy impulse. He should have found an observation point outside the bar and watched from a distance until he identified the target. Holcomb would never have allowed him to make this kind of careless mistake. Now the target had seen him. The next time he saw Moreland he would know it wasn't a coincidence.

When Hennessy went to the back hallway where the men's room and the rear entrance were, Moreland got up and walked out the front door. He got into his car and drove up the street past body shops and carpet stores and around the long block, then did what he should have done before. He pulled up near the fence at the back of a paint store, sat in his car, and watched the parking lot of the bar, memorizing the cars. He paid special attention to the ones closest to the door, where the employees, who arrived first, probably parked. Hennessy's car could be one of the four parked in the first row. There were a brownish Acura, a new blue Mustang, a black BMW, and a white Toyota SUV.

Moreland drove off and went to a restaurant for dinner, then went to a movie. He called Rebecca at ten to tell her he'd be very late tonight. He returned to the street outside the bar at eleven. The four cars in the front were still there. He had already committed himself when he'd let Hennessy see him. He had to make his move tonight.

He watched the parking lot of the bar for two hours. Men came in and went out, but none of the four cars moved. At two a.m. the bar's electric sign went out. A half hour later, two men came out, got into their cars, and left. Moreland got out of his car, walked close to the side of the building, and waited. He heard the front door open once more, and two men's voices. One of them said, "Got to get the cleaning done by ten, and the restocking done before noon."

Moreland stepped around the building, held his Beretta 92 in a two-handed aim, and fired. He put two bullets into Hennessy's chest and fired twice at the second man, whom he recognized as the bartender. Both men went down. The bartender was lying half in the doorway, and Hennessy was sprawled on his back, his eyes open to the night sky. Moreland stepped close and fired a round into Hennessy's forehead. In the corner of his eye he caught movement. He fired once more at the bartender's head, then returned to Hennessy. He took Hennessy's wallet and the key chain on his belt. He dragged the bartender inside the bar and turned on the light switch. Then he dragged Hennessy inside and locked the door.

Moreland went to the back room and looked for the surveillance system. He found the video recorder, disconnected it, and took it with him. Then he took the bartender's wallet. He turned off the light, locked the door with Hennessy's key, and drove to his apartment. He counted the money he'd taken, threw the wallets and the recorder into a Dumpster a few miles away, and then went to see Rebecca.

For the next couple of months he was extremely careful and professional. It was essential to a shooter that he be the one to choose the time and place to pull the trigger. He had made one careless mistake, and the realization had surprised him so much that he felt a residual fear whenever he thought about it.

When danger came it was from another source. He came home one evening and found Rebecca sitting in the living room. Her strawberry blond hair was washed and blown dry, but left natural and wavy so it seemed to take up a lot of space, like an aura. She wore jeans and a T-shirt, with her feet bare. He could see she had set the furniture up so the only place to sit was right in front of her.

He said, "Hi. I was afraid you'd be asleep."

She said, "We need to talk, so I waited."

"Okay. Let's talk."

She watched him warily. "I think I've been good to you." Moreland could tell she was establishing grounds for a complaint.

He decided to blunt the argument before it started. "Of course you have been. You've been great."

She said, "I think you haven't been honest with me."

"About what?"

"Just tell me the truth. Have you been doing something you haven't told me while you were here?"

"Probably," he said, and laughed. "Narrow it down."

"I found a shitload of money in that backpack you keep in the closet. Also two guns and some bullets." She started to cry. "While I'm saying it I realize how stupid I sound. What answer can there be? You've been doing really bad stuff, and you didn't give a shit if I got hurt or killed or sent to jail for, like, forever."

He sighed. "Since I met you I've been spending money in front of you. For a while I was even paying you. It's always been cash. Didn't it occur to you that somewhere there must be a shitload of cash that I got it from? And people who have a lot of cash around tend to have guns within reach so they can keep their cash." He shrugged.

"Don't act like I'm stupid." She was angry.

"I'm just doing what you asked—telling you the truth."

"I may be a dumb whore, but I'm not as dumb as this. I'm an independent person, and I don't need some john to talk to me like I was a child." Her face reddened in anger.

She swung her arm to slap him across the face, but he didn't think, just snatched her hand out of the air. She instantly swung the other hand, but he caught that one too. "Please stop this," he said. "I'll go away and leave you alone now. I'll leave you some money so you don't feel that I cheated you or something."

She began to struggle again, trying to free her hands, but he knew it was only a distraction so she could knee him in the groin. He turned his body to the side suddenly so her knee harmlessly bumped his thigh. She took her next try with the other knee, but he had known it would happen long before she did. He pulled both her arms hard to his right toward the bed. Her head pounded into the wall and she fell on the bed, dazed and possibly unconscious. He took a pistol out of his backpack, wrapped a pillow around it, and shot her in the head.

As he put the pistol away he checked his backpack to be sure she hadn't taken anything, then began to search the apartment. He found forty thousand dollars in cash hidden behind an air-conditioning vent near the head of the bed, and put it into his backpack. He covered her body with the bedspread so she appeared to be asleep.

He made sure he was leaving nothing in the apartment. He wandered through the apartment wiping every single surface he might have touched—faucets, light switches, doorknobs, counters, window latches. He knew he was being overly cautious, because there would be hundreds of male prints all over the premises, but he didn't want his to be among those collected. When he had cleaned every part of the apartment he remembered Rebecca's jewelry. There was a box hidden in the kitchen inside a set of pots and pans so none of her in-call clients would see it. He used a dish towel to open the cabinet and lift the top off the pot. He opened the box and saw that everything he remembered was there.

He pushed a few sets of earrings aside and saw one of his favorites. It was a gold chain with a gold oval disk. On the disk was a two-carat diamond she had told him was placed to show the position of the earth on her birthday.

In another minute or two he was outside, on his way to his car. This had been a shocking, unexpected night, but he had learned that he couldn't just tell a woman he was leaving her and expect her to behave rationally. He put his backpack with all the money into the farthest corner of the trunk of his car, and drove out of Los Angeles.

A year later he gave the necklace and the matching anklet to a girl in Miami named Jenny McLaughlin. He'd known he could take it back when she was through with it.

14

Jack Till spent his thirty-fifth morning in a row staring at escort ads on the screen of his laptop. He clicked on each ad that said "blond," "red," "ginger," "redhead," or "strawberry blond." He would stop every fifteen or twenty minutes to rest his eyes. When he had gone all the way through the escort ads in one major city, he would put a check mark next to it on his list and move on to the next city. Over the past month he had been through the list of major cities several times. Each time he returned to a city, he would recognize a number of girls, but there would be as many new ones he had never seen before. He had admitted to himself that he wasn't working just for Catherine Hamilton's parents now. He was working for Kyra, the girl he had hired at the Biltmore in Phoenix and then followed home. He was also working for the next Kyra, the next girl who would come into the sphere of this killer. He wanted to find her before she died.

This morning he had moved his search to Boston. After so many days it was tempting to pass over groups of ads without looking at the photographs. Then, there she was. The girl looked very much the way they all had looked. She was tall and slender and very pale, with hair that couldn't be called blond or red, but was something in between. She called herself Kelly. She presented herself in the usual poses, approximating the views a man would have of her in various sexual positions. Then he saw the glint of gold where the flash of the camera was reflected, and he held his breath for a moment. He put his fingers on the screen and enlarged the image.

Hanging from her neck was the gold oval with the diamond on it. There was the chain at the ankle. There was no question that this Kelly was wearing the custom-made necklace and anklet that Catherine Hamilton had worn in Los Angeles and Kyra had worn in Phoenix.

He closed his laptop and opened the two gun safes that were bolted against the wall in the office. He opened a couple of drawers at the bottom and found what he was looking for. He took out the two Ruger LC9 compact nine-millimeter pistols. They were only six inches long and nine-tenths of an inch thick, and each weighed seventeen ounces. He reached into the drawer again and brought out two spare magazines for each, then loaded the magazines.

Two compact pistols were the best choice for the kind of action he was expecting. Most people didn't think clearly about concealed weapons because they didn't know what worked and what didn't. The human body didn't conceal weapons well. A man walking around with a three-pound .45-caliber model 1911 under his coat wasn't hard to spot. The man's torso bent toward the weapon when he tried to hide it, and he bent away from it when he thought he might have to use it. A man carrying two small, thin polymer pistols was evenly balanced. He wasn't leaning one way or the other. The eye didn't pick up the width of the two LC9s on a man's body.

At close range there was virtually no advantage to firing a nine-millimeter round from a bigger gun. At twenty-five feet he could place his rounds within a two-inch circle. The gun would do that at a hundred feet.

Till reserved a seat on a flight from LAX to Logan airport for that evening, and a room at the Intercontinental with an estimated arrival of eight the next morning. He prepared four packages for mailing. Each contained parts of two LC9 pistols. One had the slides, recoil springs, barrels, and one trigger and sear in a metal windup toy. He put the four loaded magazines between two external computer drives. He mailed the four packages to himself at his hotel.

He didn't like doing things this way, because smuggling hand-guns around was risky. But he also didn't like his odds of finding the weapons he might need in another state within an hour of landing.

He drove to the flower shop where Holly worked, parked on the street, and entered. As he did, he saw Holly emerge from the cutting room with a vase of flowers she had arranged. Mrs. Carmody, the owner, looked at the arrangement and said, "Beautiful, Holly. But think how much fuller it would seem if you added a little baby's breath here and here." He caught himself looking at Mrs. Carmody for longer than he should have.

Holly said, "Okay" and turned to go back into the cutting room, but then saw him. "Hey, Dad."

"Hi, honey. I thought you might like to go to lunch. Do you have plans?"

"No," she said. "Mrs. Camody, can I go early?"

"Hi, Jack," said Mrs. Carmody. To Holly she said, "Finish that arrangement and you're out of here."

When Holly disappeared, he said, "Would you like to join us?"

"I'd love to, but I can't. I have other plans today—a late lunch. Besides, Holly and I are the whole shop today until two."

"We won't be long," he said. "By the way, is Holly still doing okay?"

"She's doing great. A sense of color is like an ear for music. You have it or you don't. She's a worker, and it's hard to be around her without being cheered up."

Till tried to ignore the fact that she was so attractive, with her black hair, her blue eyes, and her graceful movements as she stepped around the small store getting things for the arrangement in the front window. He knew she was a widow, but that didn't mean she would be interested in him.

Holly appeared with the vase; set it in the refrigerator case with a tag that said, "Sold"; and went to the door. "Let's get this show on the road," she said.

"See you later," he said, and Mrs. Carmody gave a little wave as they left the shop.

They walked for a block before either of them spoke, because that was Holly's rule. She didn't want to be caught walking away from people and saying something about them. As soon as they had crossed the first street, she said, "You should take her out."

"Mrs. Camody?"

"Jeanne. If you take her out you can call her Jeanne."

"What makes you think she'd want to go out with me?"

"She asks about you sometimes, and she looks at you when you aren't looking at her. At your butt, mostly. All the signs."

"I don't think that's a good idea," Till said. "If we didn't get along it might make things awkward for you."

"No problem," she said. "Mrs. Carmody and I are adults. We'll ignore anything like that."

"Well, I'm going out of town tonight, so I can't ask her out right now anyway."

"Where are you going?"

"Boston. I'd like to be home in a few days, but it could take longer."

"When you come home, then. That gives me more time to get her thinking about you, so she feels butterflies when she hears your voice. You need a girlfriend."

They went to lunch at a restaurant that was too far to walk to from the shop, so it wouldn't be a place she got to go to often, and he watched her eat a hamburger and a piece of pie, then drove her back to the store. On the way, he said, "Will you have enough money if I'm gone for a while?"

"Dad," she said. "I'm not a child."

A few hours later he got to the right gate at the airport just before boarding began, settled himself in his seat on the plane, watched the flight attendants' safety pantomime, and waited for the plane to taxi out to the runway. The plane was aloft in a few minutes, and the lights went black. He closed his eyes and slept. There were so many people on the ground who wanted an old homicide cop like Till dead that sleeping had sometimes been a risky activity for him, but in an airplane he was anonymous to the people around him, and all of them had been screened to be sure they were unarmed. He always slept peacefully on airplanes.

Daylight streaming in through the scratched plastic windows woke him. He stretched his muscles and looked at the GPS map on the screen in front of him. Many of the passengers around him were waking up too. The others looked worn and dazed as though they had worked twenty-four hours, but he felt rested. Till reached under his seat, took his sport coat out of the plastic bag where he'd kept it, put the plastic bag in the pocket, and waited serenely for the plane to land.

When it had bounced once and rattled to a stop, the plane made its way to the gate. When the lights all came on again and there was a *ping* sound, the passengers all stood, rifled the overhead compartments, and slowly lockstepped down the aisle and out. Till rode the shuttle bus to the car rental lot, then drove to his hotel. He checked in, put his bag in the room, and went into the restaurant for breakfast.

As he ate, he tried to figure out everything he would need to know about this killer. It was obvious that as soon as he murdered and robbed his current prostitute in a month or so, he would be off again. He would travel a significant distance to another city and find another girl who looked like the one before. He would shortly be so tight with her that he was—practically or actually—living with her. But what made him decide when to kill her? What made him choose the next city? Why were these girls all so willing to have him around?

After breakfast Till went to his room, took out his laptop, and signed onto the hotel's wi-fi network. He went to a couple of sites to see the escort ads posted for today. For this day, at least, Kelly was still alive, feeling well enough to advertise for work. He hadn't killed her yet. Till wrote down the phone number she had posted.

He decided it was late enough to call Ted McCann in Los Angeles. He dialed his cell with his thumb and waited.

"Hello?"

"Hi, Ted. It's Jack Till."

"What can I do for you today?"

"I'm making some headway on the Boyfriend."

"That's what you call him—the Boyfriend?"

"It's what he is. Or one of the things he is. He forms relationships with these girls. Each one seems to last a month or two. Then he kills her, takes whatever she's got that's valuable—cash and jewelry, mostly—and he leaves. He's been in Boston recently, and I'm guessing he's still here because the girl here is still alive."

"How did you trace him?"

"Catherine Hamilton had some distinctive pieces of jewelry on in some of her pictures. Jewelers have all told me it was custom-made. It wasn't listed among her belongings by the crime scene people, so I figured he took it with him when he left Los Angeles. Next time I saw it was in the photo of a girl named Kyra in Phoenix. He killed her too."

"I'm sorry, Jack."

"Me too. I think what bothers me most about this guy is that he's happy to end somebody else's life for no discernible reason. I know he's nuts, picking out girls that look the same. But I'm not detecting rage or a thrill or even regular greed. And it can't be a challenge. When he leaves he kills the girl and turns out the lights."

"What makes you think he's in Boston now?"

"There's an ad for an escort named Kelly. She's the same type as the other girls, and she's wearing the same two pieces of jewelry. It's definitely the same—a gold oval with a big diamond in a kind of off-balanced spot, and a lot of little ones around the edge."

"I'm sensing there's a problem. What is it?"

"He's here in Boston, but I don't know why he's here. I can't figure out why he chooses one place over another. I want to know if there's something going on in these cities that makes him come or makes him leave."

"Too bad you can't ask him."

"That's what I'm here to do."

"Why are you telling me?"

"I've got a feeling about this guy. He's got the skills, and he's cold. If he gets me, I want you to know what I know about him. Anthony and her partner are worse than useless. All they do is think up reasons why no lead is good enough. I know you can't go after him. But I'd hate to die and leave nobody alive who knows what I've found out."

He paused. "I also wondered if you know anybody with the Boston police."

"I know a guy," said McCann. "Met him at a vice cop convention in Las Vegas a few years ago. We talk now and then. His name is Alan Rafferty. Let me get you his number." He read the number aloud twice.

"Thanks, Ted," said Till. "I won't presume on him too much."

"Presume away. This is what the bastard's there for. He's a cop. Good luck."

"Thanks."

Till disconnected. He sat for a moment, then got up to leave. He had to find out more about Kelly as quickly as possible. Every minute was moving her closer to the moment when the Boyfriend would put his gun to the back of her head.

15

Kelly's ad included a phone number. When Till called, a girl's voice said she couldn't take a call at that moment. It also gave her address: 909 Main Street in Woburn. He took the address down and drove there. Woburn was in the northwest district outside Boston. Her apartment was in the center of a lot of roads with the names of the places they led to—Bedford, Cambridge. Main Street went right into Boston. It was a long series of one- and two-story brick buildings that housed cafés and sushi bars and other businesses, so he could see it wouldn't be hard for him to find places to loiter.

The afternoon when Till drove into Woburn he was already looking for a place to stay. He parked on Main and walked to number 909, the address on Kelly's ad. It was a gray two-story apartment building. He went to the front door and tried to enter the lobby, but the door was locked. He could see a bank of eight brass mailboxes inside. There was an intercom beside the door, so he pressed the button that said "Manager." A man with a thick Russian accent answered. "Hello. What can I do for you?"

Till said, "I wondered if you had any vacant apartments." While he talked, he looked at the names on the list of buttons. The only one that wasn't male or a couple was K. Allen in apartment 5. That had to be the second floor.

"Not right now," said the manager. "Maybe in a few weeks. If you want to leave your name and number, stick it in the mail slot." Till could see, looking past the lobby, that the door of apartment 1 was on the left in front.

"Thank you," Till said. "But I need something right away." On his way back to the car he considered what he had seen. If apartment 1 on the first floor was in front on the left side of the hall, then probably apartment 5 on the second floor would be on the left side in the front also.

He drove half a block to an old-looking but clean hotel with about forty rooms, and went to the front desk to ask about renting a room by the week. It had to be on an upper floor and it had to have a clear line of sight to Kelly's apartment building. He asked for a room high on the north side, and got it. He could look out the balcony window, up the street, and see a side view of Kelly's building; a parking lot behind it; and a small patio with several round tables painted black, where tenants would sometimes sit to smoke.

He told the people at the front desk he had business in Boston and needed to stay two weeks before he returned to Los Angeles. He drove into Boston and bought several items: a night vision scope, a sixty-power spotting scope, and a plug-in microphone that he could listen to by telephone. The microphone was small and made of white plastic and looked as though it was a plug-in receptacle. He had no idea whether he would use any of these things, but he was determined to have whatever edge was available.

He began to walk the town late that afternoon. It was a cool afternoon for summer, but still sunny. He wore black sunglasses, a baseball cap, a hooded sweatshirt, jeans, and a pair of black sneakers. Even if the Boyfriend had seen Till in a car while he was being followed in Phoenix, he would never recognize him in Woburn, Massachusetts.

But Till had decided not to bet against the capabilities of his adversary this time, so he walked without coming close to Kelly's apartment. Instead, he got to know the downtown section first, then widened his walks to both Interstate 93 and Interstate 95. He got to know the residential neighborhoods, and the convenient entrances and exits to the highways.

He slept in the hotel for the next two nights. Each night after dark, he would venture into the area closer to Kelly's apartment building. He found a small market on Main Street and bought snacks and newspapers there because carrying them served as an explanation of what he was doing out on foot.

Every time he passed the apartment building he would concentrate on learning something. He would use his phone to take pictures of the parking lot and the front and sides of the building. When he returned to the hotel, he would download the pictures onto his computer, magnify them, and study them for information.

After two evenings he had photographed the same eight cars twice. He had taken photographs of the lobby and the row of mailboxes on the inner wall. He had photographed the windows of each apartment several times, and had a good start on knowing who inhabited each unit.

He had passed by at random times between seven p.m. and two a.m. and determined which apartments never had lights on after eleven, and which had glowing windows at two. He had eliminated all four ground-floor apartments, and two of the second-floor apartments. There were a couple of toddlers in a third apartment on the second floor, and that left the one on the south side in the front. It had to be Kelly's.

Till also set up his spotting scope. It was about four feet back from the window of his room, set up on the dresser, with the curtains closed except for about four inches that allowed the lens to see out. With the lights off he could watch the apartment at the front of the second floor without being visible. On the second night at a few minutes after midnight, he saw the curtains in the second-floor window part. A girl was at the window in a white bathrobe. She reached up with both hands to lower the window and lock it. But in the three seconds while she was visible, he had seen the reddish hair against the white robe. It had to be Kelly. He watched for the rest of the evening and studied the cars in the lot, but he saw no car that he hadn't seen before, and he never saw a man leave the building. Either business was slow or she was taking the night off.

The next morning he drove to his hotel in Boston, accepted the four packages he had mailed to himself from Los Angeles, and then checked out of the hotel. He drove back to his hotel in Woburn, arranged the pieces of the two identical Ruger LC9 pistols on his bed, and assembled them, wiping each part off with his handkerchief so he left no fingerprints on any internal part. Then he wiped off the bullets, loaded the magazines, and inserted the magazines into the pistols. He cycled each one to put a round into the chamber, then put the pistols into the side pockets of the sport coat he intended to wear, then draped the sport coat over the desk chair in the center of the room where he could reach it quickly.

He resumed his observation of the apartment building. By the end of the third day he had still not seen a woman who could be Kelly leave the building. He had not spotted anybody he thought was the Boyfriend either. He supposed it was possible the Boyfriend used a disguise of some kind, but that seemed unlikely.

Till decided he couldn't wait any longer to talk to her. He couldn't just watch the apartment until the Boyfriend killed her too. The curtains were open, so he aimed his spotting scope and dialed the phone number from her ad. The voice was soft and feminine, but utterly false. "This is Kelly."

"Hi," he said. "I saw your ad online."

"Hi. What's your name?"

"Jack," he said. "I wondered if there was a way you and I could get together."

"That's what the ad is for, Jack. But you should know that I have to charge for my time. If anything happens between us, that would be up to us, since we're both grown-ups. But I'm not offering or contracting to perform any illegal acts. You understand that, don't you?"

"I understand."

"An hour of my company is two-fifty, and four hundred for two hours."

"Okay. Do you have any free time tonight?"

"You pick the time."

"How about eight o'clock?"

"Eight is fine. My address is 909 Main Street in Woburn, apartment five."

He repeated the address. "You're independent, right? There won't be some big guy standing by the door?"

"That's right," she said. "I work alone." Her throat held a laugh captive so it couldn't escape. "If you want a big guy too, you'll have to be the one to call him."

"See you at eight."

"I'll be waiting," she said.

After she hung up, she called Joey's cell phone.

"Hello," he said.

"Hi, baby," she said. "Where are you?"

"I'm working in the office I rented, trying to get it ready. What's up?"

"I'm working tonight. I just made a date for eight o'clock."

"Don't worry. I won't be in your way. I'll be here in the city until nine or so anyway. Should I bring some take-out dinner home with me around ten?"

"Could you? That'd be great."

"What would you like?"

"Surprise me."

"You got it."

"Love you."

"Love you." Joey hung up, set his phone alarm for nine to remind him, and put the phone back into his pocket. Then he looked out the window into the distance.

Joey Moreland was working on the Luis Salazar problem. When he had first seen the name on the list it had meant nothing to him. There had been all sorts of names on the Broker's lists from the beginning—Italian, English, Polish, German, Spanish. The Broker's contacts—according to Dick Holcomb a collection of lawyers, fences, fixers, and go-betweens—were in all kinds of businesses and neighborhoods in lots of cities, and he would never know who they were. Moreland had the impression that some of them were people who had done an occasional hit themselves. Some of them were probably still willing to take on a really easy job, but they passed the hard ones to the Broker.

It wasn't until after he had taken the job that he learned Salazar was worse than a hard one. He was a foreign government official. Moreland had to assume that Salazar would arrive with at least a few Mexican bodyguards. They would be hard little guys with black, suspicious eyes scanning the crowd for threats. There would also be some kind of American law enforcement, spread wider than the Mexicans because only the Americans would be expected to deal with the American public. The officers that Moreland would need to fear most were the ones who would be stationed far from Luis Salazar, probably up high to control the area with sniper rifles and radios.

Moreland would have liked to do this job a different way. But there was only one way he could think of, and that was to reach out from so far away that the cops—even if they spotted him—would need several minutes to reach him. And if they fired at him, their rounds would fall hundreds of feet short. If he felt inclined to, he could even disable any police cars headed his way. The .50-caliber projectiles were made to pierce lightly armored vehicles in battle.

Moreland had only a couple of days left before Luis Salazar would appear in Boston. There had been no public announcement that he was coming. Moreland hadn't been surprised by that. Salazar was coming to speak to local officials in Boston, not with the general public, and he was a prosecutor who had made his reputation cracking down on Mexican drug cartels. But the published schedule of the mayor and the city council agenda were curiously light beginning at three p.m. on Thursday. The mayor's office said he was taking no appointments, and the city council planned to be in session, but would consider nothing new.

Joey had spent this afternoon in the office. He had leased the space under the name ProPlay Sports after he had arrived in town. He had spoken to the rental agent on the phone, and signed the lease by mail. Today he had brought his Barrett long-range .50-caliber rifle and ammunition. They were in the hard-sided case, which he had put inside a long, narrow cardboard carton and loaded onto a two-wheel dolly. They had looked to any observer like furnishings for the office.

He had used the desk he'd rented to stand on and propped the gun case and ammunition above the false ceiling on the intersection of a set of pipes that held the fire sprinkler system. But since Kelly's call, he knew he had some extra time to spare. He locked the door to his office, took down the gun, and removed it from its case. He put it on the desk and aimed it through the big window a few feet away.

About a mile away he could see the entrance to City Hall at City Hall Plaza, a vast expanse of redbricks at Congress and North streets. He studied the building through the rifle scope. City Hall didn't look like any of the graceful older buildings in the city. It looked squat and formidable, like an alien fortress. He studied the front of the building carefully and adjusted the scope as he looked. The only place he could be sure that Luis Salazar would be visible during his visit was the one he was looking at—the entrance to City Hall at Congress and North.

When Moreland had gone to City Hall to look at the place and walk on the bricks he had needed to park in a lot four blocks away. There was no way to place a getaway car, nothing to hide behind to conceal his presence, no way to elude the police who would be on the plaza and around the building. He knew that the way he planned to do this was the only way that gave him a reasonable chance of survival. He was sure that if a government official from Mexico was shot in Boston, the police would automatically begin looking for a Hispanic with a gun. Nobody in Boston even knew who Salazar was, and certainly no one had anything against him. He was an expert on the methods of the drug cartels, coming to speak with other authorities. If anybody killed him, the police would assume it was another Mexican.

Joey had repeatedly tested his route from this office to the apartment building in Woburn. On surface streets it was about ten miles, and he'd had little trouble getting there in thirty minutes. If he wished, he could take either I-93 or I-95, and reach Woburn in fifteen minutes.

Moreland was going to do this job in a conservative suit and a tie. When it was done he would put the rifle in its case, put the case inside the cardboard carton, and wheel it to his car on the dolly. As a precaution, he would have his fake police badge with him and a Beretta 92F in a shoulder holster like a cop. In the confusion and chaos after the shooting, witnesses might report anything, but it was unlikely they'd complain because they'd seen a cop.

16

When Till arrived at the front door of the apartment building in Woburn he had already packed everything into his car. He had the two Ruger pistols—one in his pocket and one in the car under the driver's seat. He had parked a block away on Main Street near the place where I-93 and I-95 met. This time what he was after was the girl, Kelly. Once she was safe, he would turn his attention to the Boyfriend.

He pushed the button beside the door that said "K. Allen, Apt. 5," heard the buzz, opened the door, and entered the lobby. He climbed the stairs and found himself in another hallway like the one downstairs; it had light blue walls and carpet, and doors painted dark blue. The first door on the left was apartment 5. He raised his left hand to knock, but the door opened partway.

He recognized her face in the opening. She smiled at him and said quietly, "Jack?"

He nodded, and she opened the door farther, staying behind it, and let him step in. She closed the door and leaned her back on it. She was wearing an outfit that was very similar to the one she had worn for the photographs in her ad—black thigh-high stockings, a garter belt, and a bustier that was cinched to accentuate her thin waist and the white skin of her hips.

"You're more beautiful than your pictures. I didn't think that could happen."

"Thanks. Do you have something for me?"

He reached into his inner coat pocket and produced an envelope. He watched her take it. She reached in, took the money between her thumb and forefinger, fanned it so she could see the denominations of the bills, then placed it in a desk that had a lock, and palmed the key.

She led him down a short hallway to a bedroom. He could see another closed door farther down, which he decided must be her actual bedroom, where she slept with the Boyfriend. He pointed at it. "Are we alone, or is your boyfriend or somebody in there?"

She smiled and made a small production of stepping to the second door and opening it so he could see. The room was very sedate and conventional, like the room of an older woman—a dark gray bedspread, a pile of about six pillows with very clean white pillowcases. There was a woman's dresser with a big mirror, and a full-length mirror on the closet door. He saw nothing to indicate the presence of the Boyfriend, so he assumed his clothes were in the closed closet. "See? I told you before, if you're looking for a big guy, you'll have to bring him. I have a boyfriend, but you won't see him."

It occurred to Till that all the mirrors must have been comforting to a girl who looked the way she did. No matter what else happened the mirrors never had any bad news for her. She shut the door firmly. They moved into the other bedroom, which was more like what he had expected. On a platform was a king-size bed, with bright blue satin sheets and matching satin pillowcases. There were two nightstands. One held a blue china bowl filled with condoms. Behind it was a row of plastic bottles and tubes.

Kelly put her arms around him and said, "Just relax and give me a nice hug."

He complied, then sat on the bed. As he expected, she sat next to him. He said, "Can we just talk for a few minutes?"

"Sure," she said. "Talking about boyfriends has got to be a turnoff, but I'll bet you knew you're not my first date, right? When we get to know each other we'll get along fine."

"I paid to come and see you because I needed to talk to you, and to show you some things."

She was unperturbed, but confused. "Is this something special you like to do?"

He reached into the inner pocket of his jacket, where he'd had the money. "No." He removed a sheaf of folded printouts, unfolded one, and handed it to her. "This is Catherine Hamilton, in Los Angeles."

"Wow. She looks a lot like me, doesn't she? Do you always look for the same type of girl?"

"No. Your boyfriend does."

She looked irritated. "What?"

"He always seems to find a girl who has strawberry blond hair, very light skin, and blue or green eyes, between five feet seven and five ten, and thin."

"Why would you come here and tell me this?" she said angrily. "What are you?"

He held the second picture of Catherine Hamilton he had printed. "See the necklace? The anklet?"

She snatched the print and glared at it, then let it drop onto the bed.

He handed her the next picture—another tall, thin girl with strawberry blond hair. "This is Rebecca Coleman." She tossed that one aside, too, but he knew she had looked at it. He handed her another. While she held the picture she couldn't help seeing the next one he held ready. She snatched it from his hand and threw it onto the bed with the others. He said, "All of these girls were working as escorts, and three were wearing that necklace."

She stood up. "You're a creep. Get out."

"I'm here because they're all dead."

"I told you to get out."

"Your boyfriend charmed them into letting him live with them, and when he was ready to move on, he killed them."

She raised her voice. "I asked you nicely, and now I'm going to scream for the police."

"Please," he said. "Please listen to me. I'm trying to save your life. The way he'll do it is wait until you're looking the other way and put a gun to the back of your head, so you won't see it coming. Then he'll take everything you have—money, jewelry—and go to the next city."

"He doesn't need my money," she said. "He has plenty of his own."

"No, he doesn't need your money. He's got the money he stole from all of these girls after he killed them. But he'll take yours too, because that makes it look like a john robbed you and killed you. Honestly, I don't get anything for warning you. I just can't stand by and wait for him to get you too."

She stood and scowled at him with her arms folded in front of her. "You could be trying to get me to leave with you so you can kill me yourself."

"I could be, but I'm not. I trailed your boyfriend from Los Angeles to Phoenix, and both those girls are dead. I trailed him to you, and this is your chance to save yourself. Right now, tonight, while he's off somewhere, is the only chance you may get."

She had begun to look uncertain. "How can I believe you?"

"Pick up the phone, get an operator, and ask to be connected with police headquarters in Los Angeles, then ask for Sergeant McCann in

Vice. Tell him what I said and ask if it's true. If you have the operator do it, I can't be faking it."

She stared at him for a second, then seemed to realize he couldn't be lying. "Oh my God. What am I supposed to do?"

"Grab whatever is valuable to you, get in your own car, drive away, and don't come back."

"I wouldn't even know what to take."

"Take whatever occurs to you. It doesn't matter. Nothing is worth your life. Just get out. If you want help, I'll help. When is he coming home?"

"A couple of hours. But he'll come after me."

"If you don't go, he won't even have to come after you." He waited, and saw her weakening. "Come on. Get dressed."

She opened the closet and took a pair of jeans. She took a sweatshirt and underwear from the dresser. She took off the lingerie, threw it onto the floor, put on the clothes, and tied her hair in a ponytail. He watched her go to the other bedroom. She was gone for a minute, and then returned carrying an overnight bag that looked stuffed. He followed her to the living room. She unlocked the desk drawer and put Till's money into her purse.

He said, "Are you all set?"

"Yes."

"Do you want me to walk you to your car?"

"Yes."

Till opened the door for her, then stopped. "Do you have any pictures of him?"

"No. He said he hates having his picture taken. I know his name."

"No you don't," said Till. "You know an alias." He peered out the door and looked up and down the hall. "It looks clear. Walk behind me. If he appears, don't stop and hide or something. Run the other way, and keep running."

"Okay."

Till said, "Are you parked in the lot?"

"Yes. A blue Honda Civic."

"Okay." He went out into the hall. She turned back to lock the door, but he stopped her. "Leave it unlocked. I'll wait there for him."

"Oh God," she muttered, but obeyed. They walked along the hallway. Till had his right hand in his coat pocket, gripping the Ruger LC9 pistol he had brought. The Boyfriend hadn't come into the apartment, but that didn't mean he hadn't arrived at the apartment building. He could be waiting in the lot for Kelly's customer to leave.

Till stepped to the rear door of the apartment building. He pushed it open and scanned the lot. From here he could see the cars, and they all seemed to be empty. He said, "Stay here. I'll go out to Main and be sure he isn't parked out there waiting."

She didn't answer, so he turned to look at her. She was holding her telephone in her right hand and staring at it.

"What are you doing?"

"Texting my sister. I've got to have a place to go, and he doesn't know about her."

"Don't do it now. Just stay put."

She put the phone into her pocket. Till went out the door and into the parking lot. It was dark and summer-quiet. He could hear the steady *swish* of car tires beyond the building on Main, but the only other sound was his feet on the gravel: *skitch, skitch, skitch.*

As he came to the end of the lot and turned toward the front door of the building, it flew open and light splashed on the steps and the sidewalk. The girl was tall and graceful, and she took the leap down the front steps like a greyhound and kept running. The car was a white Toyota. It sped up to the curb and stopped, and the passenger door flew open, bounced against its hinges once, and the girl was there. She ducked to throw herself onto the passenger seat, and the car took off. It accelerated down Main Street, away from the girl's apartment in the direction of central Boston.

For a second Till actually considered firing at the car, but the chances of hitting the Boyfriend were slim, rapidly diminishing to none. Even if he hit the Boyfriend, at this speed the girl would be killed when the car lost its driver. As he stared after the car, he felt his frustration and irritation being overwhelmed by sorrow. The girl was sure to die. Seeing her run like that had reminded him of how young she was.

He looked in the opposite direction up Main Street, then went back inside and set the lock on the doorknob.

He spent the next half hour in Kelly's apartment searching every part of it to see if it held anything he didn't know about the Boyfriend. While he searched, it occurred to Till that tonight he'd already seen the part about the Boyfriend that mattered most.

A girl who was probably as wised-up as anybody could be in her mid-twenties had seen solid evidence that her boyfriend had killed his last five women. And the minute she'd had a chance to run back to him, she had been off—no hesitation. Probably at the last minute she'd told herself he would have an explanation as to why he was completely innocent.

As Till searched, he found lots of female clothing, but nothing that he believed belonged to a man. Kelly had a few paperback books, most of them romance novels in which young girls went to big cities and prospered. She had an iPod with hundreds of songs on it and a laptop computer that she used to upload her online ads for her escort jobs. She had taken all her money and jewelry with her. The Boyfriend would appreciate that.

Till drove into Boston and spent the rest of the night looking for the white Toyota Camry. At seven in the morning he heard a news report that told him where Kelly's body had been found.

17

Joey Moreland awoke in his hotel bed in Boston at a few minutes before noon. He had slept deeply, partly because he had been exhausted by the time he'd gotten to bed, but also because he'd taken care of some of the things that had been worrying him. He had received Kelly's text message when he was on his way to her apartment. He had told her exactly what to do. As soon as she heard his car approaching the apartment building, she should run for it.

When he had pulled to the curb in front of the apartment she was already in the lobby starting her dash toward the front door. He could see her through the glass. Then she was in the car and he was making a rapid series of turns to end up on Interstate 95 and head south. It had taken him a few minutes to get Kelly to explain what had happened on her date. She kept crying, and that made her gasp whenever she talked. It was like the voice of a person falling downstairs—"Ah, ah, ah, ah"—until finally he could hardly stand to listen to it.

The man who had come to see her had terrified her, but not because he was some kind of pervert. The man had been telling her about every girl Joey Moreland had been with in about three years, and how he had needed to leave each girl behind after a job. Who was this guy?

If he had traced Moreland in three states and across the country, he could be the FBI.

Moreland couldn't have that. He couldn't have Kelly, five feet ten, with fiery red hair two feet long, suddenly realize that the man couldn't have pictures of all those dead girls unless they were real. All she'd have to do was start a loud argument and he was a dead man. She could change her mind and turn him in just by shouting for the cops. And he had to hang around Boston long enough to kill Salazar, or the people who had paid for Salazar's life would take his instead.

So, in the end, after he had thought about it, and thought about Kelly, he'd had to kill her. He'd driven along the highway south of the city listening to her telling him the outrageous lies the stranger had told her, and then he had stopped at the edge of a field near the harbor. He told her he had stopped on the way to pick up an emergency kit he had hidden in the field, so they could leave town together. He had expected to get her to rush ahead of him to get through the hole in the chain-link fence. She would feel that she was accomplishing something, that on the other side of this dark place there would be light and warmth and safety—a whole future full of it.

But she hadn't been stupid enough. She had started to cry harder, a little wail that elongated the words. "Please" was one of them. He'd had to shoot her, whether she was fooled and looking away, or on her knees begging. So she was dead.

He would have liked to leave Boston now that Kelly was dead. Her death had deprived him of a place to live where nobody knew him and where there was no record of his presence. Now that he had checked into a hotel, this advantage was gone. He had used a false name and credit card, but he had not been able to stay completely invisible.

He had to stay in Boston and finish his job, and he couldn't rush things by even a minute. Salazar was going to arrive in town today, check into his hotel, and then appear at City Hall at three o'clock. He wasn't going to stick his head out sooner just because Joey Moreland wanted him to.

Joey was anxious. There was a kind of cop or private detective hunting for him now, and that was a big worry. He had always been careful never to draw the attention of cops and people like them. He had thought of staying with the girls as leaving no trail, but apparently the girls *were* his trail.

He wished he could leave now, but if he didn't kill Salazar here, he would have to go and get him in Mexico, and that was probably impossible. He spoke no Spanish and looked like an American. He would have to transport his own weapons across a border where the authorities were always looking for guns.

Moreland had to go through with his original plan. He would reassure himself by spending the rest of his time planning everything about the killing and the aftermath that he had not already planned and rehearsed. He turned on his laptop computer and checked for news of Salazar's visit to Boston. The news blackout was still in effect.

He repacked everything he had taken from his suitcase, checked out of his hotel, and began to attend to the details. He stopped at a gas station and filled his tank. In the little store at the station he bought water, candy bars, nuts, soft drinks, and pretzels. If he should have to end the day driving hard and trying to stay on the road, the snacks would help. If he didn't stop anywhere, then he was just another set of headlights approaching on the interstate and a pair of taillights disappearing around the next bend.

He drove to his office building and parked his car in the underground lot two floors down, even though the ground floor was nearly empty. During the remodeling there were very few tenants, so it didn't matter to the building owners where he parked, and going lower kept people from driving past his car. He got into the elevator and rode it up to the tenth floor. The construction workers doing the remodeling were on other floors today. They always worked early in the day and left before the late afternoon rush, but they must still be somewhere in the building.

Joey Moreland listened for the construction noises, but up here the air was just a steady hum of engines far below in the street. Then, as he walked along the hallway, stepping around piles of two-by-fours and leaning sheets of plywood and drywall, he heard the thuds of nail guns on the floor above, and far below him, a jackhammer. He went into his office and locked the door.

He had to do this right, and he had no control over timing. There was no way to delay or hurry the action a mile away to suit his plan. As soon as Salazar's car arrived at City Hall and Salazar got out, it was going to be time to pull the trigger. Moreland climbed onto the desk, moved an acoustic tile, and brought down the case where his M107A1 was stored.

He opened the case and set the heavy rifle on the desk. Just the gun and its scope weighed almost twenty-nine pounds. It was five feet long from the butt to the muzzle brake. He opened the legs of the bipod, then gazed along the top of the receiver, ignoring the scope while he turned the screw below the butt to raise it to the general level it would need to be. He loaded ten rounds into the box magazine. They were .50-caliber machine-gun rounds with a 660-grain bullet. They had a maximum range of 6,800 meters, but he would be nowhere near testing that figure. He pushed the heavy magazine up under the receiver until it clicked. He had a second magazine, so he loaded ten more rounds into it and set it to the right of the weapon on the desk where it would be out of his way. He supposed that if he needed the second magazine he would be fighting for his life, not completing a hit.

Firing a shot would be like starting a timer. He would have about two or three minutes to zero in on the target. The police would take a minute or two to realize what was happening. The first round would come roaring at them at 2,800 feet per second from a mile away, so it would hit about two seconds after the muzzle flash, and three more seconds would pass before the sound of the shot reached their ears. Even then they wouldn't know where the shot had come from. It might take five shots before one of them happened to see a flash a mile away.

Then they'd have to pick themselves up, organize a response, and begin to move. Returning fire would be impossible: he was out of range of their best rifles, and they couldn't just fire at a window in an office building. They'd realize they had to get into their cars and head toward the rifle. For a time Joey would be too far away for them to do anything, and he would still be able to reach out and hit whatever he could see. After his second three minutes were up, he would have to begin getting out of the building, because there would be cops heading toward it from all sides.

He went to the gun case and took out his ear protectors. They looked like a good set of earphones for a sound system. Like everything in his kit, they were of the highest quality, but they would succeed only in reducing the 180-decibel roar of the rifle to a loud noise. Because the M107A1 was based on a military weapon, the rifle's daylight scope had a hinged cap on each end to protect it from dirt and rain. He opened both caps and sighted the rifle on the steps of City Hall on the plaza side. He turned the ring on the elevation adjustment so it was set at two thousand meters, then aimed at the American flag on the high pole on the City Hall plaza. The fabric was moving a bit in a wind he judged to be about seven miles an hour. He turned the windage adjustment to compensate. A crosswind like that could move his shot a few feet to the left at this distance. He closed both lens caps.

He went to the case again, took out a thick foam pad, fitted it to the place where his right shoulder met his torso, and fastened it there with a strip of duct tape. The instant when he pulled that trigger, 11,500 foot-pounds of energy would punch that bullet into the distance and kick the rifle backward into him. There was a recoil pad, but there was no sense in getting pounded worse than he had to be.

Moreland stepped close to the open window and looked down at the street ten stories below him. The traffic in front of the building was steady but smooth in both directions. A police car passed. He could see the black "85" on its white roof. He didn't like staying in Boston after Kelly was dead. He liked to be long gone before a girlfriend was found. Maybe she wouldn't be found right away, but he wasn't going to count on it. Down below, people walked along the sidewalk, some of them having to swerve into a narrow remnant of the space by the curb to avoid the construction fence around the building. On the side where the crews were still working and might drop tools or materials, the pedestrians walked under a low scaffold with boards on top. Cars waited at intersections for the signals to turn; then other cars waited. It was a typical noisy, busy day here.

He looked up again. He was two thousand meters west of City Hall. He had a perfect view above the city and along the narrow corridor of the backs of buildings, all the way to City Hall. His building was on high ground near Beacon Hill, which was ninety-two feet above sea level. City Hall was only about fifteen feet above sea level. He sat down, closed his eyes, and mentally rehearsed everything he was going to do. Nothing would happen until Salazar's limo arrived.

18

Till had wasted much of his night driving around Boston searching for the white Toyota Camry. He had stayed out until the news at seven a.m. announced that a young woman had been found dead in a field south of Boston. The description was clearly that of Kelly.

The only train of thought that seemed plausible was to return to the speculation that the Boyfriend was doing something else besides killing hookers. And judging from his behavior and talents, there was only one really likely thing he could be doing.

Till used his cell phone and dialed the number of Detective Alan Rafferty. He listened to the ringing sound for a few seconds, and then heard a sound like a door opening. "Vice, Rafferty."

Till said, "Detective Rafferty, my name is Jack Till. Ted McCann in Los Angeles gave me your number."

"Yeah, he called me and said you might be getting in touch."

"Did he tell you anything about my case?"

"Some. He said you were trying to hunt down a guy who had been killing and robbing redhead escorts. Is that right?"

"Yes. The parents of the one who was killed in LA hired me. When I checked with Ted to find out if this was a onetime thing or a pattern, he had a list of five in other cities who fit our girl's description and had been shot with a nine-millimeter pistol."

"You're calling about the one here last night. Joelle Moody."

"Uh, I thought her name was Kelly Allen."

"Yeah, that was her work name. Same girl. Long reddish hair, shot in the head with a nine-millimeter pistol."

"The shooter was the man I've been following across the country. When I realized he was living with Kelly Allen in Woburn, I tried to warn her. I went to her apartment, and showed her the pictures of the seven murdered girls. They all looked a lot like her. They all had strawberry blond hair. Three of them had been wearing the same custom-made necklace in their online ads that she'd worn. I thought I'd persuaded her to run, but then he drove up, and she ran to join him. Now she's dead."

"If she ran to him and joined him, why kill her?"

"That's part of what I've figured out. What the girl does or doesn't do doesn't matter. He always kills them, and then leaves town. I thought at first it was a compulsion, that he was one of those guys who get so disgusted with themselves for going to a prostitute that the girl has to be eliminated along with the sin. Then I thought he was so bat-shit crazy that he got off on killing them. But now I think it's a policy. I think he kills them to keep them from talking about him."

"What's he doing that they could talk about?"

"I've tried looking at all the dates when girls were killed. I checked the papers in the cities where they died to see what else made the news in the next day or two. The only things I've found are high-profile murders, each one done right before the girl dies. I think he might be a contract killer."

"If he's a pro, and he knows from the start that he's going to have to kill the girl before he leaves town, why does he want them to begin with?"

"At first I assumed his main interest in the girls was stealing their money. That's got to be fairly profitable, since they're all pretty enough to make a lot of money over time. And they're not likely to put much of the money in a bank, where it would be reported to the IRS. So he takes the money. That makes it look to the police like the killing is a by-product of the robbery. It isn't. He kills them because they know who he is, when he got to town, and how long he's been around."

"I'm not sure about this."

"I've been tracking him. Whenever he comes into a new town, he almost immediately hooks up with one of these girls, and moves in with her. That means during the month or two it takes to prepare for his contract killing, he doesn't need a hotel, has no need to use credit cards, no need to fill out a rental agreement. He's got the cash he stole from the last girl, so he deals only in cash. If he wants to keep his car out of sight, he can leave it in a garage and use her car. Most escorts use false names and move from town to town, so not only does nobody know him, they don't really even know her. If, when he leaves, the girl is dead, nobody in town knows he even exists. He cleans the apartment, and tries to remove all prints. If he left fingerprints, they're in a room that's been visited by a hundred other men a month."

"Okay, suppose that's all true," Rafferty said. "What's going on today? What's he doing now—running?"

"If he killed Kelly prematurely, before he did his hit, then I'd say he's getting ready to do it now," said Till. "I want you to help me stop him."

"How?"

"You must have people in the department you can talk to. Get any inside info you can on anybody that's a good target for the next day or two. Some gangster in this part of the country is going on trial, or some company is about to enter a bidding war, or a rich family is having a wedding. Whatever. We've got to concentrate on anything that's only going to happen once."

"I'll do my best."

"Can I give you my phone number?"

"McCann gave it to me already. Just keep your phone on."

Till read newspapers, read local magazines, and signed onto Web sites that purported to have detailed calendars of events for the Boston area. He thought, *We are looking for a victim who may be vulnerable for today only. Or a victim who is about to do something—perform or testify or abscond or deliver. If it's a secret, or the person isn't well-known, we won't find it.*

As Till searched, he found so many possibilities that the task seemed impossible. David Farraday was filming a modern version of *Charley's Aunt* at Dunster House with exteriors in Harvard Yard. Apparently Farraday was an up-and-coming actor. Till saved the article. He could easily imagine a creep asking a movie company for a payoff or he'd kill some movie star, but he couldn't imagine the creep hiring a professional hit man to kill the star if the company didn't pay.

He saw an article about Nobel Prize winners who were or had been at MIT. He went online to see how many of them were living, and he was astounded. The answer was nine faculty members, nine former faculty members, five emeritus faculty members, one student, fourteen former staff members, and twenty alumni. He knew there was some remote possibility that somebody would want to kill a Nobelist. But if that was going on, the victim was as good as dead.

Unless they were all going to be at a party today, Till couldn't find a way to protect the intended target.

There were two well-known rock bands and a solo female singer appearing in Boston this evening. He noted the locations and kept searching.

The time was going by. He could see it always on the upper right of his computer screen as he searched. He wondered if he should be using the time to persuade some deputy chief in the Boston Police Department that a full-scale alert should be declared. Just having more cops on the street might not help, but it wouldn't hurt, either.

He searched for the heads of various companies in the Boston area. A few of them had controversial histories or products. He saved the ones accused of some environmental crime. There were extremist groups who might raise hell, but so far none had ever hired a shooter. The executives who had ordered big layoffs or were flamboyant about their riches he saved too, but he didn't have much confidence. The way to get to their money was kidnapping or extortion, not murder.

After a half hour he got to the one he had been expecting at the beginning. It was Joseph A. Peccorino, who was reputed to be the current head of the Mafia in Boston. He was a great candidate, but he had been under surveillance for years. On the days when he wasn't being questioned, arrested, or brought to court, he was probably surrounded by FBI agents who were trying to eavesdrop on him. There wasn't much Till could do that wasn't already being done.

Till tried politicians, starting with the mayor because he was based in Boston rather than in Washington. He found that an announcement had been posted only five minutes ago. This afternoon Mayor

William Meisterberg would be at a press conference to welcome a Mexican federal prosecutor, Luis Salazar, for a joint discussion of the paths of drug trafficking into the northeastern United States.

He closed the laptop and headed out of the hotel room, reaching for his cell phone. The visit of the Mexican federal prosecutor might not be the right event, but it was the only one he'd found that included a man a lot of people would pay to see dead. Till figured he might as well wait at City Hall Plaza for whatever Rafferty found out.

19

By the time Till got to his rental car, he had begun to believe that the Mexican prosecutor Luis Salazar was the victim. Salazar was probably under much less protection in the United States than he would be in Mexico. There were plenty of homicidal men in Mexico who would love to see a man like him dead. Probably most of them would not be confident about doing a killing in Boston, but they would have plenty of money to pay an American contract killer to do it for them.

He began to drive, and he redialed Rafferty's number.

"Rafferty."

"This is Till. Have you heard about the Mexican prosecutor?"

"Just now. Apparently they were keeping it quiet until it would be too late for his enemies to get here and try anything. He's just meeting with a few high-level cops here, and the security will be heavy. I was about to call and tell you."

"Did you turn up anything that seemed as likely?" asked Till.

"I turned up nothing else that seemed at all likely."

"Me either. I'm on my way there now. You might want to tell somebody in the department what we think is happening."

"I just did. That's what took me so long."

"Good. I'll talk to you soon."

It was already after two-thirty. Till drove toward City Hall, slightly faster and more aggressively than the rest of the cars, like a taxi driver in a hurry. He weaved from lane to lane when the cars began to bunch up ahead of him. He had the car radio on to listen to the news, but what he was listening for was word that he was too late.

Till glanced at the clock on the dashboard display. It was quarter to three. He wished he knew more about the Boyfriend's past jobs. The Boyfriend always seemed to shoot his girls in the back of the head. Since there were quieter, safer ways for a young, strong man to kill a 120-pound girl, he was apparently most comfortable with a pistol. Till had to rely on the little he knew. In all of the killings that could be reliably ascribed to the Boyfriend, his weapon had been a semiautomatic pistol that fired a nine-by-nineteen-millimeter round.

If the Boyfriend stayed true to the little that Till knew about him, he would be carrying the nine-millimeter pistol again today. He would have to be very close to the target to be sure of a kill. A Mexican prosecutor appearing on a public street would probably be wearing a bulletproof vest. That meant the Boyfriend had to try for a head shot. He would have to emerge from the crowd close to the prosecutor, shoot him in the head, and slip away.

It was going to be difficult and complicated. There would be dignitaries: the mayor and city council, all of them in suits. There would be Mexican state secret servicemen to protect the prosecutor, and they would be dressed in suits too. So the Boyfriend would wear a suit, and move in close. He might even attach himself to one of the locally recognizable politicians—probably not the mayor, but the council president, even the police commissioner. He could shoot the prosecutor, probably from behind, since that was his favorite angle; grab his chosen dignitary; and drag him away from the supposed line of fire. Considering the number of cops likely to be there today and the likelihood of armed Mexican bodyguards, a line of fire was sure to develop or be perceived to develop. He could drag his dignitary all the way to safety inside City Hall, then abandon him and go out another door.

Till knew so little that he clung to the few things he could surmise. There was no way even an experienced pistol shooter would want to be farther than twenty-five or thirty feet from his target, and if he was that close, the only way out would be to impersonate one of the good guys. Till now had a rough notion of what he would look for. He came to a public parking lot, swung his rental car into the lot, paid the fee in advance, then hurried toward the big redbrick cube that was City Hall.

There were steps on one side of the building, but the redbrick plaza sloped up from the street. He could see there was a wooden lectern set up just beside the entrance to City Hall. On the street were two vans from local television stations with their transmission booms extended into the air. He could see a very slight Asian woman in a tan suit standing in front of the building with a microphone. She was looking at her cameraman, who rested a large video camera on his shoulder. She moved a little bit to put the lectern with the seal of the City of Boston on it into the background of her shot.

There were sawhorse barricades to keep the entrance to the plaza clear, but so far only five police officers were visible on the plaza. Two were near the lectern and the entrance to City Hall, and the other three appeared to be wandering, but weren't. Each had taken a side on the perimeter of the plaza. There were no crowds forming, and that looked like good news to Till: with no crowd, it would be harder for the killer to hide. A foreign prosecutor was hardly a celebrity in a big American city, so most people came and went without appearing to feel curiosity about the proceedings. Those who stared at all seemed to be curious only about the television vans. A couple of them stopped a few yards from the small woman in the tan suit and watched her doing sound checks.

Then the doors to City Hall opened and a few men and women in suits walked out in small groups. A couple of stragglers stepped away from the building to make cell phone calls. Till decided they must be members of the city council.

Till stopped, held up his own cell phone, took a picture of the building, then pivoted a few degrees and took another picture. He continued around the compass, gazing in each direction for a few seconds. He was giving himself a chance to see the Boyfriend coming. The Boyfriend would have to wait until there was a big enough group to hide him, but he must be nearby already.

Till sensed that something was happening, that the event was coming together now. The men in dark suits and white shirts all seemed to make a small movement at the same time, an impulse like the one that made a flock of birds take off at once. The men looked at each other, then toward the building.

They walked toward the steps of City Hall, the first ones stopping on the lowest step so they would be looking into the television camera. The others filled in on the steps above, then just stood there to preserve their spaces to the left of the lectern, where they hoped to be in the frame.

A moment later the cops began to meet one another's gaze. They were receiving a radio transmission. Till saw one of them speak into the microphone pinned to his left shoulder, and one other spoke into a small hand radio. Four more officers came out of City Hall and stood near the councilmen.

Then electricity seemed to flow through the group again. The councilmen arranged themselves as though they were a choir standing on risers. The cops all lifted their heads at once, and the mayor emerged from the building, flanked by a couple of young aides.

The traffic in the street changed its flow, moved one lane away by a pair of motorcycle cops who had stationed themselves at the beginning of the block. Till took another look at the councilmen, the cops, the small group of onlookers. Till moved closer. Which was the Boyfriend? Was he here?

He heard a change in the traffic noise, and saw a police cruiser turn right and come up the incline onto the plaza. Right behind it was a second car, a black SUV with tinted windows. The two cars stopped forty feet from the steps. The doors of the black SUV opened, and four men in dark suits got out. They were of varying sizes and builds, but all were dark-haired and tan, with nearly opaque sunglasses and sport coats that were square-shaped from body armor and hidden weapons.

Bodyguards were the same everywhere, Till thought. Two of the men spread out, their unseen eyes scanning the plaza, the street, the nearby buildings. The other two waited. When the second SUV arrived, one of them pulled open the back door and two of them stood on either side of it while a tall, dark-haired man in a gray suit got out and walked toward the waiting group of American politicians.

The newspeople seemed to materialize in the plaza at once, the cameramen following Salazar's progress without getting close enough to him to ruin a shot, and the reporters, uncharacteristically, hanging back to wait for their moment to ask questions.

The mayor, who had been waiting near the lectern, smiled for the cameras and strode forward, his right hand extended in front of him when he was still ten feet away and Salazar could not possibly reach out and shake it.

Till's eyes strained to sort out the curious newcomers gathering in the plaza to see what was going on. They were arriving from inside

City Hall, from the street, and from other parts of the civic center. He studied faces, watched hands and arms, sidestepped to see the ones who remained half hidden in the gaggle of moving people. There was a pattering as hands applauded, a sound too small and faint for this large a space. He only glanced at the two men at the center of it, who were shaking hands now: they weren't the problem. The mayor headed for the lectern, drawing his guest with him.

Till walked closer to the crowd of passersby who had noticed something was going on. They were close to the reporters, who seemed to be the most likely source of information, but they refrained from spilling out in front of the cameras. If this was going to be an occasion for speeches, most of them were prepared to move along. He saw nothing he was watching for on any of the faces—no eyes shifting to locate cops and bodyguards, no squinting at the Mexican visitor to judge range and angle, no moving to the side in the direction of the politicians.

Suddenly the air changed, as though it had hardened. There was a disruption, like a whip crack, something faster than sound passing overhead. Till turned away from the crowd toward the mayor and his guest, both moving behind the lectern together so the mayor could—*Pow!*

The lectern exploded and sprayed splinters and fragments against the wall of City Hall. The mayor was knocked back or collapsed and fell on the pavement. The guest, Luis Salazar, seemed at first to have disappeared in the small explosion.

The instant he'd heard the impact, Till's legs had pushed him off in the direction of the lectern. He looked ahead, but saw nothing that would tell him what had happened. Was it a small—*Bang!* The noise seemed to come from off in the distance like thunder.

He caught a glimpse of the two men lying prone just an instant before the police officers and a couple of dark suits converged on them and blocked his view. Their faces and white shirts seemed to be splashed with blood. People screamed, shouted, whirled around to see where this nightmare was coming from.

Till felt the second whip crack and saw one of the men in dark gray who was kneeling in front of the prosecutor flop forward on top of him. Till stopped and looked around him.

The sound had not been a bomb. It was a projectile breaking the sound barrier as it reached the plaza. *Bang!* The distant rifle's report came to his ears. It had been at least three seconds after the bullet. The first one had slammed into the lectern, but it was hard to tell what had happened after that—splinters from the lectern, metal fragments, pieces of brick from the wall behind them, even a direct hit. The mayor was splattered with blood but he was getting up now, helped by the others, who were trying to drag him into the building.

People were running, dashing in waves away from the place where the lectern had stood. Till was not sure whether they were moving in silence or the noise had temporarily deafened him. Till moved his eyes in a semicircle to try to detect where the shots had come from, but there was nothing. The buildings facing City Hall Plaza looked just as they had before, with the bright sun behind them at three on a summer afternoon.

Then he saw it, a flash coming from the side of a building far away in the west. *That can't be*, he thought. But then he heard the whip crack again, and saw an explosion of brick above the unmoving body of Luis Salazar. He counted: *One one thousand two one thousand three one thousand Bang!* It was. He had spotted the muzzle flash.

Till began to move. He sidestepped, ducked, slipped into the crowd and through it. He didn't break into a run until he was in the middle of the sidewalk, then dodged across the street and ran toward the parking lot.

As he reached the parking lot, he called to the attendant, "Are the keys in my car?"

"Yeah."

He got in, started the engine, and drove at a steady speed out of the lot into the still-moving traffic. If the Boyfriend had been watching him through the rifle scope, he would have little trouble taking Till's car apart. It was maddening to have to turn right, going away from the shooter, then turn right again to head for the distant building indirectly. But he knew that anybody heading toward the shooter up the street the quick, direct way was probably not going to make it.

As he drove, Till looked repeatedly at the distant building where he had seen the muzzle flash. He could see that the building was about fifteen stories high, and that it was situated on higher ground than City Hall. The street he was on had an incline to it, and he judged that the end of it was about a hundred feet higher than where he was. The shooter had been able to see over most of the buildings between his and City Hall, but he must have had to sight between a few of the tall buildings. Till turned on the car radio and spun the dial until he heard speech instead of music. The announcers were talking about the stock market. They didn't know yet.

Till had been wrong about the Boyfriend. He had thought the Boyfriend would be in close with a nine-millimeter pistol. Instead he was about a mile away with something very big, probably a .50-caliber rifle. His accuracy at that distance was impressive. He had done everything right. He had chosen a high perch to the west of the target, where the afternoon sun would be behind him, lighting up his whole field of vision.

The wind was very mild and from the west today, so he had little crosswind to deflect his bullet over the long trajectory. He had fired once to zero in his rifle. He had obviously intended to use the lectern as a highly visible and convenient point to aim at, and then adjust azimuth and elevation from there. He had hit the lectern dead-on while the mayor and Luis Salazar had been behind it. The second shot had gone right through Salazar, who had looked dead to Till already.

The strategy of the bodyguards was to block a shot with their bodies and hope that they were making the victim invisible, and that their armor would help stop a bullet. The Boyfriend had made all their risks irrelevant. When the third bullet arrived it had passed through one of the bodyguards and into Salazar.

He heard a siren whoop a block behind him, raised his eyes to the rearview mirror, and confirmed what he'd feared. There was a police car speeding up behind him, trying to get ahead, weaving in and out. Till did what the other drivers were doing—he pulled over to the curb, intending to let the police car pass.

The *bang* this time was the sound of a .50-caliber bullet punching through the hood of the police car. The police car swerved to the curb and stopped. There was a haze of black smoke propelled upward by a jet of white steam, and the car remained motionless. The cop yelled something into his car radio mike, opened the door, and ran to take up a position beside a brick building. Then he realized his smoking police car was attracting the attention of pedestrians. He ran back to the street and began ushering the pedestrians into a detour behind the brick building, glancing now and then in the direction of the sniper.

Till pulled out again ahead of the police car and drove west with the rest of the cars near him. As he watched them, he could tell that none of them knew they were heading directly toward a sniper. In another couple of minutes he and the cars near him reached the vicinity of the building where the flashes had come from. It was undergoing some kind of interior renovation, with a tall wooden frame up around much of its foundation and scaffolds over the sidewalk. He looked up and saw no open windows on the east side of the building, but he knew that this proved nothing.

As he searched for a place to leave his car he dialed the police emergency number. When a woman answered he said, "My name is Jack Till, and I saw the building where the sniper was. It's at the corner of Wilburton and Holbrooke. It's got a sign that says it's the Pettigrew Building. He was up high, maybe the tenth floor."

"Please stay on the line, sir."

He hung up, put his phone in his pocket, pulled his rental car around the side of the building, and left it in the alley behind a Dumpster.

He looked up at the fire escape, but he couldn't imagine climbing it quickly enough to do anything but get stranded. He trotted around to the front of the building and went inside, taking everything in. The elevators appeared to be operating because the lights were on and they had movers' blankets attached to the inner walls to protect them from sharp loads. Hanging from the forty-foot foyer ceilings were three thick chains holding what seemed to be chandeliers wrapped in blue plastic. There was a stairwell. He opened the door, stepped into it, and listened, but he heard no footsteps.

Till stepped into the nearest elevator, selected the ninth floor, and began to rise. He got out at the ninth floor and listened. There seemed to be nobody moving. There were two-by-fours piled neatly in the hall, a couple of large coils of electrical wire, and boxes he couldn't identity. None of the rooms had doors, and the floors were dusty plywood. He stepped to the stairwell, closed the door, and climbed. He came out at the tenth floor. He walked along the hallway, and it looked different, as though it was nearly finished. On the tenth floor there were polished wooden doors on all of the offices. The only indication that some part of the floor wasn't finished was a pile of carpet rolls at the end of a corridor. He walked along trying doorknobs, but they were all locked. He heard the sound of an elevator moving up the shaft to the next floor.

Till climbed to the eleventh floor, found that the elevator had not stopped, then went up to the twelfth. He opened the door, stepped out, and heard voices. He walked toward them. He found four men working in a large office at the end of the hallway. Two were up on stepladders, running electrical cable above the false ceiling. "Excuse me," Till said. "Did you hear three or four really loud bangs a while ago?"

One man looked down for a second. "You heard that too, eh?"

"Yes. Could you tell if it was coming from this floor, above, or below?"

"I don't know. It sounded like something big got dropped."

Till didn't see any point in going on. They obviously hadn't seen anything. He moved on, looking in each open doorway and opening each door. When he reached the east side of the building he stepped into one of the empty offices and looked out the window. He could make out the plaza and City Hall from here, and he saw that the plaza looked like a parking lot for black-and-white police cars. He took special care in each of the eastern side offices, but he detected no sign that any one office was more likely than the others. He went down to the tenth floor.

And then he found it. The office was partly furnished already, and a bit more completed than the others. The place had a desk and a couple of chairs, and a second room of some kind that was locked. The room smelled like burned propellant.

He could see the place on top of the desk where the Boyfriend must have positioned the rifle. The bipod had been down, and when the rifle was fired it had scraped backward in the recoil. The Boyfriend had been sitting on a chair by the left side of the desk, then stood up when it was time to put his right shoulder to the weapon. He had raised the butt of it, letting it rest only on the bipod; aimed very carefully; and fired.

With his cell phone Till took pictures of the top of the desk, the foot depressions in the new carpet, and a place on the floor where the Boyfriend had set something about five feet long, probably the rifle case. Where was he now?

The Boyfriend had fired three times, then once more at the police car. He had apparently put the rifle back in the big case, then left the office. Till hurried to the elevator and hit the button marked "L." The man must have parked his car in the lot below the building.

Till reached the lobby level, then made it out to the street-level entrance to the garage. As he stepped into the cavernous entrance he had both hands in his coat pockets with his index fingers in the trigger guards of the two LC9 pistols. He went down the ramp far enough to be out of the street noise, then stopped and listened.

He heard the sound of a car coming up from the lower parking levels. The engine was running at high rpm, because it was climbing the incline, and the tires gave faint squeaks with every turn. He selected a car parked near the entrance to the parking lot, crouched behind it, took out his two pistols, and watched the place down the ramp where the car would appear. He flicked off the safety catches on his pistols.

The car was approaching the bottom of the straight ramp. Till steadied his aim and tightened his grip on both pistols. The front of the car slid into view, then rose up slightly on the slope. He stared at the man in the driver's seat, studying his face as he came closer.

The man saw Till and reacted instantly, hitting the gas pedal hard. The wheels spun, and Till fired. The nine-millimeter bullets hit the driver's door, but penetrated only the thin outer sheet metal. There had to be a steel reinforcement behind it. He fired at the side window, but the bullets ricocheted, leaving only a few smoky impact marks in the glass. Till's ears told him the spinning tires were about to catch, so he changed his aim. He fired both guns at the left front tire, and then at the left rear tire.

The wheels caught against the pavement, and the car shot forward, the tires already beginning to flap on the left side as the car lurched out into the street. Till fired at the rear window, but the bullets made the same white impact marks in the glass without breaking through. The car squealed out of the shadow of the building and turned to roar up the street.

Till stuck the pistols into his coat pockets as he ran to the lot entrance, but the Boyfriend's car was out of sight already. He ran across the front of the building to the alley where he had left his rental car, and got in. He had no room to turn it around, so he backed up as quickly as he could toward the street he had just left.

A big Cadillac Escalade with a pearlized paint job appeared in the entrance to the alley behind him and the man inside honked his horn. Till gestured to him to back out again. Instead, the Escalade began to move ahead toward Till's car, its horn blowing incessantly now. Till got out of his rental car and walked quickly to the Escalade.

The man in the Escalade had a look of anger on his face. He moved forward toward Till's car, leaning on the horn.

With speed that surprised the man, Till was at the side of the Escalade with a gun in his hand. He said, "You're keeping me from capturing a man who just committed a murder. If you pull back out of here fast enough, you can keep going. If you do anything else, you'll never see home again."

"Okay, okay, I'll go," the man said.

"Do it."

The man pulled back, hooking to the left so he could pull forward at an angle and edge into traffic.

Till got into his rental car and executed the same maneuver. He turned right at the first corner, but there was no sign of the killer's car ahead. He drove several blocks, but still saw nothing.

He dialed 911 and said to the dispatcher, "The sniper used a fifty-caliber long-range military sniper rifle from a tenth-floor office at 7557 Wilburton. He's driving a white Toyota Camry with two flat tires on the left side." He hung up.

As Till drove, he took the battery out of his prepaid cell phone so it wouldn't keep broadcasting his GPS location, removed the SIM card, then waited until he was stopped at a light. He tossed the phone into a sewer grating, and then drove on.

20

Joey Moreland was still feeling panicky and hyperalert. He had driven the damaged car a few blocks and made a couple of turns so he was going in the opposite direction a few streets away from his office building, and now he had to ditch it. As he drove toward a big building he could see that it had a wide parking lot entrance.

He swung the damaged car into the underground parking entrance, took a ticket from the machine, and watched the barrier rise in front of him. He drove down two floors so his car wouldn't be the first thing people saw when they entered the lot, got out, and looked at the car. He had toyed with the idea of trying to fix the flat tires, but the doors on the left side had about six bullet holes, each a puncture with a halo of bare steel where the sheet metal had been pounded in and the paint had disappeared. The quarter-inch steel plates in the doors had stopped the bullets from hitting him, but not from ruining the car. The windows looked opaque in places; there were white spots where the bullets had bounced off the bulletproof glass.

That plainclothes cop who had shot at him as he'd left his office building might very well guess that he'd doubled back. If so, the cop wouldn't be too far behind. Moreland had to abandon the car and try something else.

He opened the trunk, took out the two-wheeled dolly, set the long cardboard box containing the rifle case on it, and wheeled it up the ramp and out to the sidewalk. In the distance he heard sirens, but they seemed to be passing on their way to somewhere else. He walked along trying to look like a successful salesman delivering some piece of equipment, but his eyes were searching the area for opportunities. He passed a restaurant that looked inviting. It had freshly painted exterior woodwork and a gray stone facade. A small marquee with gold filigree letters read ETIENNE DE CHAMBORD. There was a movable sign on an iron stand that read VALET PARKING $5.00 against the side of the building in the narrow driveway to the parking lot, not at the curb in front of the building. He figured it was too early for the valet. It would be a while before the dinner customers came.

Moreland looked around him. There was no direct view from the dining room of the restaurant to the spot where he stood. He could see that the traffic on the street was moving steadily. He glanced at his watch. It was close to five o'clock. He walked up the driveway a few feet. Beside the valet sign there was a small wooden cabinet. It had a door on it, and when he opened it, he could see little gold hooks for car keys, and numbers corresponding to parking spots. There were no keys. He could see that the lot was empty, and there was no sign of a parking attendant.

He placed his dolly at the side of the building, tilted the iron stand, and rolled the sign to the curb, so it could be read from the right lane of the street. He pushed the cabinet to the curb beside it, leaving his dolly and the disguised rifle case beside the building. He stood by the cabinet for a few minutes, looking expectantly at the passing cars. He decided he would keep trying for another five minutes, and then move on.

A minute later, a black BMW pulled up in front of the restaurant. An elderly man got out of the driver's seat, and Moreland stepped up to open the door for the passenger, an elderly woman. It occurred to him that he had forgotten something. He opened the door in the lower part of the cabinet and found a roll of tickets. He tore one off and handed it to the man.

As the couple walked toward the front door of the restaurant, Moreland pulled their car into the driveway, loaded his dolly and rifle into the backseat, and drove it the rest of the way into the lot, intending to turn it around and leave; but then he saw that the lot opened onto an alley on the far end. He drove to the alley, turned into it, and then followed it out to another street.

He drove three blocks, then turned right to head for Massachusetts Avenue. He reached it and headed for the bridge over the Charles River into Cambridge. He exhibited no urgency, took no chances to gain ground in the evening traffic. Soon he was on the bridge, passing over the wide, calm river. On the other side he turned left, and slowly made his way with the commuters moving out of the most congested parts of the city. He would cross the river again upstream, and get onto Interstate 90. Boston was over for him.

He allowed himself to drive the stolen car for only two hours before he stopped at a large apartment house where the parking spaces were in a row of carports at the back of the building, and nobody could see into them from a window. He removed a set of license plates from a car and traded them with the set from his stolen BMW.

Next he stopped at a Target store and bought a large suitcase. He went to the backseat of the BMW, removed the rifle case from the cardboard carton, opened the case, and disconnected the upper and lower receivers of the rifle. The scope remained attached to the upper receiver. He removed the twenty-nine-inch barrel, so the rifle was in three pieces. He carefully set them in the new suitcase, then added the extra magazines, earphones, and cleaning kit. He emptied his old, smaller suitcase into the new one.

He put the old suitcase into the Dumpster behind the store, then drove on for a few miles until he found another Dumpster behind a fast-food restaurant. He left the dolly beside it, drove a few miles farther to another restaurant Dumpster, and put the rifle case in its cardboard carton far down under some unpleasant-smelling food.

He was headed toward Hartford, Connecticut, which was a hundred miles from Boston. Crossing state lines was good, because bulletins were generally only statewide at first. As soon as he crossed the state line, he stopped in a quiet neighborhood to steal the license plates from a car that had been pulled into its garage for the evening. He hoped that before anyone looked at the car again he'd be on his way out of Connecticut.

He drove to Hartford and found the big Hilton hotel on Trumbull Street, which he remembered from a visit about two years ago. It was the right size, with about four hundred rooms. He parked the stolen BMW, now bearing stolen Connecticut plates, in the lot and walked along the side of the building to the front entrance where taxicabs waited. He stepped up to the first one and looked in the window.

The driver looked up, got out, and lifted Moreland's heavy suitcase into the trunk. "Where to?"

"Bradley airport, the main terminal."

The terminal was only about twenty minutes away, so there was little need for small talk. The driver asked when his flight was. Moreland said, "Don't worry, I'm early. It's a red-eye."

When the cab arrived at the Bradley airport terminal, Moreland waited for the driver to pull away, and then walked inside the entrance near the arrival areas. He went to the shuttle bus desk and paid for a ride to New Haven. He had to wait only a few minutes before the driver came to the desk and called for his riders. He and three other people got into the shuttle. He made sure to get into the back of the van so the general conversation didn't have to include him, and nobody would spend enough time looking at his face to remember him. When he arrived at New Haven, he called for a different shuttle company to take him to JFK airport on Long Island.

When he got into a room at a hotel near JFK airport, he was exhausted. He had been moving constantly but slowly since morning, winning a race by being unnoticed. As he lay on the bed he reviewed his progress and evaluated it. He had checked out of the hotel in Boston without leaving any prints or having any memorable encounters. He had performed his job in Boston impeccably against terrible odds, and then had a car shot out from under him. He had stolen the BMW at the restaurant, driven two hundred miles in it, and left it with in-state license plates parked in a huge hotel lot. Then he had done two stints on shuttle buses and two in taxis without leaving much of an impression, and had paid cash for everything. The best anyone could do would be to trace him through the stolen car to the Hilton in Hartford. Through guesswork and luck, his pursuers might get some exceptional person who remembered him to pick him out in surveillance tapes at the airport, but they could not connect him to a flight because there had been no flight.

He took off his clothes and stepped into the shower. When he was drying off, he noticed that the recoil of the heavy rifle had bruised his right shoulder. And he was worried again. There was a cop who had tried to shoot him on his way out of the office building lot. And there was still the man—detective or FBI man—who had shown Kelly the pictures of all of the girls. If those two got together he would be in real trouble. He lay on the bed and tossed fitfully for two hours, and then fell asleep.

When Moreland awoke, he was alone. He wasn't used to that yet. He had killed the girl—he stopped himself before thinking *again*—and he was starting at the beginning. He had a huge worry. He had used the girls to make him invisible, but he had made the mistake of choosing a series of girls who were too much alike. He had not ever thought of himself as creating a pattern. He had simply scanned the long list of ads for escorts, clicked on one to see her photographs, then clicked on another, until he had found one who attracted him. He searched for a better word. *Attracted* was true, but not adequate. He had stopped when he had found the one who had *titillated* him the most. Each time, it had been a girl who had seemed to him not only the best choice, but the obvious choice.

But he had definitely created a pattern. The detective or FBI agent who had tried to get Kelly to betray him had seen the pattern, and shown it to Kelly. She had seen it too, agreed with him completely, and started right away to bug Moreland about it.

He had to end that pattern now. If he broke the pattern, that detective who had found Kelly could waste his time searching the country for women with reddish blond hair and light eyes. He wouldn't catch Joey Moreland doing the same. He got up, walked to a large CVS store near the hotel, and bought a prepaid cell phone for cash.

On the way back he called the Broker. After one ring the Broker answered. "Yeah?"

"Hi."

"I thought it would be you."

"That thing in Boston is done."

"I know. Where are you calling from?"

"A prepaid cell phone. I'm not in Boston anymore."

"Good. I know about the Boston thing, because it's been all over the TV news. You really had to do it that way?"

"The only place you could tell me where he'd be was City Hall, and I couldn't find anyplace else. Once he was inside, there wouldn't have been much I could do. The place is a fortress. I'd never get another glimpse of the bastard. The neighborhood around it was full of cops. All I could do was go out farther, and pop him from there. I shot him twice to be sure he wouldn't survive."

"Survive? Jesus Christ. They were picking up pieces of him. You painted the wall and the fucking mayor with him."

"I figured the kind of enemies a Mexican prosecutor had might do that."

"Right. They might. In fact, they're the ones who hired you to do it for them."

"Okay. So what's the problem?"

"They hired a pro to do it because they didn't want anything that dramatic, which would make them the only suspects."

"Seriously?"

"How you do a job is important. You don't want to draw attention to it. Mexican drug guys kill Mexican cops and politicians all the time, but they don't do it using a bazooka."

"It's a fifty-caliber sniper rifle."

"That either. Don't you see? In the United States this Salazar was a little guy. Page thirty-two, four sentences in the corner of the paper. In Mexico he was a little bit bigger than that, but just not coming home from Boston isn't a very sensational story by their standards. Boston City Hall is a lousy place to kill anybody, and using a military weapon there is even worse. The customers are not happy."

"I wasn't thinking about public relations. I didn't want to get surrounded and taken down by cops." He paused. "Look, I don't want an argument. I'm just calling so you can transfer the pay into my account."

"I don't know what's going to happen."

"Are you saying they won't pay?"

"I'm saying I don't know what they will do or won't do. Call me again in a few days. Maybe I'll know then."

"Look. I—" He stopped and looked at the display on his new cell phone. The Broker had hung up.

Moreland walked back toward the hotel feeling a growing outrage. The Mexican drug guys were pissed off. Whenever they wanted to get a politician or a police official, they always seemed to have ten guys block his car and fire machine guns into it from all sides until it looked like a sieve. If that was their idea of a good hit, fuck them. They should be delighted at the news that the guy was dead, and even more delighted that it had been done so efficiently, so far from home. When their enemies heard about it, they'd seem smarter than they were. How could they possibly be pissed off? But maybe they weren't pissed off. Maybe the Broker was just trying to steal Moreland's pay for the job.

He went back to the hotel; wiped off all the surfaces to remove fingerprints, as usual; and checked out. Then he took a cab to Penn Station. From there he took the train to Philadelphia, and checked into a hotel near the center of the city on Chestnut Street. He bought a *Philadelphia Inquirer* and looked at the car lot ads. He took another cab to the area where most of the lots seemed to be, and began to search. He found the right sort of used car after a couple of hours. It was a Nissan Maxima, and it was the gray titanium color that had been popular a couple of years earlier. It was the sort of nondescript car that he needed. Ever since the night he'd killed Kelly, he'd felt that detective who had been following him getting closer and closer. He wanted to keep moving, get far away from this part of the country, and then lie low for a while. He paid for the car in cash.

As he drove it away, he began thinking about money. He was going to need more money soon, and the person who owed him some was the Broker. Even if the customer was giving the Broker problems, they were the Broker's problems, not Moreland's. Whether the broker got paid or not, Moreland had money coming. If he had to, he would go take it. But that was a problem, because Holcomb had never told Joey the Broker's real name or his address. Maybe it was time to go visit Holcomb's ghost.

21

Till was in Boston police headquarters. The man across the table from him was a homicide detective named Mullaney. Beside him was Detective Rafferty from Vice, but Till knew he had been included only to give Till a false sense of security. If Till showed signs of being uncooperative or defensive, they'd try some other method.

"So let's go through this guy's description again," Mullaney said. "How old is he?"

"He looks about twenty-two or twenty-three to me," Till said. "But I've only seen him through tinted glass in cars moving fast, and once from a distance in Phoenix. He was wearing sunglasses that time. I have a hunch he's older. Maybe twenty-seven or so."

"Why is that?"

"He's definitely young and good-looking, with dark hair that looks kind of wavy. He seems young and slim, in very good shape. But he's really good at manipulating the escorts he's lived with."

"Manipulating them how?"

"They let him live with him. He tells them some story or other, never that he's a professional killer, of course. They all seem to buy his story, at least as long as he needs them to. He's also good at killing, and good at disappearing. Those are things that take a while to learn, so I think he's probably older."

"But you managed to follow him all the way across the country."

"He has a really strong preference for strawberry blonds. I noticed that some of the girls wore the same two pieces of diamond jewelry in their escort ads. I got in touch with jewelry companies, designers, stores, even pawnshops in the cities where the girls were killed, then in other cities. They all say the jewelry is custom-made. So whenever I saw an ad with a girl wearing the jewelry, I knew where he had been."

"What happens if the pattern ends?"

"What usually happens. I'll lose him for a while."

Till had been through this many times when he was a cop. After months of studying a killer and learning his habits and quirks, the homicide cops lost him. The killer got scared—scared of himself, in this case. After that he tried to do everything differently. The smart ones simply closed up shop for a while, and waited until all the attention had turned in other directions. The cops got busy hunting other killers, and potential victims stopped looking over their shoulders. Then the killer would come out again.

"You think he's a contract killer. Who do you think paid for the hit on Luis Salazar?"

"I don't know. If I were to guess, I would say it was one of the people or groups that he was prosecuting or had sent to prison in Mexico. I would ask the bodyguards who came with him for a list. Then I'd try to find out if any agencies, here or there, have a record of the phone calls between that suspect and anyone in the United States."

"Yeah, the FBI is working on all that." He paused. "But you've been after this guy for months, right?"

"Right."

"Do you have any idea how he operates? How does he get the jobs? How does he get paid?"

"I've never gotten anywhere on that. The victims are all over the country. They seem to be people you might expect to have enemies, but the police in the cities where I think he's done jobs haven't told me anything that forms a pattern. In Phoenix it's two city councilmen who voted on hundreds of questions a year. In New York it was a rich man who owned an art gallery. None of the victims have anything to do with each other. So I think there's probably a middleman who takes the contracts and passes them on to the killer."

"Okay," said Mullaney. "Any guess on where that middleman would be?"

"None," Till said. He spoke carefully. "Do you think I could talk to Salazar's bodyguards and ask them a few questions?"

"Not a chance," Mullaney said. "You're not a cop anymore, Till. You have no official standing, and the federal agencies are all waiting in line ahead of you. And unless you're crazy you're not going to head for Mexico to look for the client anyway. The best thing you can do is remember some detail that will help us catch the shooter."

Till said, "I told you everything I knew or suspected yesterday. If it's useful to you, I'll stay in Boston as long as you want. But I'm pretty sure he's left."

Mullaney said, "You've been cooperative. That was nice of you, considering the whole issue of what you were doing discharging illegal firearms in the middle of the city. That's been made to go away, at least for now."

"I appreciate that," Till said. He watched Mullaney for a few seconds as Mullaney brought himself to be reasonable.

"Don't get me wrong. I took a look at the guy's car, and I had to admire you for having the balls and the presence of mind to open up on him like that. If it hadn't been a tricked-out car you'd have killed him, and we could all go home. I guess we know everything from you that we're going to get. You can go. If I change my mind, I'll call you. And if I do, I'll expect you to head for the airport to get back here."

"I'll do that," said Till. "Thanks." He stood up and shook hands with Mullaney, then with Rafferty.

Rafferty said, "Come on. I'll walk you out."

The two left the interrogation room and walked down the hallway. It was lined with office doors so close together that Till thought the rooms must be the size of closets. "Thanks for all your help," said Till.

"I wish it were going better. I don't usually get involved in anything like this. My usual interest in these girls is making their business inconvenient enough so they quit. But this guy is really evil."

"Yeah," said Till. "He is." They came to the lobby. "Well, if anything comes up, please give me a call."

"I will," said Rafferty.

Till went to his hotel, called the airline, collected his belongings, and then drove his rental car back to the airport. Late tonight, he'd be in Los Angeles. Tomorrow morning he would start over again, looking at ads, calling contacts, and exploring new avenues. There couldn't be too many .50-caliber rifles around, and there were probably a limited number of places where the Boyfriend could have practiced firing one without having someone notice him. The Boyfriend had lost his car, and would be buying a new one. He would be looking for a new girl.

A week later, Joey Moreland approached Holcomb's ranch in daylight. He drove up the freeway to Antelope Valley, and then took the smaller road north and east, watching the cars thinning out, the sudden absence of big trucks, which were replaced by pickups. When he turned off onto the second county road he saw that the weeds growing in the cracks of the pavement were more prevalent this year. They generally died off in full summer. A couple of real Southern California hot days were enough to do it. He passed a few rural mailboxes he remembered at the entrances to dirt roads. After another fifteen minutes of driving he made it to the Holcomb mailbox, an oversize galvanized one with a red flag and a rounded top.

Out of curiosity he looked inside it when he got out to open the gate. There were some yellowed ads from stores, but whatever else Holcomb had received by mail must have stopped long ago. He used his pick and tension wrench to open the padlock, swung the wide steel gate open, drove in, and then closed the gate again.

He drove very slowly along the dirt road onto the ranch. He didn't want to kick up a lot of dust that could be seen from a distance. He was eight or nine miles from the nearest habitation he knew about, but being on Holcomb's ranch made him more careful. Hartmann's death had been solved at a glance, but Holcomb's had not. Since Holcomb had been killed and the police had driven all the way out here to see who and what he had been, things might be different now. All Moreland would need would be to come face-to-face with a state cop who had been assigned to see if anyone still came around to Holcomb's ranch and what he was up to.

He drove with his windows open at the speed of a man walking so he could hear or see anyone on the ranch a few seconds early. As he bounced along the dirt road, he could hear mockingbirds warbling to one another between the low California oak trees. There was a smell coming from the weeds, where wild lantana and goldenrod were swirled by the breeze into a mixture of pollen. He associated that smell with his killing lessons with Holcomb. He had not missed the scent, had not remembered it, but now that he smelled it again he loved it. The smell brought back the days of diving onto the ground, shouldering the .308 rifle, aiming and firing as quickly as possible without moving the brush around him, cycling the bolt and firing again at the distant target Holcomb had stuck on a post. The smell of burned powder and gun oil had mixed with wildflower and weed and dirt, and had made an indelible mark in his memory. When they had gone out at night, sometimes the wind was still and the smells were even stronger because the plants seemed to exhale more heavily into the hot, motionless air.

He stopped a hundred yards before the house and pulled his car in among the twisted trunks of the short, thick oak trees. The canopy of dusty leaves was only five or six feet above his head, but it was dense and almost impervious to the fierce sunshine. His car sat in deep shadow.

Moreland left his suitcase in the trunk, but he took the flashlight he had in the glove compartment. He had his nine-millimeter pistol stuck into the back of his belt under his shirt, but he didn't reach for it. He walked at a steady, leisurely pace toward Holcomb's two cinder block buildings, keeping both hands visible in case some future dead man was watching him from a distance. He resisted the temptation to speed up when he got close enough to the bigger cinder block building to relish the idea of being beside it and able to take cover. Instead he scanned the nearby brush and the high hillsides for any movement, and kept listening for sounds—a heavy foot on stony dirt, the slide of metal on metal.

The steel door that Holcomb had installed was still there, the dead bolt locked. He kept walking to the second building, and found that door locked too. There was one more way. When Holcomb had put up these buildings he had dug tunnels. There was one going from under the floor in the main house to the windowless storehouse and workshop. There was also one running from the workshop to the brush at the base of the hillside. Holcomb had said he'd used his small Caterpillar tractor to dig them as three straight trenches seven feet deep. Then he had cut four-by-four braces and set them in concrete every eight feet. Next he'd nailed a layer of four-by eight-foot plywood to roof in the tunnels, covered it with tarpaper, and then pushed the dirt back over the roof. Holcomb said he had put about three feet of dirt over each tunnel.

Moreland walked to the big tangle of brush under the hill, found the area where he had remembered the end of the tunnel; then, using his knife blade, he found the trapdoor. He used his hands and feet to uncover it. He opened it and walked down the incline into the tunnel. He took out the pocket flashlight he had brought and then closed the trapdoor behind him. He had to crouch and walk bent over for about a hundred feet before he came to the ladder. He climbed it and pushed up on the trapdoor. It was heavy, but he wasn't surprised, because they had always hidden the trapdoor by putting the rug and then the big table over it. It was meant to be an escape route, not a way in. He pushed harder, got the rug to bunch upward into a ridge, and then pushed some more so he could crawl out under it. He slithered out of the rug, and then crawled to the wall and stood up.

In the dim round beam of his flashlight he could see that the police had been thorough. They'd broken open cupboards and toolboxes and gun cabinets and taken everything. He didn't know why, exactly, except that they had searched for anything that might explain Holcomb's shooting death, and they had been required by their own policies not to leave guns and boxes of ammunition unguarded. Holcomb had maintained a full arsenal, including pistols, a few assault rifles, and a lot of parts that hadn't seemed to pertain to any weapon Moreland could see.

Guns weren't what he had come to find. Somewhere there had to be a piece of paper that Holcomb had intended not to be read by anyone. Holcomb had written things down, even if he had them memorized. There had been padlock combinations, phone numbers, names, addresses. But Moreland knew that finding the piece of paper would not be easy.

Holcomb had been aware that he was exactly the kind of man the authorities most wanted off the streets. He had lived with the possibility that he might be the target of surprise raids, or even an unexplained disappearance, so he had not made either event an easy matter. He'd built his escape tunnels before he'd built his house. He had one steel door on each building, and no windows. He'd had a series of surveillance cameras around the place so he could see what was outside, but those were gone now.

Moreland went over every inch of the storage building and work-shop. If there had ever been a piece of paper here the police had taken it. Moreland was beginning to feel hot and sticky. When Holcomb had been here there had always been a ventilation fan running, and most of the time there had been air-conditioning. The power had undoubtedly been turned off after he died.

He wanted to go outside, but he wouldn't be able to get into the other building from there. The steel doors were locked. He lowered himself back down into the tunnel, pulled the rug to roughly where it had been, and closed the trapdoor. He made his way to the main tunnel that ran past the storage building to the main house. It was only about fifty feet away. As he went he ran his flashlight along the four-by-four braces and the corrugated steel ceilings to be sure they were all still in plumb, and didn't look as though they might collapse.

He climbed the second ladder and lifted the trapdoor. This one was not as heavy as the first, because all that was over it was the rug.

Holcomb had wanted to get out fast if something happened while he was asleep. Moreland searched. He could see that the cops had taken all the paper that they could find in the house. But Holcomb would never put anything this important where cops could find it.

Holcomb had told him, "Keep your biggest secrets in your head. But make sure you also have a place where the little ones are written down—the account numbers, passwords, addresses, and phone numbers of the people you'll need on the worst day of your life. Because sure as shit, that day is going to come. It'll only be your last day if you didn't prepare for it." He had taught Moreland to keep plenty of cash around, but store the big money in banks in other states under false names. Moreland still had a piece of paper with the little things written on it—account numbers; names he had used; the addresses and phone numbers of people he would want if he was on the run. He had a second copy in a safe-deposit box in a Texas bank.

Holcomb hadn't needed to do that. His crib sheet would be here on his ranch. Moreland crawled around the floor to look under pieces of furniture, then used the round dining table as a scaffold to stand on. He reached up above the rafters to feel for the paper. Then he climbed down, moved all the furniture back, and went down the trapdoor. He moved along the tunnel back past the ladder to the storage building. Then he imagined the emergency Holcomb was preparing for.

Holcomb would have just been awakened by the sounds outside. Maybe he had even seen the lights under the steel door. He had been too smart to expect to have any hope of defending his little fortress against cops. They never had to give up and go away, and he could never kill them all. He would have taken a wallet, water, and a gun, and gone down into his tunnel.

He imagined Holcomb scuttling along the escape tunnel. He wouldn't have hesitated or stopped to collect things. He would go straight down the tunnel to the end, as Moreland was doing now.

Moreland reached the end of the tunnel, the place where he had come in. He stopped at the foot of the incline where it bent upward. He took out his lock-blade knife, opened it, stared at the walls and the ceiling, and then knelt on the floor. It would be buried under the ground.

He stabbed the dirt again and again. Every six inches he stuck the blade all the way into the ground, then moved deeper into the tunnel and tried again. When he hit something solid below the surface he pulled the knife out and used it to dig. There was a white PVC pipe, about five inches in diameter. He dug it up. There were caps on both ends. He was able to unscrew one end and take off the cap. Inside were a tight roll of cash in hundreds, a compact .45 ACP pistol, a loaded magazine, a knife, and a folded sheet of lined paper.

Moreland carefully unfolded the paper and held his flashlight close to it. There was a list of account numbers, the false names connected with them, some computer passwords, addresses, phone numbers. And there was the phone number he had been looking for. He recognized it as the phone number of the Broker. It was an 800 number, so he had never known where it was located. But beside it was the name Daniel Cowper, and an address in San Mateo, California.

He was grateful to Holcomb for the stack of hundred-dollar bills. After he had killed Kelly in Boston, he had not had a chance to drive back and search her apartment for whatever cash she hadn't taken with her, so he had arrived in California nearly broke. He put the money in his pockets. He took the .45 pistol and the magazine as keepsakes, and the paper because it was what he had come for. He restored the cap to the PVC pipe and buried it again.

He ducked up through the trapdoor, closed it again, and then pushed the dirt and rocks back over it to hide it. He could feel the fresh air wafting across his face, breathed it in, and tasted it happily. His legs had some spring as he walked back to his car under the oak trees. He was going to meet the Broker.

22

Except for his two months with Catherine Hamilton, Moreland had been away from Southern California for two years. He had lived in a succession of small apartments with women whose closets smelled like stale perfume, and who seemed to be unable to get everything picked up off the floor at one time. Driving up the coast with the car window open let him smell the Pacific air.

He had begun this drive at Holcomb's ranch in the red rocky badlands north and east of Los Angeles. He had driven farther north and west, and when he reached Valencia, the world had begun to change. Soon he was on the Santa Paula freeway to Ventura and the ocean. He stayed beside the Pacific to Santa Barbara and beyond it, and soon there were big stretches of land without buildings, grassy hillsides above the ocean that had never been ruined by developers.

He wished he could stop the car in Santa Maria or San Luis Obispo or one of the other pleasant cities along the way; buy a small, neat house a half mile from the ocean; and never leave. But he kept going, past Pismo Beach, Cambria, Morro Bay. He kept driving until he was tired, stopped at a restaurant where he could look out the window at the endless blue of water and sky, and then bought gas and got on the road again.

It was evening when he reached Santa Cruz, and he decided it was time to sleep. He was a bit older than college age now, twenty-eight, but he could still rent a room not far from the college and look enough like a student to be unremarkable. He could stay until school let out next spring, but he knew he wouldn't do it. He checked into a small hotel and slept.

In the morning he got up and lingered, walking to a restaurant for breakfast and reading the newspaper while he ate. Holcomb had taught him to travel the way he lived: "Stick to places where there are lots of people just like you." He looked young, so he spent as much time as he could in college towns. Boston had been good. The city had a college population of two hundred fifty thousand, and at least that many young people who had graduated or dropped out and stayed.

Holcomb had died before Moreland had invented the method of living with working girls. Since then it had kept him invisible for periods of a month to five months at a time. But now there was a man hunting him, turning up in each place where he stopped. The man had destroyed forever his way of staying invisible. He didn't dare go near an escort again. He knew that he was going to have to be visible for long enough to deal with the Broker, but as soon as he had his money, he would find a new way to get invisible again.

He drove on to San Mateo and began to search for the right house. He had considered checking into a hotel first, but he had decided to put that off. It was still early in the day. He might be able to finish whatever his business with the Broker might turn out to be, and then drive a distance from here before he stopped for the night.

He found the address and studied the house as he drove past. It was the right sort of house for the Broker. It was a medium-size one-story ranch house in a neighborhood of medium-size one-story ranch houses. It had a black iron fence in front surmounted with spearheads that were ornamental but also sharp. He noticed that the mailbox was at the sidewalk, built into one of the two brick stanchions on the sides of the gate. There was an alarm company's sign on the lawn, and a BEWARE OF DOGS sign on the fence.

Moreland parked his car around the corner from the house two hours after dark. As he walked past the houses on the street, he noticed that many of them had windows opened to the mild summer night. He could hear the local newscasters talking in one house and a televised gunfight in another.

He didn't stop or let himself appear to be studying the area as he walked. Uncertainty and hesitation triggered suspicion. At the Broker's house he reached in, opened the front gate, went up the walk, and kept going to the back, where he was out of sight from the street. After he got there he sat on the back steps, listening. All he could hear was the air-conditioning unit churning away. If anybody had noticed him and called the police, they would arrive shortly. If the Broker had seen him, he would hear the back door open behind him.

After ten minutes he stood and walked along the back of the house, looking in each window as he passed it. There were no lights on, but in the kitchen he could see the small green light on the refrigerator's water dispenser and the red clock on the microwave oven's controls. He stopped by the dining room window, where he could see the control pad for the alarm system. It had a couple of green dots to show the power was on, but the red display said RDY, meaning it was not engaged.

He formed a theory that was a simple preference, a hope. The alarm was off. If a person went out, or to bed, he would turn the alarm on. But if he were wide awake and watching television or reading, he might have left it off. Moreland walked to the kitchen door, turned the knob, and opened it. He stepped in and closed the door behind him.

Something was wrong. The air-conditioning was on too high. He listened without moving. The only sound was the steady hum of the central air-conditioning chilling the house to something like the temperature of a refrigerator. Even though he was wearing a jacket to cover his gun he felt uncomfortable. After a minute the air conditioner stopped blowing. Immediately he noticed that the air had a faint ugly smell, the coppery aftertaste of blood. Something in his line of work had happened here.

He moved to the bottommost kitchen drawer and pulled it wide open. He felt duct tape, a hammer, a screwdriver, a box of nails, a flashlight. He turned the flashlight on. The beam was weak, but the first thing it showed him was a bubble pack of batteries. He replaced the old ones, being careful not to leave prints on the batteries, wiped off the package, and advanced into the house.

In the living room he stopped. The man on the floor was about Holcomb's age, late forties or fifty, with a shaved head and a tangle of tattoos encircling his right arm like tropical foliage. He'd had a pierced left ear, but whatever he'd had in it had been torn out. Someone had run a straight razor or box cutter from his sternum to his belly and let him bleed out on the floor. Moreland could see that the blood was mostly coagulated around the edges and the surface, but there was still quite a bit of liquid. The man had probably been dead an hour or two.

Moreland moved the flashlight up to the equipment on the row of tables against the wall. There was an open box of prepaid cell phones. There was a pair of old-fashioned landline telephones duct-taped together, mouthpiece to earpiece, so the man could receive a call on one, dial the other, and make his own untraceable connection to a third person. He had computers he probably used as phones, because the built-in cameras had been taped over. It was hard to doubt that this man had been the Broker.

Moreland looked around. There could be information about him in any of these computers, or in the memory of any of the phones. There could be paper records around, bank records, even an address book. He looked down at the Broker and tried to fit the name Daniel Cowper to him. He wasn't even sure how to pronounce that. The Broker had bruises and abrasions on his face. Moreland shone the light on him and stood beside him, keeping his feet out of the blood that had pooled and turned sticky on the floorboards. He had been tortured—burned, beaten, cut, and finally killed. They had wanted something from him. Information. He should have given them what they wanted right away, and they might have just shot him. Maybe he had known that, but had not been able to relinquish another hour of life, even an hour of pain. Moreland banished the idea from his mind. It didn't matter.

Moreland thought for a moment. They couldn't have done this for money. The Broker was a money man. The Broker could have given them money right away and not missed it. This hadn't been a robbery. Maybe it was somebody who wanted to know about the man who had killed Luis Salazar.

Moreland didn't touch anything in the room. In here with the air-conditioning system going wild, the air was frigid. Every time the air conditioner stopped running, it started up again in about twenty seconds, so the Broker's body was like fresh meat in a refrigerator. The blood smell was strong, but soon all the blood would have dried, and the other smells would take over. But the Broker's visitors had bought themselves some extra time before anyone came by and smelled the body.

Moreland considered the computers and telephones. He had no prayer of erasing the equipment, let alone any hidden papers or disks. The experts were always pulling information off disks somebody thought were safe. Maybe the Broker had been more careful than that. There was nobody who put less faith in the safety of technology than the technologists. They all knew how easy it was to hack into anything digital.

Moreland kept trying to think of a way forward. He was pretty sure that if he burned the house down, the firemen and cops would be here before everything burned. He would have to pile all the electronics in one spot, pour gasoline on them and around them, and burn them quickly. The authorities would think the fire was to hide the murder, but he couldn't care less about the murder. First he would have to gather all the electronic devices in here.

He stepped toward the hallway just as two men emerged from it. The first man said, "Hey, Joey. You Joey?" Both men were in their late thirties, and the heavy accent was Hispanic. They were already sidestepping apart.

Moreland didn't hesitate; he simply pulled out his gun and fired, first at the man who had spoken. He was hit in the chest, so Moreland's aim moved to the other one, who was reaching under his jacket. Moreland fired four shots rapidly, and the man fell to the floor and remained motionless. Moreland knelt, flipped open the jacket, plucked a Glock 19 compact pistol out of the shoulder holster, and then approached the one who had spoken.

He kept his gun aimed at the man's face while he moved the man's jacket to find his gun. It was a Glock 19 too. He tossed it a few feet away, then studied the man. His chest was rising and falling with difficulty. Moreland drew back the gun in his right hand and hit him across the cheekbone with it. The man grunted and opened his eyes.

"Who are you?" Moreland asked.

"Somebody looking for you."

"Why? I did what you wanted."

"Not what I wanted. We're not *narcotraficantes*. We're SSP. *Policía Federal*. You killed an important prosecutor. A brave, honest man."

"How do I know you're police?"

"You'll find my wallet. It doesn't matter. I'm dead. But I think you are too. If other Federales don't get you, the drug men will."

"Why kill him?"

He smiled. "Resisting arrest."

"What did he tell you?"

"He told us who you were."

"Then why kill him?"

"He knew a lot of things. That's a disadvantage in an interrogation. There's always more." He grunted.

"Do the drug dealers know about me?"

"They'll know what we know. The world is full of informers." He coughed, and Moreland knew the blood was bubbling in his lungs. They were filling up. He said, not really to Moreland, "We stayed too long."

Moreland stood up, took two steps back, shot him through the head, and then shot the other man through the head to be sure he was dead too. He searched the dead men for their wallets, which he put into his inner pockets. He went to the door, put an eye to the corner of the small cut-glass window at eye level, and looked outside. The shots didn't seem to have been heard.

He guessed that if there were cops, or more Federales, they would have come in. He walked through the house looking at the ceilings, trying to find the smoke detectors. He found three, and disconnected them. Then he rolled newspapers and magazines into tubes and stuck them in various places among the computers and telephones. Finally, he went out to the garage with his flashlight. He found charcoal starter, turpentine, and paint thinner. He returned to the living room, doused all of the equipment, and then realized he had no matches. He went to the body of the second policeman, searched his pockets, and found a cigarette lighter.

He started the fire and saw it flash along from table to table, then rise and grow. He went out the front door, set the lock in place, walked to his car, and drove.

23

"Hi, Jack. It's Alan Rafferty."

"To what do I owe this pleasure? Does Mullaney want me back in Boston?"

"Not yet. I just called because there have been some odd developments. Vice has had a peripheral involvement in the case, and so I've been in on these things."

"What happened?"

"A couple of the Federales—the cops who came with Luis Salazar's group from Mexico—have been shot to death in San Mateo. They turned up yesterday."

"What the hell were they doing in California?"

"We're not sure. They were found in a house owned by a man named Daniel Cowper. He had been tortured and killed. The two Federales had been shot in the chest and then the head. They were both wearing shoulder rigs that had no guns or ammo in them. And the house was set on fire."

"Who was Daniel Cowper?"

"I think he was involved in the Salazar assassination somehow. Mexican cops aren't supposed to be operating in this country except as observers or consultants attached to local police units. But it's safe to assume that when their boss got turned to hash in Boston, it didn't sit well with them. I think they wanted the guy who pulled the trigger, the guy who hired him, and whoever the client was."

"Sounds likely," said Till. "The Federales must have sources in the United States, just the way the FBI does in other countries. Maybe Cowper was one of them."

"I don't know, Jack. Cowper lived there alone, and the place was full of communication equipment that seemed to the investigators to be intended to make his calls hard to trace—prepaid cell phones, computers, a couple of old-fashioned landline phone receivers taped together like they used to do when bosses in prison wanted to call out. When you were here you seemed to think there was a middleman giving the Boyfriend his jobs. Maybe Cowper was him."

"You said there was a fire. Is there enough left of the computers and things to find out what was on them?"

"Nobody knows yet, but let's say we're optimistic. There had been reports of gunshots, so the cops were on the way when the fire started." He paused. "It really seems odd that foreign cops could find the middleman before we did."

Till said, "Not necessarily. If they guessed who paid for the hit, they must have ways of finding out who he paid—wiretaps, cell phone records, informers, whatever. Can you give me Cowper's address?"

"Sure." Rafferty read the address for him, and Till copied it. "Are you going up there?"

"It's practically in the neighborhood," said Till. "I'll let you know what I find out."

"I'll e-mail you the crime scene stuff right away. Bring your computer with you."

"Thanks."

As soon as he hung up, his cell phone rang again. "Jack Till."

"Hi, Dad," she said. "I almost called on the other line so you would say, 'Till Investigations.'"

"Hi, Holly," Till automatically looked at his watch. It was nearly noon. "Is everything okay?" He knew his question was a reflex, the thing that all parents really wondered every time the telephone rang. The conversation could not proceed until that worry was satisfied.

"Everything's fine. I'm at work. I figured you might be home from Boston by now. Are you?"

"Yes," he said. "I haven't been back in town long. And actually, I'm going out of town again today. But it's just up to San Francisco, and I'll be back tomorrow."

"You're so busy," said Holly.

"Not too busy for you. What's on your mind?"

"I got Mrs. Carmody thinking about you. She's definitely hoping you'll ask her out."

"Did I miss something?" he asked. "Didn't I say I didn't want to jeopardize your relationship with your boss or take a chance on souring your job?"

"You did say something like that, but who am I to stand in the way of her social life? She thinks you're hot."

"Come on."

"She does. She wants you. You know she does."

"Don't say things like that on the phone. If somebody overheard you they might not realize you're just teasing me. Mrs. Carmody might hear you and think you're making fun of her."

"Okay. Just remember, though. She's not going to wait forever."

"All right. I'd better say good-bye now, because I've got to get my plane reservation and you've got to get to work. I'll call you when I'm home."

"Love you."

"Love you. Bye."

She hung up. He opened his computer and bought his plane ticket, then closed the office and went home to pack a suitcase.

Till was at Burbank airport two hours later, flew to San Francisco, and rented a car to drive to San Mateo, which was only a couple of miles from the terminal. As he drove, he couldn't help thinking about Jeanne Carmody. He had always thought of her as attractive, but with Holly playing matchmaker his feelings were more complicated. Holly had tried to fix him up with various divorced women or widows from time to time since she was little. She was always cute about it, and she had a bawdy sense of humor, so even though it was heartbreaking it was funny at the same time. It had always made him sad. She had been trying to supply herself with a mother. The other kids had all had one, but she never had. Now it seemed to him that it was part of her belief that since she had moved out he must be lonely.

He drove to San Mateo and checked into his hotel. He opened his e-mail and studied the crime scene information that Alan Rafferty had sent him, then went out. He left the car in a parking structure attached to a movie theater that was within easy walking distance of Daniel Cowper's house.

The house was exactly what Till had expected. It was the least obtrusive house on a quiet city block. The lawn was mowed, but it wasn't any greener than the others. The house was exquisitely disguised, a marble in a jar of marbles. It was a place that was forgotten even as the eye moved past it.

The way to learn about a scene of violence was to let the eyes and ears and muscles feel what had gone on. Till had studied the charts and photographs Rafferty had sent him, and now he was ready to rely on his senses.

It was the time of night when the Boyfriend would have come. The streets near the house were empty. The last pedestrian had probably walked his dog around ten. The last car had driven up its driveway around midnight. The night belonged to Till now.

The Boyfriend was a killer, and Till had noticed that some killers came to like the night after a while. They liked invisibility, and after they came to know the night they moved easily in it. They cruised through it, able to interpret the sounds they heard to ensure their safety, and use the silences to reassure themselves that other human beings were far away.

Till was a night walker too. He had started out hunting predators at night because that was when they were likely to be out, but in time he had come to relish the darkness. Late at night, when nearly all of the ordinary people were asleep, and most of the people out were cops or suspects, there was a kind of clarity to the world. Tonight he hunted as one of the predators, reliving what this one must have felt a few nights ago in this place.

He stopped in front of the house and studied it, looking for the ways in and the ways that merely looked safe to enter but weren't. The Boyfriend would have made this examination and then made a choice.

He opened the gate in the spearhead fence and walked close to the house. The Boyfriend would have heard the noise of the air-conditioning system as he approached. That had been in the police report—the air conditioner running at full strength, turning the place into a refrigerator. It would have puzzled the Boyfriend, at first. Till guessed the Boyfriend would have gone to the back.

As Till walked around the house he saw that the back door was covered in black dust from a police fingerprint kit. He tried the door, found it locked, and then took out his pocketknife to jimmy the latch. He opened the door and entered. He stood in the entrance with his back to the wall so he had no silhouette and threw no shadow. The Boyfriend would have stood here listening for any sounds below the whir of the air-conditioning. It was here and now that the Boyfriend would have known that something was wrong. Nobody would keep a house that cold. Till shone his small pocket flashlight to be sure he hadn't missed something he should see, then moved.

Till stepped into the middle of the kitchen, then into the dining room, which drew him into the living room. The hardwood floor was still painted with the pools of dried blood. There were outlines of the bodies marked near the bigger spots, and circles where the police had found shell casings. Till had seen the photographs. There had been Daniel Cowper, an unremarkable-looking middle-aged man with no shirt on and a sleeve of tattoos, his thorax opened from chest to belly. He had been beaten and burned and tormented before he'd died. Till considered. Would the Boyfriend have tortured and killed him? He certainly wasn't above it, but Till couldn't imagine why he would do it. People did that when they wanted some kind of information. That was more likely to have been the outsiders. Till moved ahead on the assumption that Cowper had already been dead when the Boyfriend had arrived.

If the Boyfriend had walked in and found Cowper dead, he would have been puzzled. Had this been a robbery? Had the house been searched? Was somebody still in the house? He would not have been able to answer any of his questions except by looking. The photographs of this part of the house showed a lot of telephones, bundled wires, computers, routers, and cell phones. This was the house of a man who changed lines frequently and didn't want to have calls traced. Everything had been damaged by fire and firefighting, but the home had been orderly. Till wandered, looking for anything that might give him a feel for the house's owner. The bedroom was simple and plain. There had been no pictures of relatives—or of anything else—in the bedroom. It looked like a cheap motel room.

Till could feel what had happened next, because he had been in situations like this a few times. He returned to the living room. Maybe the Boyfriend had heard a car drive up. Maybe he had heard footsteps or voices inside the house. When the two men entered the living room he was ready, but the two men were not. Maybe they thought they were just coming in to start searching the house in earnest, the way they had been taught in the Public Superior Academy in San Luis Potosí. Maybe they thought they should clean the place of their prints. Whatever they thought, it didn't prompt them to come in with guns drawn, searching for a target. That was all that mattered.

He could just about see them now. They would have stepped in, one after the other; seen the Boyfriend; and tried to recover from the surprise. Maybe they had time to reach for their guns, but probably not. Till knew that the Boyfriend had opened up the moment he had seen them—a single shot in the chest to the nearest one to drop him; and then four shots to the chest for the other, who had begun to move. Only after they were both down would he have fired shots into their heads.

Part of surviving in a world where everybody carried a gun was to be able to think through a situation instantly. Anyone in the house was an enemy. The Boyfriend also knew that there must have been some noise when the man on the floor had been cut open, but nobody had come to investigate. That meant there was no reason to worry about noise. The second the men appeared he was probably aiming, ready to fire.

So now the Boyfriend was alive, and the two intruders were dead. He must have searched them, taken their guns and money—the absence of guns and money had been noted in the police report—and learned from their wallets that they were Mexican federal cops.

Till could see that everything in sight that might hold a fingerprint or reveal anything about the kills had been removed from the house. It could take months before the technicians cracked every computer and brought back any bits of information that survived in its memory. There was no guarantee that the fire had left anything. The one who had started the fire must have been the Boyfriend.

Till closed the house again, then went back to his car. He opened the trunk and took another look at the reproductions of the crime scene photographs. The one taken in the crawl space under the half-burned house finally made sense to him. The object was a fireproof safe that the police had opened. Inside had been a gun, some cash, and a jumble of computer disks and flash drives. Till could feel the urgency that the Boyfriend must be feeling. The Boyfriend thought he had beaten back his enemies for the moment, and had obliterated the information about him by burning the computers. He would be on his way into hiding, relieved but still scared by his close call. But for the first time, what the Boyfriend had to fear most was not Jack Till.

Joey Moreland drove through the night, heading east. He had been happy when he'd thought finding the Broker would solve his problems, but he had been wrong. The men he'd killed at the Broker's house were Mexican federal cops. How had they found their way to the Broker? The Broker had told him that the Mexican drug guys were angry at him. Had they been angry enough to tip the Federales to where the Broker was? This wouldn't be the first time that a hit man had taken out his target and then learned that the client had given him up to the police instead of paying him.

As Joey drove, he had another thought that agitated him. The Broker had needed the banks and numbers of some of his accounts so he could transfer money in electronically. What if the two Mexican cops had gotten the numbers? And maybe the American cops would get the information off the hard drives at the Broker's house, though that wouldn't be easy, after the fire he'd set. Maybe Joey could slip in, get his money out, and go before they decoded everything.

He stared ahead at the long, open road and thought about how to do it. Holcomb had taught him how to use banks. A name and a social security number and a good identity were always tied to each account. When you wanted to close it, you couldn't just have the bank write a check to you for the balance and then deposit it in your next bank. You had to take some in cash, and the rest in a check to an imaginary company. Then you made the company real—filed papers to register it, opened a bank account for it, and deposited the money. Then that company wrote a check to another company. Each time, you took out more in cash. If you started with cash, you put as much as you could into a safe-deposit box instead of depositing it.

He was going to have to go to San Antonio, Texas. He didn't know San Antonio very well, and he had driven there only once, because Holcomb had told him to keep one of his hoards of money near the Mexican border, and one near the Canadian border.

Years ago Holcomb had taken Joey to a specialist to buy a Texas driver's license and some credit cards in the name of James R. Cody. He had used them in San Antonio to start a checking account. He had made a small deposit, and then the Broker had transferred money in over time. James R. Cody's address was a postal service in Chicago, which forwarded his statements to his PO box in Los Angeles. The account had grown to over a hundred thousand dollars. Converting that to cash would take time, and the money in his safe-deposit box was much more—too much to leave untouched.

The western part of the country was huge, but nothing ever seemed as huge as Texas. It took him two days of hard driving to reach the Texas border and two more to reach San Antonio. Each afternoon he paid in cash to check into a small hotel near the interstate highway, slept until the middle of the night, then drove on. When he reached San Antonio he checked into a Marriott hotel, got a good night's sleep, checked out before seven in the morning, then drove to the bank.

It was a compact, old-fashioned bank building with a concrete facade patterned and etched to look like stone, four thick pillars, and tall, narrow windows. By seven-fifteen he was outside, watching from up the street where the bank's cameras couldn't catch him or his car. Cops might be very good at hiding themselves while they waited for a suspect, but they wouldn't come to the bank three hours early. He planned to watch every one of the bank's staff arrive for the day, and then figure out who was who. There were no signs of life yet, so he got out of the car.

He went to a coffee shop across the street from the bank and bought a large coffee, a *San Antonio Express-News*, and a scone the size of a man's hand. He sat at a tiny black metal table in the front window, and watched. At seven-fifty he saw the first one, a manager type, arrive, open the door with a key, make some moves that probably had to do with the alarm system, and disappear inside.

Moreland kept pretending to read his paper from eight to eight-thirty, but didn't see another employee arrive. He was out of coffee, so he got up to use the men's room and then came out to buy another. When he turned from the counter carrying his coffee, he saw a man about his age wearing blue jeans and boots and a shirt with no collar come in, take the chair he'd been sitting in and begin reading his newspaper.

He said quietly, with a smile, "Excuse me, friend. But you seem to have my seat and my paper."

The man, still seated, looked up at him. "Oh, was this yours?"

"Yes," he said. "It is. Sorry." He could feel an ugly scene happening again, as though it were a play, and each person had to say the same things at each performance. This was happening because of the way Moreland looked. He was slim, and his face was smooth and big-eyed, and he had wavy hair. As much as girls loved the way Moreland looked, some men seemed to think it was an indication of weakness.

The man gave him a crooked smile and leaned back in the steel chair, making the chair's front legs lift off the floor. "That's a shame, son. Now, you're going to want to stop bothering me before I get irritated."

Moreland's right leg was already in motion before he had time to think. It swept the back legs out from under the man so his chair back hit the floor with a clap and his head bounced against the tile. He began to sit up.

Moreland dropped before that could happen. He came down with his weight on one knee just at the lower edge of the man's sternum. He wasn't sure whether he had caused internal damage or not, but he leaned his forearm on the man's neck to press him down.

"Stop! Stop it!" the girl at the counter shouted.

Moreland's face was near the man's, and he spoke just above a whisper. "Now that's a shame too. But you still have a choice. You can roll over, get up, and walk out the door. What's it going to be?"

The man glared up at him but said nothing.

Moreland's left hand punched the man's face hard twice, and then a third time. The man's eyebrow was bleeding, his lip torn, and his nose broken.

"All right."

Moreland stood up. The man rolled to his side and prepared to rise, but as he rose his right hand retrieved a large pocketknife from his pants pocket. He flicked it open with his thumb and swept it in a semicircle at Moreland's legs.

The girl shrieked louder. "Stop! Help!" There were no other customers, so she got no help.

Moreland jumped back to avoid being slashed, pushed the wrought-iron table over into the man's way, picked up the other steel chair, and swung it with both hands into the man's head and shoulders. The man kept coming, but Moreland avoided the knife. He raised the chair again and brought it down on the man's shoulder. He saw the right moment, threw the chair into the man's chest, grasped his knife arm, and broke it. Then he picked up the knife and closed it.

He saw a sudden movement in the corner of his eye. There were three men in suits hurrying out of the bank. He looked at them, then saw two others get out of a van parked near the bank. He could tell they were all cops of some kind. They must have been waiting in ambush, hoping he would come into the bank to get his money. He couldn't let the man go now.

In a sudden motion he flicked open the knife, stuck it up under the left side of the man's sternum to the heart, turned, and looked for the girl at the counter, but she was gone. He ran toward the back room of the coffee shop. The girl had obviously called the police, and now she was gone. He ran to the back door and looked out to the alley behind the building, but he couldn't see her.

He looked around him in the storeroom. There were shelves with bags of coffee beans, metal parts that he assumed were for coffeemakers, boxes of pastries to replenish the supplies under glass out front. And there was a green apron with the logo of the coffee shop chain and a box of paper hats like the one the girl had worn. He took off his jacket, put on the hat and apron, rolled the jacket up, and brought it with him.

In a second he was out the back door into the alley. He ran, listening for the sound of the cops bursting into the coffee shop, expecting at any moment to hear one of them coming out the back of the shop after him. At the end of the alley he threw the apron and hat into a Dumpster, walked to his car, and drove. As he passed the coffee shop he saw men in suits milling around in the front window, and a man in front who seemed to be the boss, talking on a cell phone with his free hand covering his other ear. As he talked, he stared down at the sidewalk. He never noticed the gray car going past him, and in a minute the car was out of sight, heading north out of the city of San Antonio.

24

It was night when Till reached San Antonio, and night was not a welcome prospect. Night was an interruption, a shutting down of the pursuit while the Boyfriend dissolved into the darkness again. There had been FBI agents waiting with the cops in the bank for the Boyfriend. They had learned his account number and the name James R. Cody from one of the computer disks that had been found in the fireproof safe under Daniel Cowper's house. Apparently Cowper had been some kind of agent or paymaster for hired killers.

The authorities had no idea of the real name of the man they were looking for. They knew the alias James R. Cody, which he had used at the bank in San Antonio. They also had found aliases connected with about twenty other bank accounts from that cache of computer disks. They didn't know if the accounts belonged to one man or twenty.

The cops in the bank had gotten a call from their dispatcher to say that a barista in the coffee shop across the street from the bank had called for help. Two customers were in a knife fight. The whole bunch of law enforcement officers had dashed outside. It was not clear to Till whether they thought the disturbance in the coffee shop was connected with their ambush in the bank, or they all just acted on the policeman's axiom that a gun could pretty easily end a knife fight. But by the time they made it to the coffee shop, the customer was dead, and the Boyfriend was gone.

As soon as Till had seen the report that Rafferty in Boston forwarded to him, he had driven to the San Jose airport and bought a ticket to San Antonio, Texas. He had called the local police department and talked to Ron Evans, an old acquaintance in Homicide there.

Now Till stood in the coffee shop and walked through the crime scene. He put himself in the body of the Boyfriend. He sat at a table that had been put in the place of the one used in the murder. He could tell that was the location because it had been marked on the floor.

He was surprised when one of the San Antonio cops told him the store would reopen tomorrow. All the crime scene work had been done immediately, because they had known from the beginning that the killer was connected with the murder of two Mexican cops in San Mateo, California, and was suspected of a wide variety of other killings. This was a race, and the Boyfriend had shown that he was good at breaking traps and getting away.

Till looked at the scene in the coffee shop. He could feel what the Boyfriend had felt. He'd been there early in the morning to case the bank before he went in. He had been alone, or nearly alone. He'd sat where he could see the front door of the bank, and stayed there for a while. He must have been drinking coffee, but Till hadn't heard anything about fingerprints being found. The Boyfriend had gone to the counter and had his first look at the barista who gave him his coffee. Then he had sat down.

Till could feel the anxiety that had made the Boyfriend sit here watching the bank. The report Till had seen claimed the killer could not have seen any of the cops inside the bank, but he obviously had known there could be some. He had been assuming there would be something in the computers at Daniel Cowper's house to lead the police here. He had probably hoped he had made it to the bank before the police were aware of it. If he was here before the cops, he would get his money and leave. If not, going in would get him caught. So he watched.

The police report said the 911 call from the waitress had mentioned that two men were fighting over a table. The shop had been empty of other customers. Till counted the tables: eight little wrought-iron tables, and sixteen chairs. The Boyfriend had needed to be in the center where he could watch the front of the bank. Why had the other man cared?

Till brought back the sight of the photographs of the dead man. He had been stabbed, but he had been badly beaten up before that. The police report said the knife was left stuck in the victim's heart. Till remembered the tattoo on the dead man's arm. It was old, one color, and so crude as to be barely symmetrical. It looked like a spiderweb. Prison.

Till consulted a piece of paper from his pocket and called the number on it. The man who answered said, "Detective Evans."

"Hi, Ron. This is Jack Till. I was wondering about the stabbing victim. Does he have a rap sheet?"

"I just got it. He's got a couple of convictions. Nothing recent. Assault, aggravated assault, battery. Did five years total."

"Was the knife his?"

"Right on that one too. His wife identified it."

"Thanks," said Till. He ended the call. Now it made more sense. The Boyfriend had been in the coffee shop watching the bank across the street. This guy had come in. He had looked at the Boyfriend and seen a man who was not big or formidable. The Boyfriend was alone, and there was something about him. He had a pretty face, one that made the girls all love him. He must have looked like someone this man would enjoy bullying.

The knife was the only weapon found in the building, and the dead man—Ronald Earl Barr—had brought it in with him. He was bigger, about six two. He was older, probably by five years. And when he came into this shop he made the biggest, and therefore last, miscalculation of his life. He picked a fight with a man who was good enough at killing people to do it for a living.

Till lifted the small wrought-iron chair with two hands and raised it over his head. It must have weighed forty pounds, at least. A couple of whacks with that would have changed the balance quickly. Probably the Boyfriend had used it to injure and disarm Barr, and then used the man's own knife to kill him. Till set the chair down and then guessed what the Boyfriend had thought next: *Where's the girl?*

Escaped. She saw the fight. Maybe the Boyfriend even heard her call the cops. She might have remained on the phone, as the emergency operators tried to make people do when they should have been running. The Boyfriend was moving into the back of the shop, and when he got there he saw she had run off. He had no time to chase her. All he could do was run for his car.

The police had found an apron and a hat from the shop in the trash down the street, so he had probably worn them or prepared to. It was another indication that he looked young. If Till had tried that, he'd have been shot on sight.

The Boyfriend's face made him a favorite with young girls, but it also made men underestimate him, made them think he couldn't be the mean one, the crazy one, because he looked so much like the harmless, innocent one. That was worth remembering. Till had to keep in mind that when he finally caught up with this guy, what he would see would not look like a killer. If Till took an extra second or so to see through the appearance, it would give the Boyfriend enough time to kill him too.

25

Joey Moreland could hardly believe how close he had come. When that big moron had started messing around with him, it had pushed Joey into a rage. The idiot wouldn't go away, so all Joey could do was make him die. Once he was dead, the girl should have died too. She had called the police, and he hadn't wanted to leave her alive to describe and identify him, but he'd had no choice. He'd had to run.

As he had driven past the coffee shop, he had seen the cops who had poured out of the bank's door. They must have all been in there waiting for him since before dawn. So the big psycho who had come in and taken his chair had actually saved him from the police. It wasn't a small thing. He could never have surrendered, and he couldn't win a gunfight with a dozen cops.

He drove north with determination, trying to get out of the state of Texas as quickly as possible. It was night now, and that should have made him less worried, but it didn't. What had happened in San Antonio had shocked him.

He knew he would never get the money in the San Antonio bank. Now that the authorities had connected that account to the Broker, it would be confiscated. Probably it already had been confiscated before he'd arrived in San Antonio. As he drove, he thought about the other accounts he had established. He needed to remember which accounts he had let the Broker deposit money into electronically. That had been going on for only a year or so. At the beginning the Broker had paid Holcomb and Holcomb had paid Moreland in cash. Sometimes the Broker had sent Holcomb cash and they had simply sat down and split it. But then he had gotten clever and let the Broker transfer the money. There were other times when the Broker had sent him a check, and he had deposited it in one of his accounts.

Every account that the Broker had known about would eventually be found. He had to try to save some of those accounts before the cops got to them. He had to save some of his money.

He drove steadily for the state line on Interstate 285. He went from Pecos, Texas, to Carlsbad, New Mexico, with particular care. There was no reason to get close to the Mexican border, where the cops and the drug dealers stared into one another's eyes to guess the next move. He drove at exactly the speed limit until he was past Carlsbad and heading for Roswell. He had done this trip before, and he knew that he would hit Interstate 40 at Vaughn.

He stopped at Artesia at one a.m. for gas and coffee, and then went on. He had been relying on his youth and physical conditioning to keep him ahead of the FBI agent or detective who had been following him since Phoenix. He knew he could outlast any pursuer, so he had stayed on the road. But it was getting to be time to rest. He stopped at a big motel off the highway near Roswell at two-thirty, checked in, showered, and went to bed. He had driven hundreds of miles during the day, and now he felt exhausted. He fell asleep quickly.

When he awoke at ten, he knew what had to be done. He checked out and drove toward Illinois, the northern state where he'd opened a bank account. That was the next bank account to try to salvage. It took Moreland three days to drive to southern Illinois. He stopped in a Denny's restaurant in Carbondale, and went inside to look for the right sort of person. As soon as he came in the door, he noticed a young couple who looked about right. He went to the booth nearest to their table, and sat down. As he studied his menu, he couldn't help looking over the top of it now and then, and when he did, he would see them again.

What had caught his eye was that they were just the right age—about twenty—and the right general description, attractive and clean and wholesome-looking. The girl was about five feet three with pretty skin and the kind of curves that were perfect now, but would probably turn to fat in twenty years. The boy had dark hair and a handsome, symmetrical face with intense brown eyes. He was slim and wiry. As Moreland lowered his eyes to the menu, the boy stood up and walked toward the men's room.

The girl looked around the room, a little bored, when her eyes met Joey Moreland's. She had already let her eyes rest on his for the half second when she should have kept her eyes moving, so she smiled a bright, white-toothed smile that crinkled the smooth skin at the sides of her blue eyes, then turned away to stare straight ahead, but still keep him in the corner of her eye.

"Excuse me," he said. "Do you know the best way to Springfield?"

She turned all the way around to face him, and bestowed the smile on him again. "I would say that the best way is to get on the interstate and take it north to Route 55—that's right around Centralia—and follow that straight up."

"What's the number of the interstate?"

"Oh, that was dumb. I'm sorry," she said. "It's 57. We just call it 'the interstate' because it's the only one we've got." She blushed a little and touched her hair. "Are you going up for the fair?"

Moreland had no idea what she meant. "Is the fair happening now? I've never been before, so I suppose it's time. I was just going up there on business."

"I'll say it's time," she said. "I just love the fair. We're planning to go up in a couple of days."

"We?"

She was flustered, and the blush in her cheek grew redder. "My boyfriend Gabe. Didn't you see him sitting here when you came in?"

Joey gave her his best smile. "I'm sorry. I guess my eyes couldn't get past you."

She made a swatting gesture in his direction, but then touched her hair again. "Get real," she said. "Now you're just making fun of me."

"Honest, I'm not," he said. "I'd never be mean like that. I'm just sorry you're taken, but I respect that. I'm Michael, by the way."

"Pleased to meet you." She said it and her eyes rose to his for only a second. "I'm Sharon."

"Delighted." He leaned forward, took her small pudgy white fingers in his, gave her hand one gentle shake, and then released it.

She curled her fingers into a dimpled fist, as though she had an unconscious urge to touch the place where he had touched her. She saw his eyes rise and focus on something behind her, and she spun around in her seat and pretended she'd known her boyfriend was coming all along. "Honey," she said, "this is Michael. He's going up to the state fair."

Moreland stood up and held out his hand. "Hi. Michael Grimes," he said. "I'm actually going up on business, but your girlfriend mentioned it's fair time, so I thought I'd check that out too."

Gabe had no obvious alternative but to smile and shake this stranger's hand, and Joey was pleased to see that Gabe didn't think of a way to avoid it.

Gabe sat down across the table from Sharon, and looked at her with the sort of shrewd gaze that indicated he thought she was cute rather than smart.

Moreland sensed that Gabe would start signaling for their check in a minute, so he brought out his pitch. "Sharon tells me that the two of you are planning to go up there in a few days yourselves. What are the best things for a first-timer to see?"

"We're just thinking about going," said Gabe. "Nothing definite."

Sharon interpreted the question as intended for both of them, and she was delighted to be asked. "I love the Ferris wheel, and oh, the Mega Drop, and Turbo Force."

"Those are rides," Gabe explained. "On Mega Drop they drop you a hundred and thirty feet to the ground."

"There are over a hundred rides." Sharon was more and more animated. She wiggled her hips excitedly. "There's nothing else around like the fair."

"You must like being scared," Moreland said.

"I do," she said happily.

"They have good bands some nights," Gabe offered. "Lots of chicks."

Moreland pretended to think. Then he said, "You know, the reason I'm driving up there to Springfield is that I'm a lawyer, and I've got to go file some claims to take possession of some property for a client. That's a pretty quick process, and my company is paying for everything."

"You're so lucky," Sharon said.

"I guess so. Anyway, if you two feel like going up there tomorrow, I'll drive to Springfield and my company will pay for the trip. I'll drop you off here on my way home to Texas. You can show me the way, and talk to me so I don't fall asleep at the wheel."

"Wow," said Gabe. "That sounds like a great offer, but—"

Sharon jumped in to keep the conversation from ending. "We've got to wait until I get paid on Thursday. It's only like fifteen dollars to get in, but you have to eat, you need a place to stay, and all that."

"No problem," said Moreland. "I'll tell you what. You can help me do my errand when we get there, and I'll put you on the payroll. Your pay will be whatever the trip costs."

Sharon said, "Gabe, can we, please?"

Gabe said, "Jeez, I don't know. I'm supposed to work tonight. We'd both have to take the next two days off."

"We'd have to do that anytime we go, and the fair won't be free any other time. Please."

Gabe looked at Moreland for a second, then shrugged. "I guess so."

Moreland said, "Great. We can meet here tomorrow for breakfast, and then leave from here. How about eight o'clock?"

"That'll be great," said Sharon. "I'm so excited."

Gabe looked at his watch. "We'd better get going. I'll get the check." He got up and walked to the cash register.

Sharon leaned forward toward Moreland. "Wait until you see the Butter Cow."

"The Butter Cow? What's that?"

"It's a cow. Made of butter." She stood up and gave a little wave. "Thanks, Michael. We'll have a great time."

She went to join Gabe as he was paying the check. She took his arm with both hands and walked with him to the door. She turned around and waved again. Moreland smiled and waved back.

Moreland waited for the waitress to swing by his table so he could order his breakfast, then sat at his booth and ate it. He couldn't be sure this was going to turn out well, but being one of three people would make him a little harder for all of the people pursuing him to spot.

The next morning Joey Moreland was in the same seat in the booth at Denny's. There were a few people eating breakfast on the way to work, and a few families who seemed to be vacationers just getting ready to head back to the interstate, but the place was not crowded.

"Michael!" The high, chirpy voice came from over his left shoulder. As he turned and saw Sharon in a tank top and a short white skirt, she slid into the booth quickly and stopped only after her hip had touched his. He found himself with his face only inches from hers. "Ready to go?" The minty smell of toothpaste was strong.

"I'm just finishing my breakfast," he said. "I got here early. Want to see the menu?"

"No, thanks. I had breakfast, and Gabe did too."

"Where is he?"

"He's out in the lot with our bags waiting to see which car is yours. His brother Dave drove us over here in his truck and let us off."

"Then maybe we should get going," said Moreland. "Want some coffee to take with you?"

"No, thanks," Sharon said. "It's more fun to stop for coffee on the way."

"I can see you're a worldly and experienced traveler."

She bumped him again with her hip.

He opened his wallet and set a couple of ten-dollar bills on the check beside his plate. "We'd better help Gabe load up." He slid out the other side of the booth and they met in the middle of the floor.

She looked at his hand. "No ring. You're not married, are you?"

"Nope. Never been married." He smiled the smile that had worked on her yesterday. "The good ones all seem to be taken."

"Maybe you'll find somebody at the fair."

"No heifers, though, or Butter Cows."

"You're awful."

"Probably, but I'll still stay away from the ones that are wearing blue ribbons."

She gave his arm a gentle slap, turned, and went out the door ahead of him. He led her to his car, popped the trunk with his key chain remote, and watched Gabe sling the two small duffels into the trunk and close it. He held out his hand. "Morning, Gabe."

Gabe shook it. "Morning," he said. "Would you like me to drive?"

"I appreciate that, Gabe. But I think for now I'll drive. I feel pretty fresh."

"He's not," Sharon said. "Gabe worked the night shift."

Moreland kept his attention on Gabe. "Really? What do you do?"

"I work at the big Mobil station out by the interstate. Eight gas pump islands and a store."

"Why don't you lie down on the backseat and get some sleep? If you do that you'll feel a lot better, and we'll all have a better time at the fair."

"You don't mind?"

"Of course not. Just so somebody's awake, we'll be fine."

"See?" Sharon said to Gabe.

"Thanks." Gabe climbed in the back and lay down, Sharon got into the passenger seat beside Moreland, and Moreland started the car.

"That way out of the lot," she said, "then right, then left at the first light."

He drove as she directed, and then got onto the interstate and headed north across flat farm country. He had made this trip once, when he had gone to establish the bank account in Springfield, but he pretended everything was new to him. He spoke in a low voice to give Gabe a chance to fall asleep, but he had no need to worry. Before he accelerated onto the interstate, he could hear Gabe's first slow, regular snores.

"Thanks so much for letting him sleep. If you want a good driver to spell you, well, then, that would be me."

"Are you a good driver?"

"Sure am. No tickets, no accidents, and hardly anybody ever swears at me."

"Then I'll keep you in mind."

"I'll bet you will." She smiled.

He drove for a time, keeping the car at the same speed as the rest of the traffic, and not making any sudden moves.

Sharon said, "You're a lawyer, but what kind?"

"I'm sort of a general attorney. I do whatever is necessary for each client. This job is claiming and taking possession of some assets my client owns, and bringing the money back to him. If you don't do that now and then with your financial assets, the state confiscates them, as though you died without a will and had no relatives."

"That doesn't sound fair."

"Some people stash their money away for the future, but then forget about it."

"I should have that kind of problem."

"Me too. It's pretty simple to fix, but I don't want it to spoil the fun of the fair. We can stop at the courthouse after the fair."

He could feel her staring at him for a time. The only sound in the car was the snoring of Gabe in the backseat. "Do you have a girlfriend? Anybody special?"

"No," he said. "Not lately. I've been working and traveling so much lately that it wouldn't have been fair to the girl."

"Poor thing." She patted his right shoulder, and then he felt her hand move slowly and deliberately down his arm to his elbow, and then to his thigh. She rested her hand in his lap and left it there. He turned his head to look into her blue eyes, but said nothing.

"It's a good thing we met up in Denny's," she said. "I think we'll have a good time. You'll be glad you came."

"I already am," he said. This time there was something conspiratorial in his tone. He looked in the rearview mirror to be sure Gabe was asleep. He had always loved the moment when the first step had been taken and things were no longer ambiguous. She kept her hand there, and as he began to grow hard, she gripped him.

He tolerated it for a minute or two, and then he moved her hand away. But before he could return his hand to the wheel, she clutched his hand and placed it on the smooth skin of her inner thigh, and held it there, just above the hem of the skirt.

He looked at her blue eyes again, and they were wide with innocence. He looked in the mirror to be sure Gabe was still asleep. "You hit me for teasing you, but you seem to be quite a tease yourself."

"People have said that, but I think they just weren't good sports."

"I'll try to be a good sport."

She looked at his lap. "You're doing fine."

He shrugged. "I'm looking forward to Springfield."

She nodded. "You're going to like it."

Coming into Springfield from the south brought them under exit signs that announced the fairgrounds.

"I forgot to look to see what day it was," Sharon said.

"Tuesday."

"No, at the fair," she said. "They have something every day. Agriculture Day, Senior Citizens Day, Republican Day."

"It's Sharon day."

She smiled happily and leaned back in her seat so he could move his hand farther up her thigh. "Well, maybe it is."

As though he had subconsciously set an internal alarm, Gabe stirred in the backseat, then groaned. Sharon sat up and pushed Moreland's hand away. By the time Gabe had groaned again and sat up scratch-ing his scalp, she was sitting up straight and looking prim. "Hi there, Sleeping Beauty," she said. "We're nearly there."

They drove onto the fairgrounds and parked in a huge lot that had until this week been an empty field. They walked the half mile or so to the front gate, where Moreland bought their tickets, then handed each of them a hundred dollars in cash, as though the bills were coupons that came with the tickets.

Gabe looked at the money and said, " Hey, Michael. You don't need to do that."

"It was our deal. I said I'd pay for the trip. You two will help me do my errands tomorrow, and we'll be even. Today we have fun."

"Thanks, Michael." After a second, he nudged Sharon. "How about you? Aren't you going to thank him?"

"Oh, I will. Don't rush me." Only after he looked away did she give Moreland a glance.

"Where do we start?" asked Moreland.

"Let's go on some rides right away before we eat anything," Sharon said. "I don't want to get queasy." Moreland watched her scamper ahead, her perfect white legs graceful in the short skirt she wore and her pink-lacquered toenails showing through the toes of her sandals.

Gabe hurried to follow Sharon, and Michael trailed both of them by a few feet. He never got between them or competed for Sharon's attention. For an hour they went from ride to ride. They fell 130 feet on the Mega Drop, then hurried to other machines where they were lifted, hurled, spun, rocked, somersaulted, and taken on quick turns.

When Gabe said he was going to the men's room, Sharon said, "We'll be over on the Sky Ride." She pulled Moreland to the end of the Sky Ride at gate 2, and got them aboard. They stepped onto a track side by side, and a seat like a ski lift scooped them up and a bar came down across their laps.

As soon as they were aloft and moving away, Sharon turned and kissed him. He started to pull back, but her tongue was already slipping into his mouth, and she held tight to him. He kissed her for a few seconds before he gently disengaged and looked back to see if Gabe had emerged from the men's room. "Sorry," she said. "I can hardly keep my hands off you."

He smiled. "I hope we don't get thrown out of the fair."

"People don't think that way, silly. We're young and single and cute. They don't care about anything else, and nobody looks up here anyway."

He knew they were too far away now for Gabe to see clearly, so he put his arms around her and kissed her until he had induced a kind of breathless excitement in her. He released her when the Sky Ride swooped down and stopped to let them off near the arena. They stood by the arena and he kissed her again for a second, but she pulled away. "That'll help focus our minds."

"Is that a good thing?" he asked.

"Now we go back and finish wearing out Gabe."

"He had a good nap."

"A little over two hours. Not much after he was working all night long."

When they got off the Sky Ride on the return trip Moreland studied Gabe. He was squinting and looking tired already. "I'm hungry," Gabe said.

Sharon took Gabe by the hand and made him walk quickly along the midway to a row of food shacks. She led them to one where she ordered all of them beer and barbecued pork sandwiches. Then there was another that had roasted corn on the cob and more beer. In a few minutes they were walking again, and then they went on another ride.

All afternoon she tired Gabe out. She insisted that they walk the length of the midway, stopping at each of the games where he could win her a prize. He wasn't big or heavy enough to ring the bell with the sledgehammer, but he won her a small pink bear. He had a good arm for throwing balls at clown dolls, but the dolls were on a wooden rack that made them nearly impossible to dislodge. Sharon told Gabe how good he looked throwing hard, so he kept it up until he won her a faux pearl necklace. Then Sharon insisted that he must be thirsty again, and brought him another big cup of beer.

Moreland could see that Sharon was succeeding. Gabe looked more and more exhausted as the early afternoon breeze subsided and the late afternoon sun sank lower and shone directly at him. Wherever Gabe looked, the light flared as it reflected off every metal or glass surface into his eyes. The beer was a powerful soporific, but the heat made him drink more. For a time the beer infused him with enough energy to do more walking and play more games.

As evening came, the three revived a bit. The air lost its most uncomfortable ten degrees, and they went to watch horses pulling sulkies around the track. Gabe bet and won a couple of times, so he felt elated. The lights came on at dusk and the enormous fairground glowed with a garish beauty. They went to a German beer garden, and ate dinner. Sharon made sure to buy beer by the pitcher, but only Gabe drank much of it.

By the time they were finished it was after eight-thirty. Sharon announced to nobody in particular, "Wow. This has been one of the best days of my life. I'm having so much fun. But do you think maybe we should go find a place to stay? I'll bet we have to drive a ways to find a vacancy."

"I have reservations," Moreland said. "I called yesterday."

"You did?"

"Yeah. If you've had enough, we could go anytime."

Gabe leaned against the side of a refreshment stand, and barely seemed to hear, but said, "Yeah, I think we're pretty worn out."

They made their way out of the fair to the field where their car was parked. Moreland opened the doors, and watched them get into the backseat. He drove to a hotel on East Clear Lake Avenue. On the way they passed several other hotels that seemed indistinguishable from the one he'd picked—tall and whitish with a circular drive in front, a roof over the entrance, and a large lot for guests to park their own cars.

Moreland opened the trunk and took out his suitcase. Gabe carried the other two, and Sharon handled the door openings, then waited with Gabe while Moreland registered. When Moreland returned he handed Gabe a key card in a folder with the room number written on it. As they walked to the elevator he slipped the second folder with his own room number on it to Sharon. He walked them to their room, then went on to his own room. He took a shower, lay down on the king-size bed, and turned on the television set.

It was no more than twenty minutes before he heard the knock on his door. He stood and looked through the fish-eye lens and saw Sharon's blue eye pressed to it. He opened the door.

"Surprise," she said.

"Can I unwrap it?"

"That's what surprises are for." She put her arms around his neck and kissed him. She held her body back a little so he could reach the buttons and clasps easily. He slipped off her clothes, then tossed them onto the chair by the door.

She pulled the belt of his bathrobe so it opened, then stepped inside it, put her arms around him, and held him close. "I've been waiting all day to get naked."

"So have I." He kissed her. "I assume Gabe is sleeping?"

"Yep. He felt guilty for being sleepy and said we should go back to the fair without him."

"That was nice."

"It sure made me happy." She tugged Moreland's bathrobe off and pushed him onto the bed. She kissed him everywhere, then stepped to the chair where her purse was, and returned with a small box of condoms. She tore one off the strip, put it on Moreland, and straddled him. After about a minute, she turned her head upward so her hair hung down her back, and then closed her eyes. "Still the best ride there ever was."

Moreland had spent a lot of time with young women. He had studied them carefully and soberly at times like these, and the knowledge and skill he'd obtained gave him an advantage. As the time went on he observed Sharon and assessed her changing mood by her skin coloring, movement, voice, breathing, and pulse, and the dilation of her eyes. He used the information to become her fantasy. At first she wanted him to be gentle and sweet, but as she got wilder, she wanted him to share her mood—be rougher, faster, more demanding, and so he was. She adored him for it, and soon all her inhibitions were gone.

Later, when they were lying on the bed side by side and feeling the sweat drying on their skin, she said, "Oh, I do love the fair." There was a long minute of silence, and then she said, "I've got to go back to Gabe's room now."

"I understand."

"No you don't. If there were any way not to, I wouldn't. But he's always going to be around. You're not." She got up, went to her clothes, picked them up, and took them with her into the bathroom. In a moment he heard the shower, then the hair dryer. Very soon she was out, and her hair wasn't wet. She crawled onto the bed and kissed him. "See you in a few hours."

"Call me at eight."

She got up and went out the door.

Moreland stood, went to the door, put the DO NOT DISTURB sign on the outer knob, turned the latch to engage the bolt, and put in the chain. He moved the chair in front of the door, and then went to his suitcase and took out his M-92F Beretta pistol. He checked to be sure he had left it loaded, then slipped it under the pillow beside his, turned off the light, and went to sleep.

26

By eleven Moreland, Sharon, and Gabe were in the car again. The others were wearing jeans and T-shirts, but Moreland wore a charcoal gray suit. As Moreland drove, he listened to Sharon chattering to Gabe. "I still like the Mega Drop better than anything," Sharon said. "You go all the way down thinking you're going to die. It seems to take so long to stop."

"I like it okay," Gabe said. "I like that thing where you go around so fast that you stick to the ring's walls, and then the bottom drops out under your feet." He paused. "How about you, Michael?"

"The one I like I don't know the name for." He saw Sharon stiffen, and he turned to her. "It's the one you and I were on, Sharon."

"Sky Ride," she said. "It's called Sky Ride."

"Oh yeah," he said. "Sky Ride."

He stopped on 9th Street outside the Sangamon County courthouse complex. "Here. You two drive around the block and see if there's a place to park. I'll call you when I'm ready." He got out and Gabe took the wheel.

Joey Moreland went into the main building through the metal detectors and then walked up and down the halls until he found a snack bar. He bought a cup of coffee and drank it on a bench in the hallway. Then he found a men's room. A few minutes later he called Sharon on his prepaid phone. "Okay, pull around to the front in five minutes and pick me up."

It occurred to him that it was possible they would just have driven his car off. But when he came out, there they were. Gabe was just pulling up in front of the courthouse.

When Joey got in, the others seemed impressed. "How did it go?" Gabe asked.

"The way it always goes," he said. "If you do your homework and file your motions, things go your way. Now drive to the Midwest Farmers and Merchants Bank on Sixth Street. We're on Ninth now, so it shouldn't be far away."

Gabe drove three blocks to 6th and then a few more to the bank and slowed to let him off. "Better find a parking space," Moreland said.

Gabe pulled into a space a few hundred feet past the bank, and then said, "Is this okay?"

"Thanks," said Moreland. He was busy pulling various things out of the manila envelope he'd brought—a bank withdrawal slip, a few printed sheets he had picked up in the hallway from a table.

"Is there anything we can do to help?" asked Gabe.

"Actually, there is," he said. "While I'm filling out these papers you can go in the bank and pick up the proceeds of this account." He handed the withdrawal slip and an ATM card to Gabe. On the back it had a magnetic strip, with a signature of someone named John C. McDougall above it. "Just hand them the slip, swipe the card on the reader, and then sign the signature of John C. McDougall on the withdrawal slip. Make it look at least a little like the one on the card." He handed him a driver's license from California with the picture of a young man.

"The slip says nine thousand dollars."

"I know. I just wrote that."

"That's a lot of money. And it's cash."

"They'll give you an envelope. Don't worry." He didn't look up from his scribbling on the form.

Gabe looked at Sharon uncomfortably. "Okay. I'll be right back." He got out of the car with the slip, the card, and the license.

As Gabe walked off toward the bank, Sharon leaned forward on the back of the seat. "He finally got something to do. He'll be happy."

"That's good."

"He thinks he owes you a lot for taking us and paying and all." She giggled. "If he knew everything, he might think he'd already kind of paid you back."

Moreland shrugged. "You plan to tell him?"

"Never," she said. "I'm glad we're alone for a few minutes, though. That's why you sent him in, isn't it?"

"Yes."

"I want to thank you for last night, and for the fair and everything. If you ever find yourself in the neighborhood again, call me. Here's my number." She plucked the pen from his hand and wrote her phone number on the inside of the folder on his lap, then covered it with his papers. "I'll drop everything and meet you anywhere you like."

"Thanks," he said. "I might do that."

"You can. Just hang up if Gabe answers."

"All right." He saw something in the rearview mirror. He sat up straighter, got out of the car, and walked around it to sit in the driver's seat. He started the engine, and then Sharon looked behind them.

The bank's front door had swung open, and Gabe was running hard toward the car. Two men in suits were right behind him, but Gabe was fast. As he ran he gained a few inches with each stride. There were five men out the door now, but in a moment they were all falling behind, their legs not able to pump as many times a minute as Gabe's were. They seemed to realize it, and the last three became a rear guard, falling behind their swifter colleagues, knowing they would not be the first ones in at the arrest.

Then the front-runners began to fall behind too. Gabe was still gaining speed, his head up and his arms punching like pistons, his strides still rapid and lengthening. The two men brought out their weapons and ran with them in their hands.

Moreland heard one shout, "Police! Stop or I'll shoot." Two seconds passed while Gabe seemed to be spurred on by fear. The men both repeated, "Stop, or I'll shoot." The threat seemed to terrify Gabe. He ran harder.

Some communication passed between the two men. Both stopped, aimed their weapons with the same two-handed stance, and fired. Their first shots hit Gabe in the back, but he kept on. They fired again, each squeezing off a burst of three shots. Some of them hit his legs and his lower back. His arms extended outward from his sides, and he began to tilt forward. It was not clear to Moreland who fired the next shot, but he saw an exit wound appear on Gabe's forehead. The shot turned his body limp, and he hit the pavement already dead. Sharon screamed.

Joey Moreland signaled, pulled out of his parking space, and drove up the street into the traffic at about twenty miles an hour.

Sharon was frantic. "What are you doing, Michael? They shot him."

"He's dead. If we don't get out of here, we will be too."

"Why? What would make them want to hurt any of us?"

"A horrible mistake. They must have thought he was trying to rob the bank." He kept looking in the rearview mirror, glancing at the street ahead, then back at the mirror. Two of the men who had shot at Gabe were kneeling over him, searching him for weapons. He noticed

Sharon looking through the rear window. "Keep an eye on them. Let me know if they seem to be heading for a car, or if another car pulls up the street with flashing lights."

"All right." She seemed without will, unable to think of an alternative. "Are you sure Gabe is dead?"

"He was shot in the head, Sharon."

"What did you have him doing?"

"Just picking up some money for a client. He wasn't even closing the account. It was a big withdrawal, but much more would have stayed here. There shouldn't have been any problem."

"Oh, Gabe!" she wailed. "I'm so sorry!" She watched until she couldn't see Gabe anymore, then kept watching until they were on the interstate.

"Anybody following us?" he asked.

"No. Shouldn't we go to the police—the ones at the station—and tell them what really happened?"

"Not now," he said. "We've got to get far enough away to stop and figure out what happened. The first thing is to stay alive. After that we can correct the record. We can't help Gabe now. I'm so sorry, Sharon. I never would have let him do it if I'd known there would be any trouble. I never would have let either of you come with me. This is crazy."

"What are we going to do?"

"We've got to make sure that a little time passes before we run into any police, so they don't think we're all bank robbers and shoot us too. Maybe let the Carbondale police talk to the Springfield police."

He drove in silence while Sharon cried. After a while she was leaning on him while she wept. He had checked the odometer when they had driven to Springfield. It was 168 miles. He knew when they were getting close to Carbondale.

As they crossed the city limit she knew it too. "I can't go back without him."

"Sure you can," he said. "You haven't done anything wrong. All you have to do is say Gabe told you he wanted to stop at the bank. He walked away and then came running out."

"I can't say that. Nobody will believe me."

"It's the truth."

"It's part of the truth. The rest isn't so simple." She paused. "Take me with you."

"You're practically home. You didn't do anything. This is the safest place in the world for you."

"I can't come back here."

He thought about killing her. If he did it here in her hometown, it would make the police form a really inaccurate theory, and that might be useful. Maybe if he could keep her body from being found for a couple of days, they would think Gabe had killed her. The nearest gun Joey had was in the trunk of the car, and if he stopped to get it, she might run or scream and attract attention. He could stop for a minute, break her neck, and then dump the body before he drove on.

He glanced at her, and the big wet blue eyes were staring at him, pleading. He asked himself why he wanted to kill her. She knew he had gotten Gabe killed trying to get his money out of the bank. If she was sharp, she might realize that the cops wouldn't shoot a suspect just because he was running away. They had to think he was armed and capable of killing somebody.

She wanted to go with him, so she must not have realized he was dangerous. She was upset and half crazy right now, but she was pretty and good-natured. He thought back to the night he had spent with her in the hotel room. "Okay," he said. "Here's how it is. I'd advise you to get out of the car, go to the Carbondale police, and tell them what happened. All of it. The truth. Nothing will happen to you. They'll know you didn't shoot Gabe, because the cops did. You didn't send him into the bank with someone else's identification, because I did."

"What if they ask me if I was with you last night?"

"They might, but so what? You weren't married or anything, were you?"

"They'll know I was cheating on him. Things like that always get out," she said. "It'll be in the papers. My parents will see it, and Gabe's family. And then everybody will think I made him do it, or that he was trying to get himself killed, or something."

They were wasting time. "All right. Suit yourself. I'll take you. If you change your mind, I'll bring you back. But I can't stay here with the motor idling."

"Thank you," she said, and draped herself on him, leaning her head on his shoulder and wrapping her arms around his so he couldn't drive off. "Oh, thank you, Michael. I'll make you glad you took me, I promise."

"Okay. Now let me drive."

"I'm sorry." She released him. She was still crying, but she leaned against the door, pushed herself into the far corner of her seat, and closed her eyes. Now and then he would look and see that her lips were moving. She was praying.

He drove for the rest of the day, heading west on Interstate 40. Sharon was silent and subdued. When it was dark he took her into a diner to eat. They sat in a quiet corner booth facing away from the entrance, and ate in silence. They used the restrooms, got back into the car, and went on.

As they drove toward the setting sun, he said, "I think somebody is trying to kill me. I'll never be able to forget that they got Gabe instead of me. I just wanted to give him a chance to help me. I feel terrible."

"Why would anybody want to hurt you?"

"I'm not sure. Maybe one of my clients set me up to cover something dishonest he's doing. But I've got to go someplace safe and find out."

"Where?" she asked.

"California. They'll be looking for you too, now. People know you went to Springfield with Gabe. We'll just have to lay low for a while."

"I'll do whatever you think is best," she said. "Want me to drive for a couple of hours?"

"Okay." He pulled off the interstate at the next exit, got out, walked to her side, and opened the door for her. When she got out, he wrapped his arms around her. She seemed to burrow into him. He could feel her sobbing. He waited patiently, holding her and patting her back gently.

Finally she said, "I'm sorry, Michael," freed herself from his arms, and stepped toward the driver's seat. He stopped her.

"Wait," he said. "If you're not ready, let's stop for a while."

"No," she said. "I'm ready to do whatever you want. I'm not going to hold you up and make things harder."

He got into the back and lay down on the seat. She got in, adjusted the seat and the mirrors to fit her smaller body, and drove down the entrance ramp onto the interstate.

27

Till was willing to be satisfied, but he wasn't satisfied just yet. The photographs he had received from Mullaney, the Boston homicide detective on the Salazar case, had not looked quite right. Nobody looked the same dead as alive, and alive was always better. But he had seen this transformation enough times to be familiar with it. The man who had been shot to death outside the bank in Springfield didn't seem to Till to be the one he had seen in the parking garage in Boston or driving Kyra's car in Phoenix. He had come to Carbondale to find out.

Till rented a car and drove it to the address that was on Gabriel Tolliver's driver's license. It occurred to him that the pictures he'd seen were likely to get shown on television a lot in this part of the country during the next few days. He stopped the car and sat for a few minutes looking at the house. There didn't seem to be much life. The curtains on the windows were closed, and there wasn't any motion near the house. At least there weren't any cop cars around right now.

He got out, walked to the front door, knocked, rang the bell, and knocked again. He listened for the sound of footsteps. He rang the bell again, and then he heard the thud of feet taking big strides. The door opened, and inside was a man only a little older than the one in the photograph, but related to him. "What do you want?"

"My name is Jack Till. I'm a private detective. I'm here because I don't think that Gabriel Tolliver did anything wrong."

The man glared at him for a couple of seconds. At first he seemed to be assessing what would happen if he hit Till. He seemed to decide that trying to hit Till would be foolish and painful. That thought held him long enough to make him realize that Till had said he was on his side.

"I'm his brother, Dave. Come on in." He stepped aside and let Till in. He stood on the porch looking up and down the street for someone else—reporters, probably. Then he stepped in after Till.

"I assume the police have been here already?" said Till.

"They drove over and took me to the station. While I was there they went through the whole house looking for things. They found our father's old shotgun locked in a cabinet and took it away. That's about all. The thing hasn't been fired since hunting season the year he died, like six years ago."

"Did they take anything that belonged to your brother?"

"Nothing of his was here."

"He didn't live here?"

"No. He had a place across town near the university that he lived in with his girlfriend."

"Did they interview her too?"

"No. She was up in Springfield with Gabe. Now some of the cops seem to think he and she were trying to rob banks together, and others think Gabe kidnapped her and took her to Springfield to use her as a shield or something. All I know is it's got to do with that guy."

"What guy?"

"Gabe and Sharon met a guy named Michael in Denny's three days ago. He said he had business up in Springfield. When they said they were going up for the state fair, he offered to give them a ride up and back."

"Did you see him?"

"No. Gabe told me about him."

"What can you tell me about Gabe?"

"He was a great kid. He worked in the mechanic shop where I work during the day, and did the night shift at the big gas station on the edge of town four or five nights a week. He and Sharon were saving up to get married and then put together a down payment on a house."

"Did he get a day off to go up to Springfield?"

"He got two days. They were going to stay overnight and come back today."

"When was his last day off?"

"Hell, I don't even remember. He was sick one day last winter. I guess that was the last one."

"Have you talked to his girlfriend?"

"She wasn't with him when they shot him, and she hasn't come home. The cops are trying to find her."

"What was Gabe doing in that bank?"

"I don't know. Maybe that Michael guy put a gun to Sharon's head and told Gabe he had to rob the bank to keep her alive."

"Can you tell me anything about Sharon?"

"I think she's probably been good for Gabe. She's pretty and has a kind of cheerful way to her. They've been together since, like, eighth grade. She's a little loud and flirty sometimes, but I think she means well."

"Can you tell me where they were living?"

"Over on Washington. 6363. Top floor is their apartment."

"Thanks. Have you told the cops all of this?"

"Yeah. Like three times."

"Then they already know your brother wasn't the bad guy. They'll be devoting all their time to finding Sharon now."

"How do you know?"

"I was a cop once, and that's what I'd be doing," said Till. "The guy they were expecting at the bank doesn't work nine or ten shifts a week, and he was in Boston a week or two ago." He stood up. "I'm sorry for your loss." He walked toward the door. "Was it regular cops who interviewed you?"

"No. There were a couple of Carbondale cops, but there was another guy in a suit who said he was FBI and another guy who had a Spanish accent. He never said who he was."

"Do you happen to have a picture of Sharon?"

"Quite a few of them. She and Gabe always came to family celebrations together. Hold on a minute." He went to another room and came back with a shoe box. He set it on the dining room table and began to finger through the photographs stored in it. Now and then he would pull one out and toss it onto the table. "This is her."

There was a picture of his brother and a short blond girl about twenty years old with blue eyes and a bright smile. Next to Gabe's tanned skin, hers looked like white makeup. The two held up beer bottles in a toast. In another shot, they were sitting at a picnic table with paper plates full of food. There was one of her alone in front of a cake.

"Do you think I could borrow one of these?"

"These three are copies." He picked them up and handed them to Till.

"Thanks. I'll try to find the guy who did this to your brother."

"I hope you do."

Till walked out and went to his car. He set the three photographs on the seat beside him. This girl was in trouble. He hoped when the cops found her, it wasn't the usual way, with a bullet through the back of her head.

28

Joey Moreland drove for three hours and then slept while Sharon drove for the next three hours. For two days they went on this way, never stopping for more than a few minutes to use the restrooms in gas stations and at truck stops, or to buy take-our hamburgers or tacos to go. Most of the time Joey was the one to show his face, because the police would be looking for Sharon.

As they got into the car in Albuquerque, Sharon stopped him in the parking lot and held his arm. He looked down at her and she stood on her toes to kiss him. Then she got into the car again.

He took a moment to look around in the lot to see if anyone had noticed. An old truck driver sitting in his rig at the end of the lot smiled at him and gave him a thumbs-up sign. Joey waved and got into the driver's seat.

"You've got to be a little more careful," he said gently. "That trucker saw."

"I'm sorry," she said. "I figured everybody was so far away it didn't matter. Some girl gave a guy a peck on the lips in a dark parking lot, and a driver who's going to be in God Knows, Arkansas, tomorrow saw it. Not sure what the cops will do with that."

He started the car. "You're right, of course. But what keeps people safe is safe habits." He drove along the ramp to the highway entrance.

"Safe habits?"

"I've had a couple of people in my law practice who had to travel without being noticed, and that's what they told me. You have to just automatically behave in all the least risky ways. You act like you're being watched even if you think you're not. You only stop as long as you have to. You use cash whenever you can. Pretty soon you do all that without thinking about it. And you don't do anything that makes people think about you."

"We've been doing that like crazy," she said. "We're not in Illinois anymore. This doesn't even seem like the same planet. It's like Mars. There's, like, nothing and nobody out here but rocks."

"I know," he said. "It's a good place to get comfortable with the right habits, before we're in crowds of people and it matters." He paused. "You should probably get some sleep instead of listening to me nagging you."

"I want to talk just a little bit first, okay?"

"Sure. What about?"

"You know that I can't go back to Carbondale, right?" she said. "My parents already kicked me out, so I was living with Gabe. When the police find out you and I slept together, my family is not going to be interested in knowing me. Once the police think you're a bad person, anything can happen. Gabe has a huge family. They all think he's the best little boy, and I'm just the skank that snagged him because he was too shy to go after anyone better. There's nobody left for me. I can't live there anymore. I've used up that life." She looked at him out of the corner of her eye. "Seems to me you've used up yours too."

"I certainly can't go back to Texas without getting in a terrible mess. I'm beginning to think my client did something really bad, and the police were just waiting for him to come in and claim that bank account."

"We're both in trouble," she said. "We're going to have to be everything to each other." She waited, listening to be sure she caught every syllable of his answer, but then too many seconds passed for the kind of answer she wanted. She rapidly changed her hope to a hope that he wouldn't contradict and deny her. She pulled her feet off the floor and curled up on the rear seat to sleep through his shift. At least he hadn't rejected her or pushed her away. All he had been was silent. She took that with her into sleep.

Late the next night they crossed over into California. She saw the place on the road where the painted lines changed from white to yellow with raised blue reflectors, and soon there was a sign about not bringing fruits and vegetables. She said, "I'm waking up. I'm about ready to drive. We're in California, aren't we?"

"Yes."

"Thank God. I'm getting a little tired of travel. When I take over, where do you want me to drive to?"

"I think I'll keep driving for a while. I have a place I want to check on while it's dark."

The night was amazingly huge in the eastern California desert, but the roads were not empty. They were in the Mojave, on the route between Las Vegas and Los Angeles. Every twenty or twenty-five miles a sign announced how far away Los Angeles was. And there were lots of trucks sharing the road with them, grinding along at a steady speed, while dozens of cars swarmed up behind them and shot past like projectiles. It didn't matter that it was long after midnight. The traffic in both directions was constant.

Near dawn they were northeast of Los Angeles. The land was still desert, but there were clusters of houses that looked identical from a distance and sat on their own grids of streets. Some of the developments had brick fences and metal letters that said something oddly out of place: Estancia de la Playa, Rancho del Mar, Villas di Firenze.

"What do people way out here do for a living?" she asked.

"They commute. Houses got so expensive around LA that people kept building new, cheaper houses farther and farther out. People were willing to drive a couple of hours to work—a hundred miles, sometimes."

They came to an exit onto a road leading straight into the desert. A hundred yards along the road a metal sign reading WELCOME TO SIERRA LOMA reflected their headlights, but the blue on the sign was faded and weathered. Sharon could see that most of the dirt along the road was the same as the desert. It was tan, not the black moist dirt under people's lawns back in Illinois. This dirt was a mixture of sand, pebbles, and hard cake with cracks in it like a dried-up pond bed.

When the road ended in a network of residential streets, she began to feel a bit more hopeful. Most of the houses were twice as big as the one where she had grown up. They had roofs made of pink tiles that looked like drainpipe split down the middle. They were just about all stucco, but some of them had facades of flagstone or brick. Nearly all had a two-story section in front, and double wooden doors the size of the church door at home. Above the door was always an oddly shaped window—an octagon, a fan, or a circle. There were often a few gables to make the houses' silhouettes look more complicated. Nearly every house had, on its dried-up lawn, a sign on a pair of thick, sturdy posts.

"Are they all for sale?" she asked.

"They're way beyond that," he said. "Most of the houses in this development got foreclosed on three or four years ago."

"Why?"

"For a long time the price of houses anywhere near Los Angeles went way up. It had been about twenty years since the last price drop. People got bigger and bigger loans to buy them. Houses were selling, so the developers built them farther and farther out. This was probably one of the last developments built. The houses are big and flashy, but they're in the middle of nowhere. All of a sudden one day, the whole world realized that houses couldn't keep going up forever. And then they realized a lot of people had borrowed a whole lot more to buy them than the houses were worth."

"Sounds pretty stupid."

He shrugged. "They were doing what everybody told them was the smart thing to do."

"This place looks like everybody left the same day. Like a ghost town."

"It took a couple of years. Some people held out because they thought house prices would go back up. They didn't. Some people lost their jobs, and they were so close to the limit that they stopped paying their mortgages the first month. There were a whole lot of foreclosures. Other people didn't wait. They stayed for as long as the bank let them, and then walked away. The people who bought their houses last had bought for the highest prices and borrowed the most, but they hadn't had the time to sink much into payments. Near the end they had a loan called the 'liar's mortgage,' where you didn't have to prove you had a big enough paycheck to pay."

"Everybody did the same things at the same time?"

"Pretty much. The value of your house is what somebody will pay for it. If the guy next door walked away from an identical house, nobody would buy yours. Eventually even the holdouts left."

"Then all these houses are just sitting here empty?"

"I'm guessing there are a few people in some of them," he said. "Squatters. We'll have to figure out which ones."

"Why?"

"So we can avoid them."

"Do you mean we're going to stay here?"

"For a while."

"Why?"

"I think we need to know how hard the police are looking for you before we go into a city where a thousand people a day will see you."

Sharon was silent for a couple of minutes, then said, "Okay. What are we looking for?"

"We want a nice house. It doesn't have to be big, but pleasant. I like the ones with brick or stone on the front. We want a garage, not a carport. We want a house in the middle of a row of five or six empty ones. And look for sale and foreclosure signs with the names of big eastern banks. They won't be sending anybody out here to look at all the properties in foreclosure. They'll leave them empty and untouched until the year comes when they can get something for them."

They drove up and down the deserted streets, past houses that looked like little Spanish haciendas and houses that looked like little Italian palazzi. Now and then Sharon would get tired of looking at houses and look instead at the high, dark mountains that had not even the smallest electric light on them, or look the other way at the vast desert, where the only life she could see was the distant freeway. Occasionally a set of headlights would make its way across the horizon to become a set of red taillights. Then she would say, "How about that one?"

"It's got the right kind of signs up, but there are squatters in it. See the corner of the house? Right behind it is an SUV."

Another time when she asked he said, "No. The plants aren't dead. That means somebody's been watering them."

Another house that had the right silhouette made him slow down, but he didn't stop. "The windows are boarded up. The copper hunters have been here, I guess." He sped up and went by.

"What are copper hunters?"

"Scavengers. They come in and take everything they can—sinks, toilets, pipes, light fixtures, anything you can tear out and carry off. People call them copper hunters because copper pipe is their favorite."

Sharon decided to keep quiet and wait. After nearly an hour he said, "This looks good." He turned into the driveway of a house with a high silhouette, stopped in front of the closed three-car garage, got out, and disappeared. After a few minutes one of the three garage doors opened and he stepped out of the garage and drove the car in. He turned off the car and then pulled the garage door down to close it.

"The power isn't on, but you can disconnect the electric motor and it opens easily." He stepped to the door that led into the house, and Sharon got out of the car and stood watching. He reached into his pocket, took out a knife, and then jimmied the door lock. Once he had the blade in, he gave the door a bump with his shoulder and it opened inward.

He stepped in and felt his way around. "Sharon, get the flashlight out of the glove compartment."

She was torn between her fear of being alone and her fear of the dark. She decided it was best to obey, and so she got the flashlight. She resisted the strong urge to turn it on, because he hadn't told her she could.

He took the light, switched it on, and swept the beam around the room. Off the foyer and down a short hall was a big kitchen. There was no refrigerator and no stove or dishwasher, only a space for each. But there were two big stainless steel sinks, and there were light fixtures.

Moreland left the kitchen and she followed the flashlight. There was a big living room with a fireplace and a lot of built-in cabinets and shelves. No furniture. She wondered about the fireplace. Did it ever get cold enough here to light a fire?

She followed him to a grand entry. The floor was a pattern of black and white squares that looked like stone. She slipped off one sandal to step on them. She felt the cold of stone. There was a big, thick wooden door with stainless steel hardware on it like the outer door at her doctor's office—a kind of lever that came out of a big steel plate, and a dead bolt with a bar that went into the floor. Far above the door was a circular window with struts in it that made it look like a pie.

Moreland turned off the flashlight. The high windows and the skylights in the ceiling let a dim gray glow of moonlight into the house, so they could see where they were walking.

He went to the circular staircase and climbed, so she climbed too. The second floor had three small bedrooms and one huge bedroom with a couple of walk-in closets, each with an island in the middle and built-in dressers and shelves. He said, "Not bad."

"Not bad," she agreed.

He looked around the room, opening drawers and closing them. Finally he found some padded movers' blankets on the floor of one of the bedrooms. He took one, sniffed it, seemed satisfied, and handed it to her. "It seems okay. The movers just forgot them, I guess." He spread one on the floor, then the second. "You like a blanket on top?"

"Sort of."

He spread the third, then rolled the top one down a bit. "Should be fine. We'll sleep here."

They slept, and in the days that followed, they fell into a routine. Every night he wandered. Every morning he made improvements. He found a hibachi and a big bag of charcoal in a garage in an abandoned house nearby, so they could cook. Then he drove to Bakersfield for groceries, and brought back lots of things—a cooler and ice, two thin twin mattresses, sheets, and two pillows. On the first night they had used the toilet by putting a big plastic trash bag in it because there was no water to flush it. The next day he used a big wrench to turn on the water in the meter box at the curb. He filled the downstairs bathtub with cold water and then he carried buckets of boiling water to it so they could take a bath. He had bought candles and flashlights, so they didn't miss electricity much. Once they could cook, bathe, wash clothes, and sleep, she wasn't unhappy. And every day, he seemed to think of new ideas.

He ranged through the empty houses in the development, looking for things that the families who had been evicted left behind. On the fifth night she said, "Can I go with you?"

He stood very still and stared at her for a moment, as though he were actually considering it. Even though she knew he would say no, she appreciated his making it look like a decision. Then he said, "Okay."

She was so happy she jumped up and kissed him. "What should I wear?"

"Something dark. And sneakers, not sandals. We shouldn't be bumping into people, but if we do, we'll want to avoid them, or even run."

"Okay," she said, and hurried to get ready. She wore black jeans and a blue T-shirt, put her hair in a ponytail, and pushed it over the strap in the back of a baseball cap he had bought in Bakersfield.

Today he had found a set of keys to their house. They had been hidden in the garage on a horizontal stud over the small window. When they left he locked the doors.

The night was hotter than usual, with a faint breeze that felt like the blast out of an open oven. "East wind. It'll be hot tomorrow," he said. "I've been hoping it would stay cloudy and cool."

"We'll just have to get through it."

He smiled. "Do you have any idea how hot it gets out here?"

"Not really."

"You'll see tomorrow."

Sharon loved walking along the dark, deserted streets exploring the development. He had already found a few streets where there were no people at all, and five houses with stubborn people still living in them.

The swimming pools were a problem. The yards were dark, and most of the pools were still half full of tepid water even months after the houses had been abandoned. It would be easy, if she wasn't paying attention, to step into one. Once she caught the reflection of the moon and saved herself, and another time she smelled the dead water and began to search for it.

As they walked they searched for treasures. After a couple of hours he found a very long heavy-duty extension cord in the garage of an abandoned house. He carried it over his shoulder. Later he found most of a set of hand tools. But the best thing he found came at dawn. They were nearly home, coming along the backs of houses on their street, when he stopped.

"Ssh," he whispered. "Listen." He held his hand up and put down the treasures he had found.

Sharon froze and stood there for a time while he moved slowly toward the back fence. Then she realized what he was hearing. It was a pool motor, running at very low speed. He went behind a section of the wooden fence, found the motor, touched it to feel the vibration, then stood up and pointed at the roof.

The roof was covered with solar panels. "Here are the keys," he said. "I'll be home in a little while."

"Can't I stay and help?"

"Okay," he said. "Go to the corner of the house and act as a lookout. If anybody comes, run to get me. We'll hide by the pool motor."

"All right."

She found a good vantage point and watched the nearby streets and the cars passing on the distant interstate.

He walked from the pool motor to the back of the house. He found the circuit box, turned off the power, and then took out his knife and began to splice the wire from the extension cord into the circuit for the pool motor. Then he began to walk toward the house he and Sharon occupied, uncoiling the electrical cord as he went. When it ran out, he went into the house, where there was another cord plugged in. He unplugged it, took it outside, plugged it into the first cord, and kept going. "Dig a trench and bury the line," he said.

Sharon found the work wasn't difficult. She could have done it with a stick. The ground was loose sand and pebbles. While she worked, he was at their house splicing the extension cord into the circuit box. She worked until every bit of extension cord was buried, and nothing could be seen except the cord running up the side of the house a few feet. When she was finished he turned on the switch at the other house.

Later, when the sun climbed high and the middle distance in every direction was wavy with mirages, and the ground was too hot to touch with bare hands, he turned on the air-conditioning. It ran slowly and quietly, but they closed all the vents except the two in the master bedroom and shut the door. They made love on the mattresses and then lay there peacefully, feeling the cool air tickling their sweaty skin, and then fell asleep until dark.

29

Nobody in Carbondale remembered the man who had gone to the state fair with Gabe and Sharon. One waitress at Denny's remembered seeing Sharon and Gabe talking to someone seated nearby, but had no memory of who it was. She thought he might have been Gabe's brother.

Sharon's relatives were difficult to interview. She had a father named Walt who had pretty much given up on her shortly after she had reached puberty. When she was twelve he had put her to work in his hardware store for a few hours every Saturday, sweeping up and washing windows. By the time she was thirteen she would breeze in for an hour or so in the morning, take an advance on her pay from the register, and then come in on Sunday when the store was closed to make up the time. That way she didn't have to do as much actual work. She spent her evenings on the phone, not doing homework.

Sharon's mother, Matty, was essentially the opposition. When Walt said the girl was lazy, Matty said, "Sharon is a dreamer."

Till had learned many years ago to ask questions and then show nothing but attention to the answers.

Walt said, "She did inherit one thing—her mother's looks. She's a very pretty girl, but it wasn't a great advantage for her. When she was really young, I could see older guys had an eye on her. With some of them, you could see all they were waiting for was for me to stop watching."

Matty said, "Sharon had to work in the hardware store as soon as she was in middle school. She had to learn to get along with grown men, understand what a torque wrench was and a socket wrench, and still learn to grow into a fine young woman."

Behind Matty, Walt was rolling his eyes. He said, "Sharon grew up. We had great hopes for her. We wanted her to go to college, but what she accomplished was to be Gabriel Tolliver's girlfriend." He sighed.

"What do you think happened in Springfield?" Till asked. "They met this man and went to the fair with him, and then what?"

"I don't know," Walt said.

Matty said, "We're not so sure there was a man. Where do we get him from? Gabe's brother says Gabe told him there was a man who would drive them to Springfield. Who does that?"

"You doubt the story?"

"I mean it doesn't sound likely. Gabe had a car."

Till said, "Gabe and Sharon apparently left it at Gabe's brother's house while they were gone."

"Did they? Who saw it there?" Matty said. "I mean besides Gabe's brother."

"It's still there," said Till.

"I think maybe he didn't take his own car because he was going to rob a bank."

Till said nothing.

"Who do you think robs banks?" she asked. "Losers like Gabe Tolliver. Men who never will amount to much, who work in their brother's auto shop and pump gas on weekends. And I think he took our beautiful Sharon and got her in the worst kind of trouble."

"What do you think happened?"

"I think he took her with him to sell her to somebody. That's the only other man in this." She was beginning to produce tears at the thought of it. "I think he decided this little town was too small for him, and that he could start over again as a big shot. I think he was changing his life, rolling the dice. I think he gave his brother his car in exchange for lying about him and Sharon. I think he took all the money they had, and then went to Springfield to sell her and rob the bank. You can check all of that. The police found no money in their apartment. None."

"Do you happen to have some photographs that I could take and reproduce? I promise I'll give the originals back."

"What do you want to do with them?"

"I've been looking for a man for months who might be the one who went to Springfield with Sharon and Gabe," he said. "If he has her, then she's in danger."

"What good is a picture of Sharon?"

"I don't know his name, and I don't have a picture of him. But if he's with Sharon, then a picture of her might be just as good."

Matty stood and went to a large sideboard and pulled out a family album. She opened it and browsed. He could see that it was full of pictures. Now and then she would choose one, look at it, and set it aside. Till was struck by how similarly she and Gabe's brother behaved.

Till accepted the pictures without looking at them. "Thank you. I'll do my best to get to her as quickly as I can." He walked to the door. "I'll have her call when I've got her."

Till drove out of town toward Springfield. The three of them had gone to the fair, and there might be some news footage or a security camera on the cashiers' booths. If they had stayed at a hotel, there would certainly be some captured images there. Nearly all hotels had cameras mounted in their hallways.

If there was footage from the hotel's cameras, he knew what it would be. At some point during the night, the Boyfriend and Sharon would be seen entering the same room.

Till sat in a hotel office watching the videotape for the tenth time. He watched the young man come out of the elevator, look at the sign on the wall telling him which hallway room 680 was on, and walk that way, toward the camera. He was wearing a thin nylon windbreaker and a baseball cap.

He was the man Till had seen in Phoenix and again in Boston, always as a blur or a shadow, or in this case, a black-and-white image with half-defined boundaries. He had the squared shoulders and the swimmer's build, but Till couldn't make out the face. This man had already walked around the state fair for a whole day, but his gait looked like the step of an athlete who was well-rested. He kept his head down most of the time, and the baseball cap shielded his face. The weather in the upper Midwest had been hot all week, so probably he was wearing the windbreaker to conceal a weapon.

The next video Till watched answered a few questions he'd had. It was the girl, Sharon. She stepped out of the elevator, walked up the hall to the same door, looked behind her to be sure she was alone, and then knocked. She put her ear to the door, and then knocked again, a little harder. She tried to look in the peephole, but the door opened, and she slipped inside and the door closed again. Later, she came out alone and went to the elevator.

The hotel security man said, "Would you like any copies of this?"

"No, thanks," said Till. "I didn't find what I was looking for. But thanks very much for your help." When he had asked to see the tape he had given the man five hundred-dollar bills.

Till left the office, and walked up the corridor to the hotel lobby, thinking about how he must look on the cameras right now. He went out and got into his car. It was as he had supposed. This girl was another one who had seen the Boyfriend and thought, "What the hell. It wouldn't do any harm," and slept with him. She had probably been the one to talk Gabe into walking into that bank to withdraw the Boyfriend's money for him.

Till took out the collection of photographs of Sharon and looked at them. She was pretty enough, and if she wasn't innocent, at least she looked naive and uncalculating. People would see the pictures and feel an instant sympathy. He selected a few of the best, and then put them away so they wouldn't get bent. He looked at the road map that had come with the rental car, started the engine, and drove north toward Chicago.

Tonight he would check into a hotel and begin working on the first Web site. Tomorrow he would begin getting appointments with the advertising departments of the largest cable television companies in the Midwest. Then he'd fly to Los Angeles and start getting appointments there. He could see the ads now—the beautiful skin, the blue eyes, the shining blond hair: "Have you seen Sharon?"

30

Joey came in the back door of the house, locked it, and drew the curtains that Sharon had opened to give herself light.

"Something wrong?" she asked.

He stood with his back to the wall for a few seconds, and then appeared to have found the answer. "Yeah. I saw some guys while I was out. I'm almost positive they didn't see me, but they were looking."

"What do you mean?"

He slipped out the door to the garage. She could hear him open the car trunk and then hear him rummaging around in there for a few minutes. He came back in and closed the door. "Have you ever fired a gun?" He was carrying a small hard suitcase, like a carry-on bag.

"My dad took me out once when I was a kid, and let me shoot an old twenty-two he had. Then Gabe's brother took us out once to shoot his gun. That was a thirty-eight something. Special."

"Good. That's a start. You know that you have to hold the gun steady, and that when you pull the trigger it will make a noise and jump in your hand."

Sharon was frowning, and the sight reminded Joey that she was really a child. She looked about ten right then, with her big blue eyes wide and her lower lip quivering a little. "Why are we talking about this? What happened, Michael?"

He reminded himself that Michael was the only name he had given her to use. "I told you, I saw some guys driving around the development."

Her voice started low and went higher, becoming almost a lamentation. "Can't we just go?"

He said, "You don't have to be hopeless. They may not have noticed this house. From a distance there's nothing different about it. We buried the power line, so they won't know we have power. The car has been hidden in the garage since we got here. We don't use the lights."

"But you said they were looking for something."

"Yeah. I'm saying they're thieves. They'll break into some house and take what they can tear out and carry, and go back where they came from. There are dozens of houses. We'll just get ready, then sit tight and wait. Most likely we won't see them again."

He reached into his bag, moved a couple of objects aside, and came up holding a dark gray semiautomatic pistol. "I want you to have this with you all the time tonight."

"But I can't—"

"I have no time for that. We're here in the first place because you wanted to come with me. I'm trying to keep you safe. So do what I ask."

She looked down at her feet, and then up at him. "Okay."

He took her hands and put them out in front of her. He pressed the handgrips of the pistol into her right palm and set her left hand to help her right hold the gun.

"Get your trigger finger outside the guard like this." He moved it. "Leave it there until you're aiming it at somebody. This is a Glock 19. Just like cops use. It's light and reliable."

"Okay."

"See the white dot on the front sight? Get it on your target and be sure it's in the middle of the two rear sights."

"How do I get the safety off?"

"When you apply pressure to the trigger the safety disengages. Then *Bang!* When you release, the safety engages again. Now aim."

"At what?"

"I don't care. The door."

She held the pistol out in front of her and closed one eye.

"Here," he said, and put his hands behind her knees.

"Cut that out. It tickles." She waggled her hips.

"Bend your knees a little. Keep your arms straight, and lean forward just a little. Breathe normally. Good. Much better. Forward a little more. Imagine there's a guy coming in that door. He really can't wait to knock you down and hurt you. We're in the middle of nowhere, there's no help coming, and now here he is. There. Perfect."

She lowered the pistol, smiled happily, and presented her cheek to him for a kiss.

He pecked her cheek absently and took the gun from her. "Okay. Here's the part you have to remember. You're sitting around with the magazine full of bullets in the gun. You hear the guys pull into the driveway. What you have to do while you're still alone is pull the slide back until you feel the spring push the first round up into the chamber, and then you let go. Where's your finger going to be?"

"Outside the trigger guard."

"Good. Now the guy comes in the door. Make it three guys. What do you do?"

"Stop, or I'll shoot," she said.

"I'm glad I asked. You say nothing. You just shoot. Get the nearest one, then any others. You've got seventeen rounds. Keep firing until they're down and not moving."

"But I don't know if they're even criminals."

"If they get to you, they've already killed me. They're looking for you. If you don't shoot them, you're in for a long, ugly night that only ends with you dead. They won't come in the house unless they really want trouble."

"I don't want to shoot anybody."

"Probably you won't have to. But you have to be ready."

She looked at him, pouting. "I still don't know why we have to do this."

"We don't," he said. "We can leave and go someplace where there are lots of cops to protect us. If one of them recognizes you, they'll be happy to take you back to Illinois."

"I can't go back. What could I say? Why am I way out here? They'll think I helped Gabe try to rob a bank."

"Then we'd better stay here." He went upstairs, got their blankets, and moved them down to the living room carpet. He brought in some of the bottled water he had in the car. While he was out during the day he had bought a shotgun. He sat in the living room alcove with it aimed at the door.

They had sex until they were tired, and then fell asleep on the blankets. It wasn't until three o'clock that they heard the cars. He woke up first, and shook her. "Wake up."

He sat up and turned his head to listen. He whispered, "Stay right here in the alcove. Anyone comes in, you know what to do." He clicked the magazine into the handgrips of the Glock 19, charged it, and handed it to her.

She saw his silhouette cross her vision in front of the window for a second, and then he was gone. She pulled on her jeans and her T-shirt, but kept a thin blanket over her partly because it was dark blue, and partly because when she had it around her shoulders she felt hidden, sheltered. She kept the pistol in her hands.

She'd heard the car in front of the house and heard a couple of male voices, but since Michael had left, there had been silence. She wondered if they had somehow realized there were people here and gone away. That would be the most sensible thing. Maybe she should have put a NO TRESPASSING sign out front. She could have left it at dusk each night and brought it in at dawn, so only the people who needed to be warned would see it. That would have been better than what she was doing now. There were lots of things that were better than sitting alone in a dark room waiting either to shoot somebody or get raped. As she scared herself with the thought, it occurred to her that this was the way she'd always thought the end of the world would be.

After about fifteen minutes she began to think about Michael. He was a lawyer. She wondered why he had been traveling around with a pistol and a shotgun in his car trunk. He was from Texas, she knew, and apparently that was the way a lot of people in Texas were. The gun laws were more lenient in the parts of the country that used to be the old West. Then she remembered the bank where Gabe got killed. Michael had been planning to pick up a load of money at the bank for a client. He had expected to be driving it all the way back to Texas. She supposed he had the pistol to guard that money. It made sense.

She had used up all her distractions. Where was Michael?

Suddenly there was a loud smashing of glass, a bang as though somebody had hit the glass with a crowbar, and then a crash and tinkle as the person cleared off the smaller pieces held in place by the glazing. She pulled back deeper into her alcove.

She heard the front door latch rattling, and a person coming from the opposite direction. She began to feel panicky and trapped. Maybe they had caught Michael out there alone, and killed him quietly.

She stood, the blanket still around her shoulders. She walked toward the place where the glass had broken—the kitchen. There he was. He was shorter than Michael, but broader. He appeared to be floating toward her like a ghost.

Sharon was grateful that Michael had told her what to do. *Don't say anything, just fire.* She went into her firing stance and pulled the trigger. The gun flashed, and the man staggered backward. *Keep firing until he's down and stops moving.* She aimed at the tottering silhouette and fired three rounds. He looked as if he was being punched. His legs collapsed under him, and he was down.

There was somebody throwing himself against the front door. Then it sounded like two men: *Boom-boom, boom-boom.*

The shotgun gave a much louder sound than her pistol: *Blam!* She heard the shotgun being pumped, and *Blam!* again. After that, silence resumed. She aimed her pistol, stepped into the living room, and saw the front door. There were two ragged holes where something had punched in some of the wood.

The door opened and Michael stepped over two bodies lying on the porch. She could see that on the outside of the door the two holes looked worse. There was a shiny reflection on the door as though it was wet. Blood? "Jesus," she said. He closed the door.

He said, "It's me."

"I know."

"There are two more, I think. At least one." He went to his suitcase. "We have to take care of them." He went to the door, and she followed him out into the night. The air was hot and still, and she could hear the emptiness of the place in the heaviness of the silence. Michael had made sure the nearby houses were all unoccupied foreclosures, so no sound emanated from any of them. She gulped to clear her ears, but she still didn't hear anything.

A car's headlights appeared a mile or two away on the interstate, and then passed along the horizon from one side to the other. When it was about halfway, the faint hiss and hum of the car passed into audibility and out again to nothing.

He went to the front porch and patted the bodies of the two men he had killed with the shotgun. He found two sets of car keys. Then he went into the house again and found keys on the third man.

He and Sharon went around to the rear of the house. She had noticed he always walked along the backs of the houses. She had always known it was because he didn't want anyone to come along the street, see him, and wonder. But now she knew that he also did it so he could see anyone else who was skulking around the development. She followed as he walked along from yard to yard, avoiding pools and barbecue pits and hot tubs. Sometimes he would stop for a second to listen. He would pass close to taller structures to mask his silhouette. They went along parallel to the street for a time, and then he stopped and suddenly turned.

She watched him dash out of a backyard, run between two houses, and sprint across the street. She ran after him, some distance to his right and already far behind. She had no chance of catching up to him or even keeping his lead from widening. He wasn't like a man anymore. He was like a dog after a rabbit.

The last street of the development appeared, a street with houses only on the near side. Across the street was a vast empty field that went all the way out to the interstate highway. He crossed the street, taking the asphalt pavement in about four steps. A man rose up from the field and ran a few steps, and then Michael plucked him out of the air with an arm around his neck. Michael brought him down and hit him with the shotgun butt once, twice. He knelt by him, reached into his pocket, and made a motion that looked to Sharon as though he was cutting the man's throat.

Sharon stopped, backed away, and turned toward their house. She didn't run. It wasn't because she was too tired to run anymore. It was that as long as she walked and didn't make the noise of running, she felt invisible. She walked along the side of their house to the back. She opened the back door and stepped inside. It was then she remembered that the man she had shot was still in the kitchen. She reached into the kitchen drawer beside her, grasped the flashlight, and turned it on.

He was young and wore a dark wife-beater T-shirt with jeans and black work boots. His hair was blond. There was a pool of blood. She turned off the flashlight. She thought she heard Michael coming back, but then the footsteps seemed to be sounding in her imagination. She hoped the sun would be up soon, but then the sights would be worse. There were dead men on the porch and in the kitchen.

She found it was bearable only outside. She went out to the yard and sat in a lawn chair with the gun on her lap. In a few minutes Michael arrived. "Come on. I'll need some help."

Sharon went with him. She had not thought about the two trucks parked in the driveway. There were a van and a pickup with a shell over the bed. He said, "We'll put all four of them in the van on the floor. I have the keys. Let's start with the one from the kitchen."

They rolled him onto an old section of carpet and dragged him, then lifted him through the side door of the van. She was surprised that she was able to lift his feet if Michael lifted the top of him into the van, then climbed in and pulled. They repeated the process with the two on the porch. Then they got into the van's seats and drove out to the last street and put that man into the van with the others. Michael took some time finding the four wallets and then searching the van for useful things. Next he drove back to the house.

"You drive the pickup. Follow me closely."

Michael drove out onto the interstate, kept going about twenty miles, and then turned onto a smaller, narrower road, and a smaller dirt road after that. When they reached the end of the road, he drove to the edge of a hillside to a narrow canyon, got into the driver's seat of the pickup, and pushed the van off into the canyon so it rolled downhill into the darkness. She could hear it moving through heavy brush, and then the sound stopped. There was no crash.

Michael drove the pickup home. He opened the garage. He made her get into the car and follow him while he drove the pickup twenty miles in the other direction on the interstate. He found a deeper arroyo, farther from the highway, and pushed the pickup into it.

During the trip back to the house, neither of them spoke. They locked the doors, and he nailed a piece of plywood over the broken window. They lay down and Michael slept. Sharon lay there beside him, her eyes open in the night.

Jerry Escobar was nearly ten miles away from the house by then. He had hidden in the weeds only fifty feet away while that guy had gone chasing after Juan Cabrera. He had heard the *pow-pow-pow* of the pistol killing Jody Kelleher inside the kitchen, and heard the roar of the shotgun at the front door.

After the massacre Jerry had alternately run and walked through ten miles of chaparral, but it wasn't over yet. He had come out to this deserted housing development tonight with his friends trying to make a quick buck salvaging stuff from abandoned houses. He and the others had not been armed and had not expected any kind of trouble. They had pulled up in their two trucks, had gone to find the easiest way into the house, and the guy opened fire.

Inside the house, where he and Jody Kelleher had gone in through the window, the woman had opened up with a pistol. It was insane. If they'd known anyone was there, they wouldn't have gone in.

Jerry was jogging along the shoulder of the road, heading for the next town, or the next rest area. He couldn't remember which was going to come first. He had to get there before the sun came up and he died in the heat.

He had left his cell phone at home because the police could use the record of the towers that had recognized his phone to prove he'd been out here. As soon as he got to a pay phone he would call his cousin to come pick him up and drive him back to Bakersfield. He would remember this night for the rest of his life. And the girl. Especially the girl.

He had first seen her in the muzzle flashes from her pistol. A girl so young and pretty, with blond hair and milky skin, like an angel, and she was killing Jody Kelleher. Then, when she was standing in front of the van with the headlights lighting her up as if it were day, he had gotten a long look at her. He would remember her until his memory shut down and he died.

31

Till's ads ran on cable television. They were played as public-service announcements on network affiliate stations. There were articles on Web sites that tracked kidnap victims and fugitives. Every police department or sheriff's department in the country had a collection of photographs of Sharon Long and a "Wanted" bulletin.

Each day Till kept sending Sharon's picture to more and more sites, more and more organizations. He had been searching for the Boyfriend for several months, and he was determined not to let this advantage slip away. Till believed that if he didn't succeed within a few days, Sharon would be dead, as the other girls were. She would have a nine-millimeter round through the back of her head.

It was only a few days later that Till noticed the other ads. They offered a reward if a witness would call a telephone number with information leading to the capture of the man who had kidnapped Sharon Long. The number didn't belong to a regular police agency, but it wasn't a hoax. When he tried the number from a pay phone, there was a cheerful, efficient young woman on the other end. He wasn't sure whether he imagined a slight Spanish accent or just suspected that the Mexican federal police would not have entirely pulled out after losing two cops and a prosecutor.

He called Detective Mullaney in Boston, but Mullaney had no idea who was behind the ads. Till tried calling other police departments—Carbondale, Springfield, Phoenix, Los Angeles—but they didn't know who it was either.

Till called the number that Catherine Hamilton's parents had given him, waited through seven rings, and then heard the phone lifted. "Yes?" It was Mrs. Hamilton's voice.

"Hello, Mrs. Hamilton. This is Jack Till."

"We've been hoping to hear from you, Mr. Till. I understand the authorities believe the man who killed Catherine is the one with the girl in Illinois."

"He is."

"No maybe, no uncertainty?"

"It's him," said Till.

"Are they going to catch him?"

"If we leave them alone, probably not. I think he's taken the girl—her name is Sharon—far from Illinois, and police efforts that require departments all over the country to cooperate don't usually work very well. I've been trying to keep the pressure on, putting this new girl's pictures online and getting the cable TV networks to put them on the air. And now somebody else is doing the same thing, and offering a small reward for information leading to his capture."

"Is there anything else we can do?"

"Well, I've been thinking. If we could offer a reward too, it might be enough to get people to start looking for Sharon."

"We've already given you a hundred thousand dollars to pay for your expenses and services. We don't regret it, but we're not wealthy people."

"If you can't afford a reward, then don't worry. I'll try some other ways. I can even ask people to contribute to a reward fund."

"Give me a moment to talk to my husband." Till heard the phone being muffled, and very faint voices beyond that. Then the hand was removed from the receiver. "How about fifty thousand dollars?"

"That's plenty," said Till. "If you're sure you can do it, then today I'll start offering fifty thousand for information leading to this guy's arrest and conviction."

"I'm sure. If you'd like us to put it into an escrow account, we can do that."

"That's not necessary," Till said. "And thanks. I think this might do it."

Jerry Escobar was in Bakersfield again, lying on his single bed with the air conditioner mounted in his window blowing cold air across his body. The other night, while he was running for his life through the dark, empty desert to escape that crazy man and his crazy girlfriend, he had thought he would never make it to safety again. When his cousin Miguel had arrived at the rest stop to take him home, Jerry had been as tired and worn down as he had ever been. He had thought he might still die of heatstroke.

Jerry was a strong man. He had worked with a crew of gardeners from the age of eleven, and when he'd turned sixteen he'd started as a mason's helper on a construction crew. He'd loaded bricks by hand into a wheelbarrow, then pushed the wheelbarrow on top of a track of narrow boards across uneven ground to the wall his boss was working on. He would mix the mortar for his boss and keep the bricks and mortar coming all morning and all afternoon when the days were so hot that people hid indoors. He had lost that job when the housing market went away.

He had worked as a plumber's assistant after that. There was no plumbing for new houses, but there were always tree roots in the ground to crush sewer pipes. He was the one to stand above the broken pipe and begin digging, sometimes going down five feet, sometimes more, up to his ankles in sewage. He had lost that job too.

His friend Jody Kelleher had talked him into salvaging metal from empty houses. Jody had said, "It's not even stealing from anybody. Who even owns them?" Construction projects that had been started wouldn't ever be finished. Houses that had been built far out from the city would never be sold. By the time anybody got interested in them again the banks would have to bulldoze them and start over. Nobody would notice that plumbing fixtures and pipes and wiring had been taken out of them until then—and who would know or care what was taken and didn't have to be bulldozed? Had the bankrupt contractor even installed them? It wouldn't matter. There would be sand blowing through open windows by then.

So Jerry had begun to go with the others, even though he knew stripping the houses was stealing. They always had to go out into the dry, hot country northeast of Los Angeles, but the air got cooler at night, so the work was tolerable.

He had made a little money, enough to rent this apartment in an old motel. He'd even had the money to take Gloria out on real dates a few times. Then those two people had started shooting.

Afterward, Jerry had slept for twelve hours. Whenever he woke up, he would go pee and drink a full glass of water before he fell asleep again. And every time, he would lie there for a couple of minutes until he remembered the horror in the night—the blond girl's face, looking scared while she pulled the trigger again and again. After a while he would retreat back to sleep.

Jerry was a coward who had not done anything to fight back or save his four friends. He was an ingrate. Even as Kelleher was dying, the shots piercing his body, Jerry was hating him for persuading him to go steal things from houses. Jerry was a fool for going along, and a weakling for hiding in the spare, dry bushes while that maniac soldier or whatever he was killed his friend Juan in the field practically with his bare hands. He felt such disgust at himself that he never wanted to get up.

The next evening Miguel called, then brought him some food. At first the sight of it made him sick, but after a few minutes he realized that what was bothering his stomach was hunger. There were a couple of big sandwiches from Subway and a six-pack of beer.

He and Miguel sat in the small room and ate. On the way home twenty-four hours before, he had told Miguel what had happened in the desert, so tonight he didn't talk about it. Jerry really felt bad about it. He had no idea what he would say to the families of the four guys on the crew.

Miguel kept looking at Jerry, and finally picked up the remote control and turned on the television set. Jerry felt a second of irritation, but then it went away. He wasn't going to be able to afford his cable bill next time, so he might as well watch while he could.

Miguel clicked through a few channels. There were old kids' shows that he and Miguel and the other kids in the family had watched years ago. They all looked faded and cheesy now. There were a couple of old movies—one a western, with guys shooting at each other in the middle of a desert as they'd shot at him; and another, a black-and-white detective thing where everybody was wearing a hat and a suit that didn't fit him. There were bad new bands, a couple of good old ones, a couple of women on the shopping channel selling lotion that looked enough like sperm to make him feel creepy to watch them rubbing it on. There was a commercial for a body shop.

Then the man came on. He was tall, kind of lanky, with hands that seemed all knuckle. His hair was light brown, almost blond. His eyes seemed sinister to Jerry because they were a flat gray, and the pupils were tiny black dots in the center because of the bright lights. "My name is Jack Till, head of Till Investigations. Please look closely at the pictures of this young woman. Her name is Sharon Long. She was abducted from Springfield, Illinois, on July twelfth." The screen showed slides of the girl, who was very blond and friendly-looking—smiling, laughing in practically every picture. "She was last seen in the company of her abductor, a man in his twenties. He has dark wavy hair, and is unusually good-looking. If you have seen Sharon Long, please call the number on your screen immediately. Do not speak to either of them or try to approach them. The man is an armed and extremely dangerous homicide suspect. Call the number on your screen. There is a reward of fifty thousand dollars for information leading to his apprehension and her safe return to her family."

Jerry sprang to his feet, pointed at the television screen, and shouted, "That's her!"

32

"Homicide, Detective Anthony."

"It's Jack Till," he said. He moved his chair closer to his desk and sat up straighter. "Remember me? I'm the private investigator working on the Catherine Hamilton murder. I called because I got the tip I've been waiting for."

"Are you sure it's *the* tip?" she asked. "What is it?"

"A copper thief on a crew stripping foreclosed houses in the desert northeast of LA stumbled on them two nights ago in one of the houses. His name's Jerry Escobar. He says Sharon Long was there alive, but the boyfriend killed his four friends and drove the bodies off somewhere to dump them, and ditched the two trucks they were going to use to haul off the pipes and wires and things."

"You're planning to take the word of a copper thief?"

"He's positive about the girl. And his four friends really seem to be missing. I called their houses."

"Suddenly a scavenger, who probably has never seen five hundred dollars all in one place, sees you're offering fifty thousand for information leading to the arrest of a kidnapper from Illinois. The thief is stuck here in Southern California. But that doesn't stop him from making a bid for the reward. He sees this Midwestern kidnapper right here, with his living victim."

"This is the same man who killed Catherine Hamilton here, and a few others in other places. I believe that Jerry Escobar is telling the truth."

He heard her sigh. "All right. Bring Jerry in, and we'll talk to him. Can you get him here tomorrow afternoon at, say, two o'clock?"

"Tomorrow?"

"If you can't round him up by then, the next day is fine."

Till said, "Look, Detective Anthony. I was a homicide detective for twenty-three years. I broke a lot of cases, got a lot of convictions. I'm not a naive person or somebody who doesn't know what it sounds like to be lied to. This suspect is a heavily armed, experienced killer who has a twenty-year-old girl as a hostage. You don't think it's worth going out there right now?"

"I understand your impatience. But please let's not insult each other. Even if this man exists, and is out in the Southern California desert, and is actually the kidnapper from Illinois, we still have lots of groundwork to do. Is the abandoned house in Los Angeles County? Or is it in Kern County? Or some other county? We'd need the cooperation of the local police, probably the state police, or even the FBI. We'll need to make a plan and execute it so that if he is there, no law enforcement officers get shot. All this takes time and effort."

"It's four in the afternoon. We've got nearly five hours before dark."

"I repeat my offer. Bring Jerry in to see us tomorrow afternoon, and we'll see. Nothing is going to happen tonight." She paused. "Now, if you'll excuse me, I'm on my way into a meeting."

She hung up.

Till sat at his desk for a full minute before he moved. He wasn't sure why he was doing this, but he had an instinctive urge to do something that made sense. He dialed the number of the flower shop where Holly worked. The phone rang a couple of times, and then, "Flower Basket, good afternoon."

"Hi, Jeanne," he said. "This is Jack Till."

"I recognized your voice, Jack. I'll get Holly."

"Wait. If you have a second I'd like to talk to you first."

"Sure. What's on your mind?"

"I wondered if you had an evening free this week. I'd like to take you to dinner."

"Well . . . okay. I'm free tomorrow night. Or Thursday. Does either of them work for you?"

"Tomorrow night sounds best," he said. "I was thinking of Banque in West Hollywood."

"Wonderful. I read about the place all the time, but I've never been there."

"Great. Can I pick you up at seven-thirty?"

"That's fine. It gives me time to get the shop closed up." She hesitated and then said, "Jack, I just wondered. Is this about Holly?"

"Only to the extent that she keeps telling me that you and I should go out."

"Good," she said. "Oh, I didn't mean I don't want to talk about her. It's just that—"

"I know," he said. "I'm glad you asked. It's not about Holly; it's about you."

"Then I'll see you tomorrow night. You know where I live, right?"

"Yes."

"Did you want to talk to Holly too?"

"I'd better," he said.

There were some unidentifiable sounds, and then Holly's voice. "Hi, Dad. I hear you finally got around to asking for a date."

"She already told you?"

"Well, we had discussed it before. You know, how if it doesn't work out, we'll still be just as close friends. Or if it works out too well."

"That's reassuring."

"Was that all you wanted?"

"Not exactly. I wanted to call because I'm going out on a case tonight. You won't be able to reach me for a few hours. I'll be back in the morning sometime, probably. If I'm gone longer, you have a key to my apartment."

"Dad, are you worried about getting your plants watered, or afraid you'll get killed?"

"Why would I make a date for tomorrow night if I thought that?"

"You're right. That would be pretty stupid."

"But if that did happen sometime, you would know that I love you very much. And I'm proud of what a nice person you grew up to be. And you have a key, and know where the important papers are, and where the emergency cash is hidden. Right?"

"Right. And I love you too."

"Then I'll talk to you tomorrow, after I'm back."

"I'll look forward to it. Love you. Bye, Dad."

"Bye, honey."

Till walked from his desk into the second room, which was his private office. He had a pair of locked gun safes along the windowless outer wall. He worked the combinations and opened them. He placed on his desk two .45 ACP pistols and a short M-4 rifle with a sling. He took from another cabinet a heavy body armor vest.

Till was aware that if the Boyfriend brought out the Barrett .50-caliber rifle, the vest would do no good.

He picked up the rifle and shouldered it. The rifle was just like the old M-16 A2 that he had used in Vietnam, except that the M-4 had a four-position stock and an eleven-and-a-half-inch barrel, and the "Auto" position of the selector lever didn't restore it to full auto. It weighed a bit over five pounds, and a thirty-round magazine added a pound. Till took out four full magazines and set them on the desk too.

Till brought out camouflage pants, shirt, and baseball cap; a "camelback" water carrier; and a small backpack. He took an infrared night scope out of the last safe, and attached it to the rifle. He loaded the gear into two duffels, carried them downstairs and out the rear entrance, and put them into the trunk of his car.

He went back upstairs, went to the desk, and picked up the road map. He had brought it with him when he'd gone to visit Jerry Escobar. He had listened carefully to Escobar's description of the housing development, and then put a mark on the map. He had shown it to Escobar, who had said the mark was in the right place. Till had planned to use it to direct Detective Anthony and Detective Sellers and a SWAT team to the place. On the back was a pencil drawing of the development, with the house marked. He folded the map and took it with him.

He went back to the desk, opened his bottom drawer, and removed two sets of handcuffs. Not to bring handcuffs would have given his actions a different meaning.

33

Till knew it was a long drive out into the rough, craggy badlands to the desert housing development, but even as he covered mile after mile, everything was happening fast for him. There should have been more time to think about what he was doing, more time to make mental good-byes. But he knew that was just the mind speaking for the body, wanting any excuse to delay or avoid the risk of death. He saw the sign for the exit.

He went past the exit on the long straight interstate, because he wanted to see what it looked like first. There was a road leading away from the interstate toward some distant jagged hills. In the flatland between the interstate and the hills, the road led to an unlit stone sign with metal letters on it. Just beyond the sign there were maybe seventy-five or a hundred lots along a network of streets paved and with curbs, all of them occupied by practically new homes.

Jerry the copper thief had said the Boyfriend and Sharon were staying three streets from the near edge of the development in a two-story house with a circular window above the door, and a three-car garage.

He took the next exit a minute later, then took the overpass to the entrance going back, and got on and then off again at the proper exit. Just past the straight road into the development, there was a winding road that led up into the hills, probably put there by crews erecting utility poles. Till took it. As he climbed the road he would stop every time he could look down and see the development.

There were no lights on in any of the buildings, even though it was only around eleven at night. The street lamps were dark—they must have been paid for by monthly assessments on the vanished home owners.

After a half mile up the road there was a flat place at a turn where Till could park his car. He got out; walked to the trunk; took out the duffel bags; sorted out the rifle, pistols, ammunition, and gear. Then he put on the camouflage clothes, the armor vest, and the boots. He closed the trunk, locked the car, and then loaded the weapons. Each time he finished loading one, he set it on the car roof. He put on his camelback water carrier, then the small backpack that held only ammunition and a spare pistol, put the sling on his shoulder to hold the rifle, and began to walk toward the house.

He made his way along the hill road in the dark, stopping again whenever he had a view of the rows of houses below. There were still no signs of life. Once he stopped, took a drink of water through the tube that ran from the water carrier, and looked up at the sky. He wished that he had taken Holly out to remote places like this more often during her childhood. There seemed to be many more stars out here, shining more brightly than they ever shone in Los Angeles. There were so many things he should have shown her but somehow forgot, and she would have enjoyed them so much.

When he was near the lowest part of the road, he sat on the ground and used his night scope to try to find any human being he could. The scope images showed bare walls, empty streets.

It occurred to him that the Boyfriend and Sharon were probably living like desert animals, moving around at night when it was cooler and sleeping during the day when the sun was fiercest.

He went over the whole development again. There wasn't any electric light that he could see. He counted three streets up from the highway, two houses in from the corner. That was where Jerry Escobar had seen them.

He studied the house. He could see the back window by the porch, where Jerry the copper thief had said he and his friend had climbed in. The window was covered now, with a sheet of plywood over it. Till decided to give himself more time to find the occupants. He turned on the infrared night scope and searched for body heat.

Till stayed in place on the stony hillside a hundred feet above the development, hidden by rocks and brush. The thermal scope showed hot spots from the heat of the sun all over the outside of the houses, as they slowly cooled from the edges inward, but he saw no human presence.

He stood, kept low, and began to walk. At first he was high enough on the hill to keep his eye on the house where the Boyfriend had been living with Sharon Long, but soon he could see only the house behind it.

Till walked steadily and quietly through dry chaparral and gravel that would have been the next phase of the housing development if there had been one.

Every few minutes he would stop, kneel, and use the night scope to try to read the neighborhood. He would find nothing, and advance. As he came closer to the house he consciously resisted the temptation to hurry to get out of the open.

Till reached the house, then stood with his back to the rear wall of the building, waited, and listened. After a few minutes, he stepped to the side of the door and quietly tried the knob, but found it locked. Till took out a knife, knelt beside the door, and pushed the blade in between the knob and the door. He carefully inched it up and into the crack where it could depress the latch, then pushed the door inward.

Till waited a couple of seconds for the Boyfriend to panic and shoot at the open doorway, then stepped around the jamb to the inside with his rifle ready. He moved steadily but quietly from room to room. Till stopped at the front door. He could see big holes in the wood with moonlight showing through.

He climbed the stairs to the second floor, but there was nobody left in the house.

"They're in the other house," said Moreland. "Good thing we moved over here." He sat on the floor in the living room of their new house watching their old house through the window. He had seen a man's silhouette in an upper window.

"Who are they?"

"I can't tell. Maybe friends of those thieves."

"What are they doing?"

"I'd guess looking for us," he said. "First thing is to go get the pistol I gave you, and the suitcase I brought from the other house. I'll stay here and watch them."

"What if it's the police?"

"Then we'll have to be sure we kill them and get out before the other cops get here. Now do what I said."

"What I mean is, if we're unarmed and don't try to hurt anyone, the police will arrest us," said Sharon. "If we have guns they'll shoot us."

"That's true, but they aren't the police. If I'm wrong, they'll yell it out: 'This is the police. Come out with your hands up.'"

She dragged the heavy suitcase to him, and he opened it and began selecting things and pulling them out. She said, "Can't we just leave? They don't know where we are yet."

"Just be quiet now. I've got to hear what they're doing."

Sharon stood in the empty living room, not certain what to do. Being quiet seemed to be an unassailable idea, so she obeyed. He seemed so busy and preoccupied with the men that he didn't care what she did.

She had been feeling depressed since the night the men had come for the pipes and wires. One thing she and Michael had not even talked about was that those men had not actually come here to kill him and rape her. When Michael had made her go outside to help him drag the bodies to their van, not one of them had been carrying a gun. In their van and their truck had been wrenches, screwdrivers, a couple of hacksaws, and some power tools.

She felt terrible that she had shot the man coming in the window, and thinking about him had somehow broken the mechanism that had kept her from doubting Michael. For a couple of days she had been asking herself why she had trusted Michael. At first it was because she had a big old crush on him. And after Gabe was killed, she needed to trust somebody, and Michael was all that was left. She had tried to cling to him, to believe in him, to do everything he said. Each time she'd wanted to turn back, what had kept her from doing it was her shame at what she'd done so far.

And now, tonight, she was going to get killed. She deserved it, she knew. She was terribly sorry for what she'd done, and she knew the bad things had been destined to catch up with her. She watched Michael crawling around below the window with a gun in his hand. He was peeking out at the house where they used to live and trying to assemble a big long rifle of some kind at the same time. She had never seen anything like it. When he attached the barrel, it looked as long as an old flintlock from a museum.

Sharon put the pistol he had given her on the counter between the empty living room and the empty dining area and walked into the foyer. She thought about saying good-bye, but she knew that was a bad idea. She didn't take anything but her purse. She quietly opened the door and stepped outside.

Sharon felt the warm, still air as she walked down the front path, stepped off the curb, and started across the street. Suddenly, she heard footsteps coming toward her from behind. She sensed it was Michael, so she ducked and ran hard to the side. He grabbed for her, but over-ran her. He stopped and turned to her.

His voice was a whisper. "What are you doing to me? I saved your ass. I took care of you." He held out his hand to her, but kept his pistol pointed in her direction, apparently unaware of the contradiction. "Get back inside."

"I can't, Michael."

He aimed his pistol at her head and began to step backward away from her, moving to get closer to shelter before he made the noise of shooting her. Sharon could see that there was no reason for her to run, because he couldn't possibly miss.

Behind him, he heard the garage door of the house he'd just left rise on its squeaky springs, and he turned. A voice called out, "You're going to want to do something else."

"What?" Moreland kept turning, tilting his head, searching franti-cally to spot his target. The voice had to be coming from the garage. "Who are you?"

Jack Till shouted a second time. "What do you think, boy? You up to pistols at sixty feet?" He stepped forward from the shadowy rear wall of the garage of the house where Moreland had come from, and stood beside where Moreland's car was parked facing outward. He had his pistol in his left hand hanging down by his thigh. "Come on. Just you and me. Bring your weapon down to your side, and we'll play quick-draw."

Moreland couldn't believe it. This was the man he'd seen in Boston, the one who had shot up his car. Behind him, Moreland heard Sharon push off and begin to run, trying to get away from him.

Moreland's mind judged the timing instantly: take the pistol shooter down, hit Sharon before she made it to cover, and then dash back to the house and wait for any others in ambush.

Moreland didn't lower his weapon; he just crouched, pivoted, and raised his arm to aim at the man with the pistol.

As he did, the car's headlights came on. After hours of the desert darkness, the glare was searing, blinding Moreland. He fired to the right side of the left headlight, where he figured the man must be.

Till had leaned into the car's open window to reach the switch. He heard the bullet dislodge air by his leg as he raised his pistol. He held his sights on his brightly lit target and squeezed the trigger while the Boyfriend fired again hastily, trying to make up for the first miss. Till's bullet passed through the Boyfriend's head, and his body fell to the street.

Till left the headlights on, stepped down the brightly lighted driveway to the body, knelt, and felt the neck for a pulse. He stood and saw the girl walking toward him tentatively, as though she might decide to run again. She gave a long, despairing sob, and he held her, waited it out, and then said, "Are you Sharon Long?"

"Yes."

"Are you hurt?"

"No," she said. "Why did you do that? It's crazy."

"To make him think about me instead of you."

"To save me."

"Yeah." Till took out his cell phone, then looked down at her, frowning. "Sharon, I'm calling for help now. But before anybody comes, you need to listen to me. You got kidnapped in Springfield, and that man made Gabe go into the bank. Then he dragged you out here. That's all you know. Never say anything different to anybody."

"Why do you want to help me?"

"It's for all of us—you, the families of the girls he killed, a bunch of cops you don't know, and me. You're the first one we could get to in time," Till said. He turned away as he put the cell phone to his ear. "Hello. My name is Jack Till, and I would like to report a shooting."